I0831787

Indigenous Writers of Taiwan

MODERN CHINESE LITERATURE FROM TAIWAN

Modern Chinese Literature from Taiwan

Wang Chen-ho,
Rose, Rose, I Love You

Cheng Ch'ing-wen,
Three-Legged Horse

Chu T'ien-wen,
Notes of a Desolate Man

Hsiao Li-hung,
A Thousand Moons on a Thousand Rivers

Chang Ta-chun,
Wild Kids: Two Novels About Growing Up

Michelle Yeh and N. G. D. Malmqvist, editors,
Frontier Taiwan: An Anthology of Modern Chinese Poetry

Li Qiao,
Wintry Night

Huang Chun-ming,
The Taste of Apples

Chang Hsi-kuo,
The City Trilogy: Five Jade Disks, Defenders of the Dragon City, Tale of a Feather

Li Yung-p'ing,
Retribution: The Jiling Chronicles

Shih Shu-ching,
City of the Queen: A Novel of Colonial Hong Kong

Indigenous Writers of Taiwan

AN ANTHOLOGY OF
STORIES,
ESSAYS,
& POEMS

EDITED BY
John and Yingtsih Balcom

TRANSLATED WITH AN INTRODUCTION BY
John Balcom

COLUMBIA UNIVERSITY PRESS NEW YORK

Columbia University Press
Publishers Since 1893
New York, Chichester, West Sussex

Columbia University Press wishes to express its appreciation for assistance given by the Chiang Ching-kuo Foundation for International Scholarly Exchange in the preparation of the translation and in the publication of this series.

Library of Congress Cataloging-in-Publication Data

Indigenous writers of Taiwan : an Anthology of stories, essays, and poems / edited by John and Yingtsih Balcom ; translated with an introduction by John Balcom.
p. cm. — (Modern Chinese literature from Taiwan)
ISBN 978-0-231-13650-1
ISBN 978-0-231-50999-2 (ebook)
1. Folk literature—Taiwan. 2. Taiwan aborigines.
I. Balcom, John. II. Balcom, Yingtsih. III. Series.
GR338.I57 2005
398.2'089'9925—dc22 2004065671

Designed by Lisa Hamm

Contents

Stories

Essays

Poems

Acknowledgments

I WOULD LIKE to express my heartfelt thanks to the following people and organizations. First of all, I would like to thank David Wang, who proposed this project a number of years ago, for his unstinting support. Sun Ta-ch'uan has been a most helpful teacher in educating me about Taiwan's indigenous literature. A number of people have been helpful in securing materials and author contacts: Wu Chin-fa of the Council for Cultural Affairs and his assistant Natalie Chen, Sarah Hsiang of the PEN office in Taipei, as well as Dominic Che-ming Chang of Dong Hwa University and Woo Kam Loon of Rye Field Publications. I would like to thank Hsiang Yang, poet and friend of many years, for helping to arrange a visit to Dong Hwa University as part of a research trip to Taiwan in April 2004. Kuo Ch'ing Tu provided me with the romanization of Japanese names in these translations. Michelle Yeh, friend in Taiwan poetry, read and commented on the poetry section, for which I am grateful. My wife, Yingtsih, editorial collaborator on the present volume, read and commented on the entire manuscript and saved me from many a blunder. I want to thank Susan Pensak, my terrific editor, for a superb job. I want also to thank the Chiang Ching-kuo Foundation for International Scholarly Exchange for their generous support of this project as well as funding a research trip to Taiwan. I should also like to thank *Chinese PEN*, *Manoa*, and the *Taiwan Review* in which some of these translations originally appeared.

Sources

STORIES

Topas Tamapima, "The Last Hunter" ("Zuihou de lieren") from *Zuihou de lieren*, pp. 45–74 (Taizhong: Chenxing chubanshe, 1987).

Kowan Talall, "Tears of a Fledgling" ("Chuniao lei") from *Beiqing de shanlin,* pp. 263–269. (Taizhong: Chenxing chubanshe, 1987).

Badai, "Ginger Road" ("Jianglu") from *Shanhai wenhua,* nos. 25–26 (Taipei; October 2000): 25–34.

Yubas Naogih, "Out of the Brush" ("Chucao") from *Tiangou buluo zhi ge,* pp. 137–169 (Taizhong: Chenxing chubanshe, 1995).

Lekal, "Elegy" ("Wange") from *Shahai wenhua,* nos. 25–26 (Taipei; October 2000): 36–40.

Siyapenjipeaya, "The Last Days of Ikafaduan" ("Ikafaduan de mori") from *Diao dao yuxie de yameiren,* pp. 101–102 (Taizhong: Chenxing chubanshe, 1992).

Liglave A-wu, "The Legend of Gubachane" ("Gubachane de chuanshuo") from *Shei lai chuan wode meili yishang,* pp. 220–223 (Taizhong: Chenxing chubanshe, 1996).

Husluma Vava, "The Hunter" ("Lieren") from *Qingmian,* pp. 254–279 (Taizhong: Chenxing chubanshe, 2001).

It Ta-os, "The Thunder Goddess" ("Lienu") from *Shanhai wenhua,* nos. 25–26 (Taipei; October 2000): 79–87.

Auvini Kadresengan. "The Eternal Ka-balhivane" ("Yongheng de Guisu") from *Yebaihe zhi ge,* pp. 249–279 (Taizhong: Chenxing chubanshe, 2002).

ESSAYS

Pa'labang, "Mother of History" ("Muqin de lishi, lishi de muqin") from *Jiu jiu jiu yici,* pp. 9–21 (Taipei: Living Psychology, 1991).

Paiz Mukunana, "Wooden Clogs" ("Muji"), from *Shanhai wenhua,* nos. 25–26 (Taipei; October 2000): 118–121, repr. *Qinai de A'ki—qing ni buyao shengqi,* pp. 127–139 (Taipei: Nushu wenhua, 2003).

Rimui Aki, "The Sound of a Flute in the Mountains" ("Shanye disheng") from *Shanhai wenhua,* no. 12 (Taipei; February 1996): 29–32, repr. *Shanye disheng,* pp. 37–43 (Taizhong: Chenxing chubanshe, 2001).

Adaw Palaf, "Let's Go for a Big Feast Outdoors" ("Zou ba, dao kuangye chi dacan") from *Wenxue Taiwan,* no. 4 (Taipei; 1992): 34–36.

Syman Rapongan, "A Large Stingray" ("Da hongyu") from *Lenghai qingshen,* pp. 173–183 (Taipei: Lianhe wenxue, 1997).

Sakinu. "Wind Walker" ("Zoufeng de ren") from *Shanhai wenhua,* nos. 25–26 (Taipei; October 2000): 98–101.

Neqou Sokluman, "Father and the Land" ("Fuqin yu tudi") from *Zhongguo shibao* (Taipei), September 12, 2001, p. 18.

Topas Tamapima, "Fish" ("Yu") from *Layu xingyiji,* pp. 45–50 (Taizhong: Chenxing chubanshe, 1998).

POEMS

Monaneng, five poems from *Meili de daosui* (Taizhong: Chenxing chubanshe, 1989).

Walis Norgan, three poems from *Xiangnian zuren* (Taizhong: Chenxing chubanshe, 1994); "He Makes Another Survey" ("Yi neng zai diaocha") from *Zhongguo shibao* (Taipei), October 17, 1996, p. 19, repr. *Yi neng zai diaocha,* pp. 174–178 (Taizhong: Chenxing chubanshe, 1999).

Tasi-ulauan Pima, poem from *Shanhai wenhua,* no. 25–26 (Taipei; October 2000): 140–141.

Adaw Palaf, two poems from *Chuangshiji,* no. 123 (Taipei; June 2000): 29–31.

Lavulas Geren, "Fists and Tears" and "Withdrawn" from *Shanhai wenhua,* no. 1, p. 84; "The Plum Rains Still Not Here in the Sixth Month" and "Through Hwa Dong Valley by Train at Night" from *Shanhai wenhua,* no. 2 (Taipei; January 1994): 82, 84. "Zipper Song" from *Shanhai wenhua,* no. 6 (Taipei; September 1994): 75; "On Rereading Bei Dao's Poem 'Let's Go'" from *Chuangshiji,* no. 123 (Taipei; June 2000): 36.

Haisul, five poems from *Shanhai wenhua,* no. 10 (Taipei: May 1995): 68–71.

Maishu, poem from *Shanhai wenhua,* no. 18 (Taipei: March 1989): 64.

Guyou Hsilan, poem from *Shanhai wenhua,* nos. 25–26 (Taipei; October 2000): 148.

It Ta-os, poem from *Shanhai wenhua,* nos. 25–26 (Taipei; October 2000): 143.

Purdur, song/poem from *Chuangshiji,* no. 123 (Taipei; June 2000): 37.

Darkanow Ruruang, song/poem from his CD "Alright" (*Haode . . .*).

Siepep, poem from *Chuangshiji,* no. 123 (Taipei: June 2000) p 38.

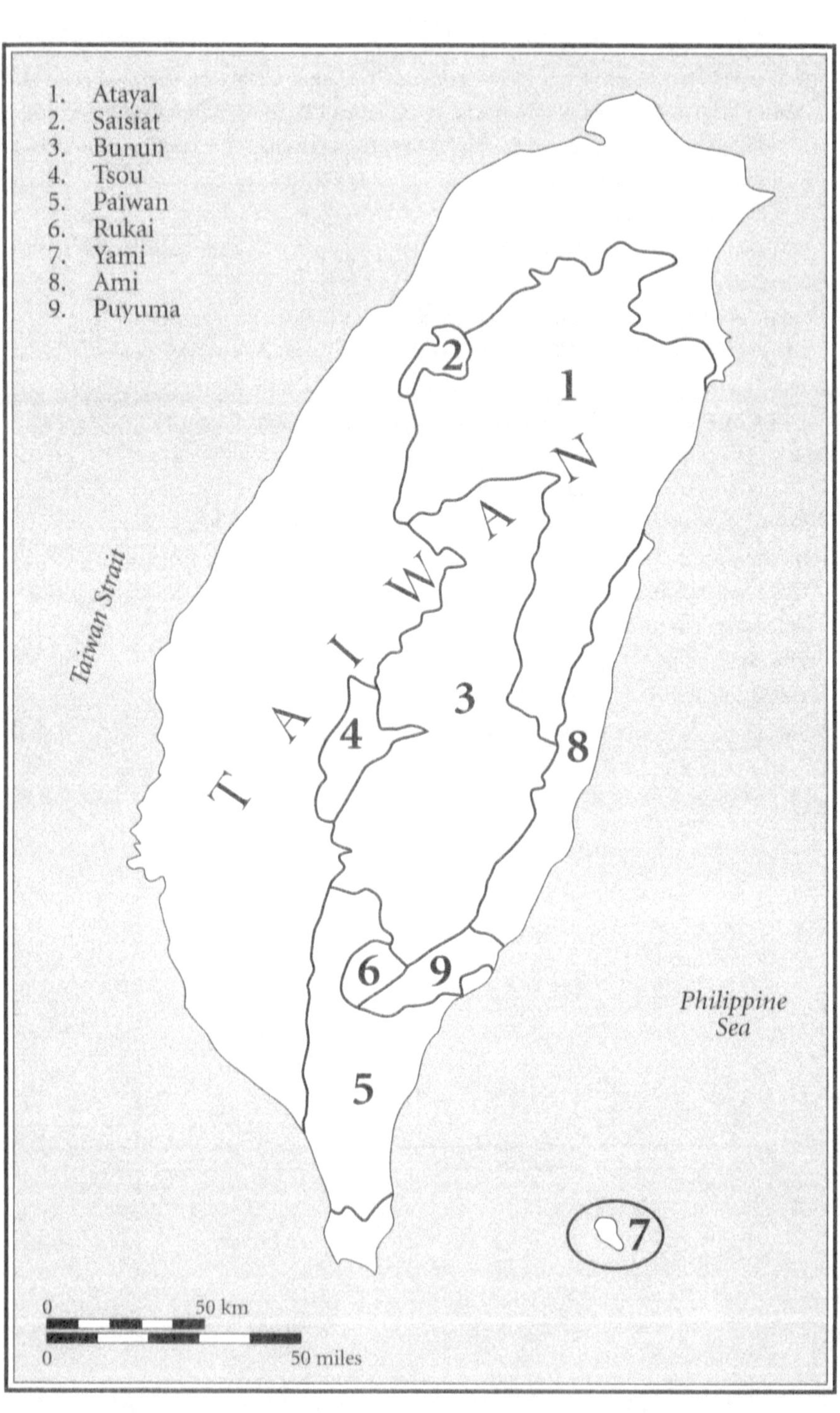

1. Atayal
2. Saisiat
3. Bunun
4. Tsou
5. Paiwan
6. Rukai
7. Yami
8. Ami
9. Puyuma
TAIWAN
Taiwan Strait
Philippine Sea
1
2
3
4
5
6
7
8
9
0
50 km
0
50 miles

Translator's Introduction

JOHN BALCOM

FEW PEOPLE BEYOND the shores of Taiwan are aware that the island is home to a population of indigenous peoples; but with a total population of less than four hundred thousand, they constitute less than 2 percent of the population. They are the earliest inhabitants of Taiwan and, like many indigenous populations in different parts of the world, they have been displaced and marginalized. In the last twenty years, for a number of reasons that will be discussed, indigenous literature written in Chinese has witnessed a boom of sorts. The present anthology is the first to introduce these works to an English-speaking audience. As such, the series editorial board felt that an introduction to provide the cultural and historical background of Taiwan's indigenous peoples to readers with little or no knowledge of the subject was essential.

General Ethnographic Background of the Nine Tribes

The indigenous peoples of Taiwan are Austronesian peoples, and evidence suggests that they have lived in Taiwan for at least fifteen thousand years.[1] There are three theories as to their origins. The first, the theory of southern origin, suggests that they originated in Southeast Asia and spread north and east. The second, the theory of northern origin, suggests that they originated in China. The third and more recent theory suggests that Taiwan itself is the Austronesian homeland. This theory rests largely on linguistic evidence: Taiwan has the greatest concentration of Austronesian languages—about a dozen extant and a dozen extinct.

Taiwan's indigenous peoples are generally divided into two main groups: the plains peoples and the mountain peoples. The plains peoples, who are now extinct, once consisted of fourteen tribes. They lived on the coastal plains and were exterminated and assimilated by the Han Chinese. There are eight mountain tribes in Taiwan—the Saisiyat, Atayal, Ami, Bunun, Tsou, Puyuma, Rukai, and Paiwan. (The only surviving nonmountain tribe is the Yami, a tribe that lives on Lanyu (Orchid) Island, one of Taiwan's offshore islands.) Living largely in the mountainous regions of the island or the more sparsely populated east coast, they were able to maintain, to some extent, their cultural identities.

The languages spoken by the indigenous peoples belong to the Proto-Austronesian linguistic family, an agglutinative language type to which both Malaysian and Hawaiian belong. Most of the Austronesian languages spoken in Taiwan are categorized as Formosan Austronesian languages and are subdivided into three branches: Atayalic (Atayal), Tsouic (Rukai and Tsou), Paiwanic (Ami, Bunun, Paiwan, Puyuma, and Saisiyat). The Yami speak a Malayo-Polynesian Austronesian language related to Ivatan of the northern Philippines. The Austronesian languages of Taiwan are mutually unintelligible and there is a great deal of dialect variation. None of the languages possesses a written form; however, missionaries have developed romanized forms to facilitate their work.

There are many differences among the tribes in terms of material culture, social organization, and religion. According to Chen Chi-lu, the indigenous peoples of Taiwan earned their livelihood mainly through agriculture, stockbreeding, and hunting and fishing. In addition to a host of wild plants that are gathered, the indigenous people of Taiwan cultivate about fifty varieties of plants, eight of them common to all tribes—millet, which is considered sacred, sweet potato, taro, banana, ginger, ramie, sugarcane, and bottle gourd. Land is cultivated most often using the slash-and-burn method. Stockbreeding is the work of the women. All tribes keep pigs and chickens, but these animals were mainly raised for sacrificial purposes and the eating of chicken was once taboo. As such, hunting is second only to agriculture in the lives of the indigenous people. Important types of game include deer, muntjac, wild boar, civet, and pheasant. A great number of taboos are observed in hunting, and omens are important. Hunts can be by individual or group. Fishing is really important among the Yami. The flying fish is the most valued fish, followed by the dolphin.[2] Despite similarities in material culture, the tribes are often very different in terms of social organization and religious beliefs.

ATAYAL (POPULATION 78,300)

The Atayal are distributed over much of the northern part of Taiwan's central mountain region and are divided into three branches. The Atayal kinship is ambilineal with a tendency toward nuclear families preferring patrilocal residence. All three branches of the Atayal have patriarchal social systems. Leaders from community ritual groups controlled the political and economic authority. In general, Atayal society was closed and did not readily accept outsiders. Considered the fiercest of indigenous groups, they were the last group to submit to Han and later Japanese rule. The Atayal believe in spirits and unnamed supernatural powers called *utux* as well as spirits of the dead.

SAISIYAT (POPULATION 4,200)

The Saisiyat are divided into two groups: northern and southern dialect groups. The northern group lives in the mountainous regions of Hsinchu County, while the southern group lives in the highlands of Miaoli. The tribe was the first to be acculturated by the Han Chinese and adopt Han names. The basic structural unit of Saisiyat society is a totemic clan linked by geographical and family ties. Three of four households constitute a settlement, and several settlements might unite to form a village with shared farmland, fishing territory, and mutual assistance units. The Sasiyat continue to observe a unique ceremony called *Pastaai*, or Ceremony of the Little People. According to legend, the dark-skinned little people taught the Sasiyat how to farm, sing, and dance, but they also harassed Sasiyat women. The Sasiyat retaliated by pushing them into a narrow ravine as they crossed a narrow footbridge. The ceremony is meant to appease the souls of the little people.

BUNUN (POPULATION 37,900)

The Bunun live in the mountainous regions of central Taiwan. The tribe is divided into six groups. The Bunun social organization is patrilineal, with extended family households grouped in small villages. Usually, the extended families consist of twenty members living in one house. Patriarchial rule is absolute, but every member has equal access to the settlement's resources. Because of this group sharing, wealth was not individually accumulated and social stratification never developed. They are relatively accepting of outsiders. The Bunun believe in guardian spirits and have both male and female shamans who are responsible for treating illnesses.

TSOU (POPULATION 5,700)

The Tsou are found in Chiayi, Nantou, and Kaohsiung counties. They are divided into three language groups. The Tsou languages have the least in common with the other indigenous languages, suggesting that they broke away from a common ancestral language in the very distant past. The Tsou are patrilineal and high positions such as chiefs, war leaders, and elders are differentiated. The men's meeting hut, or *kuba,* is a religious and political center. Unlike the Atayal and Bunun, the Tsou have many particularized names for gods and spirits.

PUYUMA (POPULATION 8,000)

The Puyuma live in the flatland area of Taitung county. The Puyuma have a multilineal kinship system with ritual groups. The extended family inheritance goes to the eldest daughter. The positions of chief and shamans are patrilineal. Puyuma society was stratified into noble families and commoners; marriage between the classes is not prohibited. Shamans come from the leading clan's ancestral worshiping groups. A chief's power is symbolized by his role in ancestor worship and the transfer of tribal knowledge, not from the monopolization of land.

PAIWAN (POPULATION 59,700)

The Paiwan inhabit the southern part of the island. Paiwan kinship was originally matrilineal but is now ambilineal. Most marriages are matrilocal. The position of chief was hereditary. The Paiwan observed class distinctions and intermarriage between classes was prohibited. Chiefs held power by virtue of monopolization of land. The Paiwan were famous for wood and stone sculpture. Ancestral figures were often carved in shallow relief on house posts, slate, and plank panels.

RUKAI (POPULATION 7,800)

The Rukai inhabit south-central Taiwan. They are closely related to the Paiwan in terms of material culture and social structure. Like the Paiwan, they are also noted carvers, especially of ancestral images.

AMI (POPULATION 122,800)

The Ami are the largest group of indigenous people. They are mainly plains dwellers, living in valleys from Hualien to Taitung. The Ami are further divided into five groups, based on geography, customs, and language. Ami society is matrilineal, and the oldest woman in the extended family is generally the household head. Men, however, exercise authority at meetings of leading men from different villages. Villages tend to be large—between two thousand and one thousand people. The Ami have elaborate cosmogonic myths that can only be recited by trained male lineage shamans.

YAMI (POPULATION 4,200)

The Yami live almost exclusively on Lanyu, or Orchid Island, which lies forty-four miles off the eastern coast. Culturally, the Yami are closely related to the inhabitants of the Bataan Islands of the Philippines, with whom they trade. The Yami language and that of the Ivatan dialect of the Batanes are mutually intelligible. Yami is also related to the Paiwanic languages of Taiwan. Fishing is central to the Yami economy, and fishing groups of kinsmen in villages from the same region form the basic cooperative and distributive units of Yami society. The Yami are fearful of ghosts and blame them for all evil and mischief. They do not have shamans but do believe in magical amulets for protection from ghosts. The Yami are justly famous for their gorgeously decorated dugout canoes.

History

Prehistoric human habitation of Taiwan, according to archaeological evidence, dates back fifteen thousand years.[3] Historical connections between Taiwan and China go back to the Three Kingdoms period (A.D. 221–263). But significant settlement by the Han Chinese did not begin until about the fourteenth century. Most of the early settlers came from nearby Fukien Province. The island also provided haven for fishermen and pirates. Records from the imperial period refer to the indigenous inhabitants of the island as *Eastern Ti* or *Eastern Fan,* terms that can be translated as "Eastern savages." The Dutch maintained a colony in southwestern Taiwan from 1624–1662. But the Dutch occupation was not without incident: in 1629 warriors from Matou village massacred a Dutch force. It wasn't until 1635 that the Dutch defeated Matou village, establishing peace in the area. The Dutch traded with the local plains peoples and were primarily interested in deerskins. The trade so depleted the deer population that local inhabitants turned to farming.

The collapse of the Ming dynasty in 1644 had a profound effect on Taiwan and its indigenous inhabitants. The Ming loyalist Zheng Chenggong (also known as Koxinga) and his followers fled to Taiwan in 1661. The following year he expelled the Dutch, and over the next two decades he and his followers set up their own government and ran the island. The indigenous peoples in the coastal areas were taxed and subject to a corvee labor policy. Assimilation was beginning. Taiwan fell to the Qing dynasty in 1683.

The Qing court imposed a partial quarantine on the island to prevent dissidents from gaining a foothold there but also out of concern for the effects of Han settlement on the indigenous population and possible conflicts. The government continued Zheng Cheng-gong's policies of taxation and corvee labor on the coastal indigenous peoples, known as "cooked" or "civilized" savages, but could do nothing with the so-called raw or uncivilized savages who inhabited the mountainous areas beyond government control. In 1731 the indigenous people rebelled against the Qing government and its policies. The government, in the aftermath, instituted a policy of assimilation through education. By 1740 the immigration quarantine on the island was lifted and settlers began to pour in to the island. The government prohibited the Han settlers from encroaching on the lands of the indigenous people, but the scarcity of coastal land pushed more settlers into the mountainous areas where they often entered into land tenancy agreements with the tribes. It was not until 1884, when Liu Mingchuan became governor, that the mountainous tribes were finally forced to submit to Han rule.

China went to war with Japan in 1894 over Korea. The war ended the following year with China's defeat. The Ch'ing court signed the Treaty of Shimonoseki on April 17, 1895, ceding Taiwan and the Pescadores to Japan. Thus began fifty years of Japanese rule. When the Japanese first arrived, they decided that the indigenous people would be isolated on reservations and forbidden to have any interaction with people on the plains. They were expected to wear indigenous clothing and maintain their traditional ways. It was hoped that by preserving their ways the government could maintain their identity and thus bar them from making any claims on land and resources. Japanese researchers began the ethnographic study of Taiwan's indigenous peoples. The first Japanese ethnographic research was undertaken in 1897 by Ino Kanori and later with the help of Torii Ryuzo. Population studies, research on the material culture, and the collection of oral literature were undertaken. In addition, textual research was done on the vanished coastal peoples. It was the Japanese who formalized the current classification of the indigenous people into eight tribes.

The Japanese demanded submission, which was not often forthcoming; between 1898 and 1909, the colonial government launched eleven punitive expeditions against the indigenous peoples. The colonial government built roads in an effort to open up the mountainous areas and the east coast. The indigenous people rebelled against Japanese rule on more than one occasion; the best-known perhaps is the Wushe incident, which occurred on October 27, 1930. Beginning in 1910 the Japanese also provided rudimentary Japanese education as part of a larger assimilation policy. Schools were established in the mountain areas. The schools were run by Japanese police officer/headmasters and math, ethics, Japanese, and vocational studies were taught. By 1941 71 percent of indigenous children were attending Japanese schools and the tribespeople were generally termed *Takasago zoku*, or Formosan race. In 1920 a system of reservations was established. In 1930 the Japanese government suppressed the practice of head hunting by some tribes. Tribal life changed dramatically under the Japanese. Many indigenous people quickly adapted to Japanese ways and learned to work within the Japanese system. Education and cooperation was the stepping-stone to a better life. Many of the older indigenous people still identify with the Japanese.

In 1945, with Japan's defeat in World War II, Taiwan was returned to China. Immediately after Retrocession, the government forbade the use of Japanese and instituted universal education in Mandarin Chinese. In 1949 the ROC government moved to Taiwan. Fearful that the remote mountainous regions might become home to communist or subversive elements, the Nationalist government immediately replaced the Japanese schools with Chinese schools with a curriculum emphasizing Chinese language as well as history and a good deal of propaganda. However, few teachers were willing to teach in such remote schools. In 1951 a major assimilation policy was implemented. The assimilation policies resulted in the erosion of indigenous language and culture as well as the creation of a double standard within society in which indigenous peoples were treated as second-class citizens. The 1970s saw the beginning of an influx of young Han Chinese teachers into the mountainous areas. This was an idealistic movement dedicated to serving the mountainous areas after Taiwan found itself politically isolated in the world. It wasn't until after the lifting of martial law in 1987 that a really vigorous indigenous rights movement emerged.

Since the mid-1990s, as part of a larger localism movement, the government has taken steps to raise indigenous awareness and expand rights. Since 1998 the standardized curriculum has been recast to contain positive and favorable mention of indigenous people. A good deal of money has also gone to building museums and centers of indigenous culture as well as on infrastructure projects to open up the mountainous regions. Courses on indigenous literature are now offered in many universities, and the trend has so far culminated in the establishment of the College of Indigenous Studies at National Dong Hwa University in which all students (approximately half of whom are Han Chinese) are required to study an indigenous language. There has been much discussion of more autonomy for the tribespeople as well as mandatory offerings of indigenous languages in school. In 2003 a draft National Languages Development Law was proposed that would make the indigenous languages official languages of the ROC and thereby mandating their use in education and government. It should also be noted that Taiwan has a cabinet-level Council for Aboriginal Affairs as well as similar councils on the provincial and municipal levels.

Indigenous culture has seriously eroded. Many of the younger people have not been educated in traditional ways. Although strides are being made to correct the situation, the indigenous people still are often found living on the margins of mainstream society, with better than 35 percent now living in urban areas, further accelerating the breakdown of traditional society. But there is also a movement among indigenous people to return to their lands and attempt to continue their cultures and languages as well as earn a living in ecotourism and the selling of indigenous goods. Some have hoped to cash in on hotel and resort activities in their areas.

Indigenous Literature

The indigenous literature of Taiwan is typically divided into three "stages."[4] The first stage covers the traditional oral literature in the form of myths, legends, and ballads as handed down through the ages. It was not until the Japanese Occupation Period (1895–1945) that efforts were made to record this extensive collective literature. For example, in the early thirties two Japanese linguists, Ogawa Hisayoshi and Asai Erin, collected nearly three hundred indigenous legends and stories. The stories were published in 1935. In 1991 a collection of forty-nine of these stories was published, translated into Chinese by the Taiwan poet Chen Qianwu, who was educated in the Japanese system.[5] In this stage outsiders often functioned as "ghost writers" for the indigenous people as they recorded such materials. In other words, the indigenous peoples were the object of study by others, be they anthropologists, linguists, travelers, or missionaries. However, in the last twenty years many indigenous writers and scholars (as well as Han Chinese) have undertaken collections and recordings of what remains of the oral literature. Sun Ta-chuan commented that there is an urgent need to do such work on a large scale because the oral culture is disappearing rapidly as older tribal members, the repositories of this oral culture, pass away.[6]

The second stage of indigenous literature is a bit more complicated as it includes not only works by Japanese and Han Chinese authors based on the indigenous oral literature but also original work about the life and plight of indigenous people. During the occupation period Japanese writers such as Oshika Taku, Nakamura Chihei, Sakaguchi Reiko, among others, wrote about Taiwan's indigenous people. Lai He, the "father of Taiwan literature," who wrote during the occupation, penned a famous poem memorializing the Wushe incident. Chung Chao-cheng and Lee Chiao, both Hakka writers, have written eloquent stories about indigenous people.[7] In recent years the poet Chen Li has written poems based on indigenous myths, and Hsiang Yang wrote a narrative poem about the Wushe incident.

In the second stage the indigenous people are still the object of the research of others; in this case Han Chinese writers who appropriate indigenous culture and history to create imaginative works of literature. Wu Chin-fa, editor of *Beiqing de shanlin* (Sad mountains and forests), an interesting 1987 short story anthology that was the first to juxtapose works by Han Chinese writers with those by indigenous writers, made the useful distinction between "aboriginal literature" (*shandi wenxue*) and "indigenous literature" (*yuanzhumin wenxue*). Aboriginal literature, as defined by Wu, is writing about the indigenous peoples by nonindigenous writers; whereas indigenous literature is all writing by indigenous writers, which typifies the third stage.[8]

The third phase of indigenous literature includes the literary works written by indigenous writers in Chinese. The writings of this period are often retellings of traditional myths and legends as well as individual creative works written in Chinese. This is the phase of primary concern in this book. The earliest work of this stage, a collection of short stories by Kowan Talall titled *Yuwai menhen* (Traces of dreams in foreign lands), was published in 1971. But it was not until the1980s that indigenous literature really blossomed, particularly after the lifting of martial law in 1987. The indigenous peoples of Taiwan had always been silent; someone else had always spoken or written for them. Why, then, did they seem to find a voice in the 1980s and indigenous literature in Chinese blossom? There are many reasons.

This recrudescence was in many ways an outgrowth of the social, political, and cultural changes of the 1970s and 1980s. In the 1970s Taiwan suffered numerous setbacks internationally as countries moved to recognize Mainland China. Taiwan's inferior position internationally forced the ruling party at home to make concessions to the disenfranchised Taiwanese majority, beginning a trend of Taiwanification politically and culturally. Nativism in literature and art emerged and a greater interest in local things developed. This trend deepened into an intense localism (*bentuhua*) of politics, society, and culture in the 1980s that further helped to awaken the indigenous peoples. The local Taiwanese and Hakka were the principal proponents of this regionalization and they looked to overturn decades of political, economic, and, to a lesser extent, cultural, oppression. The indigenous peoples took this localism a step further in that they sought to resist/oppose the authority of a dominant Han culture, regardless of when it arrived from Mainland China, in the 1940s with the KMT exodus to Taiwan or earlier with the local Taiwanese, or Hakka. At this stage a still burgeoning indigenous identity was tied to resistance and opposition. Identity politics and minority rights emerged as prominent foci in Taiwan's public discourse after the lifting of martial law in

1987. The vigorous ethnic politics as well as the coming of age of a generation of writers who had received a complete education in Chinese as a result of the government's long-term assimilation policy helped to fuel the boom in indigenous literature.[9]

In addition to the ideological factors, increased economic prosperity also afforded more opportunities for publishing: newspapers, magazines such as *Shanhai wenhua* (Taiwan indigenous voice bimonthly), perhaps the most important magazine devoted to indigenous culture, was established in 1993 and in 1987 Morning Star began publishing a series of books devoted to indigenous literature and culture that now numbers well over fifty titles. Literary awards for indigenous literature were established too: in 1995 Taiwan Indigenous Voice Bimonthly Literary Awards were set up and 2000 saw the creation of the China Motor Indigenous Literature Award. In 2003 INK published the seven-volume *Anthology of Taiwan Indigenous Literature in Chinese*. Edited by Sun Ta-ch'uan, it is the single most comprehensive collection to date and a must for anyone seriously interested in the literature.

Needless to say, much of the indigenous literature focuses on identity issues such as the encroachment of the outside world on traditional society, the erosion of culture due to assimilation, and a feeling of nostalgia for the old ways. Ironically, this literature is all written in Chinese, the dominant language of the "oppressor." One might ask whether this does not further diminish the viability of indigenous culture. Despite the apparent gains made by indigenous literature in Chinese, some scholars and thinkers warn that the indigenous people should avoid allowing the issue of identity to be framed by the logic of the dominant Han culture; instead, the indigenous peoples should move beyond a simple challenge-and-response sort of logic and look to themselves and their own cultures and languages to establish their identities.[10] Simply resisting the dominant culture does not necessarily define who one is. Some authors such as Adaw Palaf, Syman Rapongan, and Auvini Kadresengan, who initially found a voice for themselves in the climate created by the indigenous rights movement, later found that they only really began to understand themselves when they returned to their roots. Some have also warned that by using Chinese, the dominant language, the indigenous peoples are actually in greater danger of deepening and strengthening the dominant culture.

Most indigenous writers only began the formal study of Chinese when they entered primary school at the age of six or seven. When asked why he writes almost exclusively in Chinese, Walis Norgan, voicing the opinion of many indigenous writers, said that there was no audience for literature written in the indigenous languages. Monaneng said that he had never learned the romanized form of his language developed by missionaries and that Chinese was better suited to describe life in the cities. Rimui Aki, who teaches the Atayal language, said that there wasn't much of an audience and that she had a greater proficiency in written Chinese than in her native language (probably because her father was a primary school teacher and her instruction in Chinese began early). She did say that she is gaining proficiency in Atayal by communicating with friends via the internet.[11] Writers such as Syman Rapongan and Wallis Norgan, in a nod to preserving and promoting their own languages, have published bilingual books.[12]

This situation might raise questions about the notion of "authentic voice" and to what extent these works are conditioned by the literary conventions and audience expectations of the dominant Han ethnic group, in whose language they are written. Clearly a language offers a worldview, and in this case the authors stand in two worlds—their own indigenous culture as well as the dominant culture, albeit in a perhaps marginalized position. What will not be obvious to the reader of the translations in this volume is the nature of the language in the original texts. Quite often the native language of an author impacts or "interferes" with the style and grammar of his or her writing in Chinese. (In terms of word order, the Austronesian languages are largely V-S-O as opposed to the Chinese S-V-O structure.) Therefore, even when reading an award-winning story such as Topas Tamapima's *The Last Hunter*, the native speaker of Chinese will find the work almost fluent, but not without some awkwardness. In the case of Adaw Palaf, Mandarin structures are so distorted that what is printed on the page often means the opposite of what is intended. Reading such texts is a slow process that requires a good deal of unpacking on the reader's part. One wonders to what extent the violations of Chinese grammar are a conscious subversion or in fact a remaking of the language. In addition, most indigenous literary works are also filled with an extensive indigenous vocabulary, much of which is often explained for Han readers, but not in all cases.

However, despite the boom the indigenous cultures have entered what has been described as a twilight phase. Sun Ta-ch'uan and other champions of indigenous culture are generally pessimistic about the future.[13] The cultural gap between generations today is expanding at a rapid rate; customs and language are disappearing as assimilation continues apace. The cause of indigenous people today is widely considered lost to genocide or assimilation; what remains of their culture is often nothing more than an exotic cultural commodity to be sold to tourists. For Sun Ta-ch'uan and others, it is impossible to strategize for an ill-defined future. In looking at the use of Chinese, Sun has commented that naturally some beauty and expression of the indigenous languages has been lost, but the use of a single language has provided the means for a dialogue between tribes as well as between the indigenous tribes and the Han Chinese ethnic majority. This communal language is allowing the indigenous people to engage the possibilities of the future, to enter into a dialogue with the rest of Taiwan society to create a new dawn for the island as a whole.[14]

Text Selection and Translation

Bearing in mind that this book is the first such anthology of its kind in English, the editors have attempted to provide a survey of the representative works from the three main literary genres—short story, essay, and poetry—over the last twenty-plus years. Both the editors read the corpus of indigenous literature available—a stack of books, magazines, and newspapers about four feet high. Both noted works that impressed and made the final selection from the combined pool. We have tried to provide, when possible, equal representation of literary works by writers from all tribes. This was not always possible; some tribes have produced a larger number of writers than others, often with little correlation to the actual size of the tribes. In the case of fiction we attempted to give an idea of thematic range as well as variety of narrative style, from the retelling of traditional oral tales to more contemporary pieces of individual creative writing. The essays tend to focus more on a realistic depiction of the dilemmas faced by indigenous people in contemporary Taiwan; the same can be said for most of the poems. However, there are writers such as Lavulas Geren, who tend to situate themselves more within the context of contemporary Chinese literature than under the rubric of indigenous literature. Each writer's indigenous name has been provided where possible. As is the case with any anthology, many worthwhile works could not be included. Readers interested in reading more in the original language are encouraged to consult the comprehensive seven-volume *Anthology of Taiwan Indigenous Literature in Chinese*, edited by Sun Ta-chuan.

A couple of things should be said about the translation. First of all, all words and phrases in an indigenous language or languages have been retained. When the original contains an explanation or a footnote, such information has been worked into the translation. If the original author provided no explanation or footnotes, none have been added. Of greater importance, perhaps, is that for the sake of readability all nonstandard Mandarin constructions in the original texts have been smoothed out into normal American English in the translations. The rationale for this is that if nonstandard Mandarin were translated into nonstandard English, the translator, and not the author, would be blamed. The reader is therefore left with what is said and not particularly with how it is said, and for that decision I must bear full responsibility.

Monterey/Taipei/Hualien 2004

Notes

1. Most of this section has been drawn directly from the *1999 Republic of China Yearbook* (Taipei: Government Information Office, 1999), chapter 2, titled "People," especially pp. 27–34; also see Michael Stainton, "The Politics of Taiwan Aboriginal Origins," in Murray A. Rubenstein, ed., *Taiwan: A New History*, pp. 27–44 (New York: Sharpe, 1998).
2. See Chi-lu Chen, *Material Culture of the Formosan Aborigines* (Taipei: Taipei Museum of Art, 1968), especially section 2, "Means of Subsistence," pp. 19–48.
3. Our summary of the history of the indigenous people has been drawn directly from Wen-hsiun Hsu, "From Aboriginal Island to Chinese Frontier: The Development of Taiwan before 1683," in Ronald K. Knapp, ed., *China's Island Frontier: Studies in the Historical Geography of Taiwan*, pp. 3–28 (Honolulu: University of Hawaii Press, 1980); I-shou Wang, "Cultural Contact and the Migration of Taiwan's Aborigines: A Historical Perspective," in Ronald K. Knapp, ed. *China's Island Frontier: Studies in the Historical Geography of Taiwan*, pp. 31–54 (Honolulu: University of Hawaii Press, 1980); and the "Taiwanese Aborigine" entry at *Wikipedia*: http://en.wikipedia.org/wiki/Taiwanese_aborigine (consulted August 20, 2004).
4. Tu Kuo-ch'ing, "Aboriginal Literature in Taiwan," in *Taiwan Literature: English Translation Series,* Santa Barbara: Forum for the Study of World Literature in Chinese, no. 3 (June 1998): xiii–xx.
5. See Chen Qianwu, trans., *Taiwan yuanzhaumin de muyu chuanshuo* (Legends of Taiwan's Indigenous People in the Original Languages) (Taipei: Taiyuan chubanshe, 1991).
6. Interview with Sun Ta-ch'uan by the author on April 20, 2004.
7. See Tu, "Aboriginal Literature in Taiwan," p. xv; and Shimomura Sakujiro, *Taiwan yuanzhumin wenxue xulun* ("An introduction to Taiwan's indigenous literature") trans. Nian Xiuling and Zhang Xuxuan in *Shanhai wenhua* no. 8 (Taipei; January 1995): 85–99.
8. Wu Chin-fa, *Taiwan yuanzhumin wenxue taolunhui* ("A roundtable on indigenous literature") in *Wenxue Taiwan* no. 9 (Taipei; September 1992): 43–52.
9. See Sun Ta-ch'uan, *Yuanzhumin wenxue de kunjing: huanghun huo liming* ("The difficult situation of indigenous literature: Twilight or dawn") in *Shanhai shijie* (Mountains and sea), pp. 142–162 (Taipei: Unitas, 2000).
10. Fu Dawei, *Bailang senlin li de wenzi lieren—shidu Taiwan yunazhumin de hanwen shuxie* ("Word hunters in the bright forest: Reading Taiwan's indigenous literature in Chinese") in *Dangdai*, no. 83 (Taipei; March, 1993): 28–49.
11. Interview with Monaneng on April 18, 2004; interview with Walis Norgan on April 24, 2004; interview with Rimui Aki on April 25, 2004.
12. See, for example, Syman Rapongan, *Badaiwan de shenhua* (The myths of Badaiwan) (Taizhong: Chenxing chubanshe, 1992); and Walis Norgan, *Taiya jiaozong* (Footsteps of the Atayal) (Taizhong: Chenxing chubanshe, 1991).
13. See Sun's comments in "The People of Song" in *Free China Review* 42.6 (Taipei; June 1993): 20–33.

14. Sun Ta-ch'uan, "Bianxu: Taiwan yuanzhumin wenxue chuangshiji" ("Editor's preface: The genesis of Taiwan's indigenous literature") in *Taiwan yuanzhumin hanyu wenxue xuanji* (An Anthology of Taiwan Indigenous Literature in Chinese), pp. 5–15 (Taipei: INK, 2003).

Stories

The Last Hunter

TOPAS TAMAPIMA

BIYARI SQUATTED IN the woodshed at dusk chopping firewood. His dull eyes were those of an old man. He no longer chopped the wood as cleanly as he did in the past; the wood looked more like a piece of raw pork gnawed by a rat. Sometimes his chopping ax would stray and strike the ground. He became increasingly more irritated. Finally he stopped chopping and squatted there holding the ax in both hands with a vacant look on his face.

"Biyari, hurry up. The fire is going out."

Biyari's hunting dog that had been dozing by his side woke up, its big ears erect, its front legs bent and its hind legs straight, poised to attack. Biyari kept his head lowered, looking at the chips of wood. His dog stretched and shook itself several times then lazily lay down again.

Pasula sat on a small bench watching the scene. She wanted to laugh, but when she saw that her man did not respond she angrily returned to the stove to warm herself.

"Biyari, who are you thinking about? Are you deaf? If you had listened to me and gone down to the flatlands to work as a temporary packer and bought some sweaters, then you wouldn't have to chop wood to fend off the cold. Hurry up and toss me a couple pieces of wood." As she spoke, she threw a small chair at his feet. She stood with her right hand on her hip, grit her jaw, showing her big front teeth that the children made fun of. The dog continued to laze around on the ground.

"What are you mad about? Pasula, you threw the kid's chair on the ground and if you broke its legs God will punish us by giving us a child born with broken legs. Biyari picked up the chair and tossed three pieces of wood to Pasula.

Last summer she had been pregnant for the first time, but after taking care of herself for two months she had a miscarriage one night. Biyari had built the chair at that time as a gift for the baby. Looking at the chair now, he felt very sad. He checked the legs of the chair to see if they were OK.

"I'll put the chair away. Next time you get pregnant, we'll get it out again." He put the chair up on a rack used for drying millet. Then he put on his jacket and went over to where Pasula was sitting and stretched out his fingers to warm them by the fire. His jacket was old—it no longer looked the way it did when he had first taken a fancy to it in the shop window. The sleeves had lost their original milk-white color and there were two large holes in the back—when he was out hunting, he had fallen and snagged his jacket on a piece of wood, ripping the holes in it. He never thought about throwing it away and had in fact come to cherish it.

"If it weren't for this curse handed down by your ancestors and the devil in your body, I wouldn't have to squat next to the fire to stay warm. My little girl would be this big by now and I could squeeze her between my breasts. Hunters, hunters! It's all because of your ancestors," she scolded, her voice quavering.

"Stop, don't start that again. The past is over and done with. We will have children someday."

As he finished speaking, Biyari called to his dog and took off, nearly kicking the wood he tossed in, and was soon out of sight beyond the light of the fire.

"Get out and stay out and don't come back!"

They had been unable to find the reason for Pasula's miscarriage. As a result, they started to live like enemies and exchanged harsh jibes—he blamed her womb for its impatience, and she blamed his seed for its inability to adapt. She was also afraid of his family, who had been shamans for generations, and their curses. In the last six months she had grown accustomed to Biyari going out at night and coming home alone after midnight.

The fog began to shroud the tribal village; the damp air entered the room through cracks in the walls. Pasula hugged herself but could not fend off the cold. She locked the door and buried herself under her quilt.

The clouds grew thicker and rolled savagely down the mountains like an avalanche. Biyari walked behind his dog, afraid of straying off the small path and falling into a ditch. One time he had fallen into a ditch and it took three days to recover from the cold he caught. It had been a terrible experience. He peeked through the window to see if Pasula was asleep. He went slowly and pushed open the door but found the bedroom door locked. He stretched out on the bench and was joined by his dog.

Biyari couldn't sleep. He kept thinking about avalanches and the icy chill.

Wasn't that when the animals came down the mountain? He made up his mind to go hunting up on the mountain the next day. He felt suffocated and discouraged at home. He closed his eyes and thought about what he had to take with him hunting—the bullets were in the storeroom, wire, bag, and matches. Once he had prepared all of these things in his mind, he fell asleep.

Before dawn the clouds and fog gradually withdrew from the valley as if they feared being blamed for the cold of the night. Here and there a rooster could be heard crowing. Men chopping wood and barking dogs could also be heard before the sun rose. Fires had already been lit in a number of houses and black smoke could be seen rising from the chimneys. No one thought of the black smoke as pollution; it was believed that smoke rose to become clouds. Pasula sat by the stove making a fire with dry bamboo and charcoal in which to roast purple sweet potatoes. She did not want to wake Biyari, who was sleeping on the bench. The flames grew hotter. But as she was turning the nearly blackened sweet potatoes, the steam from the rice cooker sent the lid clattering to the floor, waking Biyari and his dog with a start.

"Yifan, go to the kitchen to see if a rat is eating our leftovers."

"Come here, Yifan, it's me. So you're going to be mean to me too!"

"Pasula, you're already up. I'm going up the mountain today. Last night I had a dream, and hunter's dreams always come true. It was just like the *bahyu* omens my father believed in. Will you get rice and salt ready for me? I'll probably spend two nights in the forest." Biyari stood behind Yifan and spoke to Pasula, who was about to faint from fear.

"Forget it. Don't bring up your dreams. Your ancestors never send you a dream about having kids."

Biyari packed the things he needed himself. Pasula removed a cooked sweet potato and blew on it as she tossed it from hand to hand.

"Take this to eat. I hope you catch a mountain deer and sell it to the Hakka shopkeeper at the foot of the mountain. The walls of the house need patching—if it can't be done this spring, I'm going back to my father's house. Don't say I didn't warn you."

He smiled coldly. He slung his knapsack over his right shoulder and put Yifan on the gas tank of his motorcycle. He started his motorcycle and rode away.

Early mornings in December were cold. The tree leaves were yellow, adding some color to the mountain slopes. From the lower slopes to the peak, the colors changed from black, to brown, and finally to white, just like in a painting, but one lacking a neat and uniform design. Instead it was rather messy but, still, it delighted the settlement and everyone enjoyed the beautiful composition. The ground was parched and cracked. The villagers had been hoping for rain for a long time. They didn't care if the weather was cold, they just wanted the clouds to darken and break the drought. The pink eastern sky gradually turned white. Biyari shuttled across the small roads. He was a big man and had a beard much like a field allowed to go wild by a lazy farmer. His eyes were set deep and wide apart, forming to dark ravines on either side of the bridge of his nose. His eyebrows were thick and bushy and shifted as his expression changed, but more often than not he looked sad. He was the only boy among seven sisters in his family and had received the most nutrition from his mom and had very strong arms. He lived alone now with his wife. Wearing a long-sleeved blue sweater and patched green pants and yellow rain boots, he disregarded the cold as he sped along.

Biyari took a deep breath, inhaling the moist air. Crossing the suspension bridge, he left the settlement. Happily, he increased speed, his motorbike jumping along the rocky road. He purposely sped over the uneven ground and, when his front tire left the ground, he stood up. Yifan sat perched precariously on the gas tank but was happy all the same.

He pulled up at a small store run by a Hakka couple. There wasn't much in the dusty case, but wine and betel nuts were always there to be had.

"Give me two bottles of rice wine and three packs of betel nuts," said Biyari in the Hakka dialect.

"What do you want? Turn off your engine and tell me," said the owner, poking his head and wrinkled neck out the door, much like a tortoise, to timidly eye Biyari.

"Two bottles of rice wine and three packs of betel nuts. Did you hear me?"

"OK. Why don't you buy some Gaoliang wine, I've got some Quemoy Gaoliang. I like it myself—rice wine is too plain."

"Not for me. The strong stuff is for those who are dying. Keep it and sell it to those sad people to wash away their suffering. I just want plain old rice wine. Here's thirty yuan." Biyari felt around in his pockets. Fortunately he had the thirty yuan.

Before starting out again he checked his bag for salt, matches, rice wine, and betel nuts. Then he nodded his head, approving of his own prudence and satisfied with the things that would keep him alive in the forest. He felt alive, strong, and happy as he started his engine again.

Prior to the seasonal frost the rice had been put in the granary and all the young people had left the mountains in search of temporary work to buy things to keep them warm in the winter. For years Biyari had stuck to his father's idea that one should be either a farmer or a hunter. He knew that it was on account of their unwavering adherence to this principle that he never had a pleasant winter. He never forgot his chapped, broken skin, and he hated his father even more when he recalled how his friends played among the stones on the grassy fields in their tennis shoes. At the end of autumn he worked hard to collect firewood because winter would find the whole family huddled with their eyes closed around the smoking stove just to stay warm. Even though they had wild boar and flying squirrel to eat, he would always sit at the window looking outside. He once had an idea about getting back at his father when he was old and helpless. He would go hunting all winter and never worry about having enough firewood in the house. But he never got the chance.

The year before last, Pasula wanted him to save money to buy some things for the baby who was expected in the winter. He got a temporary job as a packer in a shipping company. He worked for five days but was laid off because the boss wanted to save money. Biyari was angry because he was strong and worked hard. When he left he forgot a pair of pants and the eight hundred yuan in wages. Since then he had never forgotten his father's deathbed words: he was destined to be a farmer or a hunter.

The sun had risen to forty-five degrees. In the forest, two thousand meters above sea level, warmth was not determined by latitude. Whenever he passed through the shade, he would speed up.

"Are you cold, Yifan? You won't be lonely in the forest—every sound will stir your wild nature. Oh, Biyari, will you regret leaving that foolish woman at home alone? Poor Pasula," he shouted to the valley. That's what he liked to do. Or sing songs he made up to curse at others or take a leak or fart down the mountain. He insulted all his enemies and hate vanished.

There wasn't a trace of anyone along the road, just tall cypress trees. He felt good. Human beings disgusted him, especially women. He stopped by a dilapidated workers hut that seemed to cower at the side of the road. The sheet metal roofing had long since rusted, and while the cypress-log walls still appeared strong enough to support the roof and to keep out the rain, they didn't look like they would keep out the cold. Biyari's dog hopped down off the motorbike and went to investigate the inside of the hut—perhaps there was a wild boar inside hiding from the cold. A continuous gurgling trickle of water could be heard nearby—the water ran in a course as thick as Biyari's calf. The spring water flowed through the snow, making it cold and sweet. Biyari plucked a taro leaf and shaped it into a funnel-shaped cup to dip up some water to drink. Then he sat down in the middle of the road to soak up the sun.

The sun shone directly above the forest. Biyari sat quietly. He reached into his knapsack and felt around until he felt a bottle. Warmth surged through his chest. He took the bottle out of his bag and removed the cap with his teeth. Before the cap hit the ground, the wine was already flowing down his gullet.

"No, I can't drink too much. I won't get drunk, but it will make me hungry," said Biyari to Yifan.

He took another swig, swished the wine all around in his mouth, and then swallowed. He took another swig before capping the bottle. The continuous warmth fired him—his ears gradually turned red and his eyes even redder. From his neck up he showed signs that he had been drinking—no wonder he had never been able to hide it from his woman.

Yifan suddenly began to bark and ran forward.

Biyari's face showed a hunter's caution, which is not the same as the terror or anxiety one experiences when facing death, but rather the fear that one is perhaps not fully prepared to face an attack. With a nimble jump, he went after Yifan, who stood by the roadside barking at the forest. It was just a red turtledove.

"Stop it, Yifan. Shooting a red turtledove is bad luck for a hunter. We have to cross this peak by noon if we are going to get to the cave before nightfall."

He called his dog and walked back briskly, feeling very light. He was pleased with his own speed and Yifan's alertness. He believed there was no hunter as smart, certainly not in his village. He jumped to avoid a mud puddle but slipped on some wet green moss. If he hadn't luckily caught himself with his left hand, he would have tumbled in the mud like a child. He hurriedly straightened himself up and, taking a look around as if afraid someone had seen him, he smacked the mud from his left hand. He quietly returned to his motorcycle, fearful that he might have broken a hunter's taboo. If, for example, he had fallen, he might just as well have called off the hunt, because he would never catch anything regardless of how many days he spent in the forest.

As he navigated the steep, winding road, the air grew colder and the ground hard with ice. It seemed to be sleeting and the cold moist air turned Biyari's cheeks all red. His whole body shivered as he pulled his clothes tight. The mountaintop off to his right was covered with snow; the moisture-laden clouds produced more snowflakes. After twenty-five switchbacks up the mountain, the sunlight no longer penetrated. Biyari turned on his headlight and slowed down. He could see what was left of the snow that had fallen the night before by the roadside; the road was wet with melted snow, making it difficult to drive. His hands never stopped trembling.

Crossing the industrial road at three thousand meters, he turned off on a mountain road headed west. The sun was already there waiting. He started to descend, which proved even more difficult than the ascent but faster. He passed a police checkpoint and saw that no one was around so he boldly sneaked by. The checkpoint had been set up to catch people illegally removing timber. After hunting was banned, the checkpoint was no longer a rest stop for hunters. The attitude of the police changed: they no longer greeted the hunters passing by. This puzzled the hunters. Biyari pulled off to the side of the road; two other motorcycles were already parked there.

Biyari took stock of the things in his bag. The road led directly down into a valley so he had to be especially careful. He entered a hunting trail and scanned the bamboo grove, the underbrush, and the black bark of the pine trees that looked more like telephone poles. Ten years before a huge forest fire had decimated the forest here. It was now brush land. Only the burned and blackened tree trunks indicated that a forest once stood there. The older hunters told the young ones that after the Forestry Bureau had cut the expensive timber a fire had been set and the area later replanted. The young hunters couldn't believe that the Forestry Bureau could be so foolish, but they were certain it hadn't been the hunters who had caused the fire. They knew life in the forest accounted for half the life on earth, most of which was closely bound up with the hunters. Biyari knew that his father would never have done such a stupid thing.

He whistled as he jogged; occasionally he would break into a mountain song. His quick and light footsteps maintained a fixed rhythm. He stopped below a huge boulder—it was the only cool, shady place amid the brush. From a crevice in the rock he pulled a wine bottle that was half full of water. There was no spring water in the brush, but there was always dripping dew—the water in the bottle was that accumulated night after night.

He took two swigs and glimpsed some larvae wriggling in the bottle, but pretended not to notice them. Those two swigs would help him cross the brush land. He sat down to cool off in the mountain breeze, took Yifan by two legs, and then lay down out of the sun.

"Human beings are bad, but women are the worst. Women are less loyal and obedient than you, Yifan. Of course I can't marry you, but I want to always be with you," he said, scratching the dog's head.

"But I am still interested in women. I prefer the sentimental ones and hate cheerful ones. Pasula is never concerned about me when I leave the house. Once I swallowed a betel nut and she rolled her eyes and said that it would come out in the shit hole the next day. It would be great if women were like the forest—quiet and solemn. From inside and from outside, but especially from above, the beauty of the forest is harmonious and green, just like the Garden of Eden mentioned by the minister in his sermons. But Pasula is more like maple leaves that turn red in autumn and lose all their charm in winter," thought Biyari to himself.

He then lowered his head and mumbled to himself: "If I really get fed up with that woman of mine, I still have the forest."

Yifan suddenly awoke with a start and dashed headlong down the slope. Biyari also jumped up. Yifan was scared of snakes, and Biyari thought that a snake had appeared nearby. Before he could figure out what was happening, he saw a man approaching up the slope with long strides. His gait was unusual and exaggerated. Biyari thought he was good looking and probably had a lot of women coming after him. His fleshy chest made him look soft so he had to be tender hearted. Biyari stared at him and thought that his thin legs made him look young but that his haggard expression made him look like an old veteran road worker.

"Hey, peace. Oh, it's Biyari, the great hunter." Yifan accompanied the man.

"Peace, Luka. Have you stopped breathing? I can't hear you huffing and puffing, Chief of the Forest. My Yifan is panting. Your knapsack must be filled with meat." Biyari looked out of the corners of his eyes at Luka's knapsack, which appeared to be empty.

"Did Pasula throw another fit? Poor Biyari. Can't those big chest muscles of yours tame her? You shouldn't have married her."

"Luka, don't change the subject from your bag. Are you trying to test the curses of my ancestors? The hunter walking uphill should share his meat with the hunter walking downhill. You ought to know my grandmother's story. Five hunters personally delivered meat to her door to remove the curses from themselves."

"All I've got in my bag is one squirrel. It's only about a year old so it's too small to divide. Even if I share it with you, it wouldn't be enough to feed your dog. Forget it."

"Did you have any dreams before coming to the forest? Were there any *bahayu* in your dreams? I can explain why the hunt has been so embarrassing."

"I dreamed that we were having a banquet and my people were feasting and drinking. We were eating food out of china dishes like city people and drinking brightly colored wine. That was a good dream, so I thought I'd catch several deer."

"People should not call you Forest Chief. The things in your head aren't those of a forest chief. Touch your ears and tell me, are they the same shape? They look like shelf fungus growing on rotten wood—soft and weak."

Biyari took another swig of water and continued: "Feasting and drinking, and in the city, how could you serve game on china dishes? That's disrespectful."

"Recently, I've been down on my luck. Perhaps . . . "

"For a quick hunter, luck doesn't matter!"

Maybe on this hunting trip you'll be like me—you'll go home exhausted with an empty bag. There's nothing in the forest." Luka was livid at being scorned by Biyari and cursed him in his heart.

"Your curses are of no use, they don't scare me. Ever since I was small I followed my father and his hunting gun all over. Never once was his bag empty. Wild animals don't have their tubes tied on account of family planning, so you don't have to curse me. Let me take a look at your squirrel."

Luka knew that Biyari wouldn't let him off. He couldn't escape his clutches so he put down his bag and let him have a look.

"Luka, are you going to take that little thing home? If we eat it in the forest, that will save you from taking it home to be a laughingstock of the village. You can say you went to the forest for fun."

"It's for the kids to eat so it doesn't have to be a big one."

"It's smaller than you said before. Forget it, I don't want my share."

Luka was so upset he was on the verge of tears. He knew Biyari was a famous hunter in the tribe and he didn't want to argue about it.

"I have to go, Biyari. I don't have time to argue with you. We'll see." Luka quickly picked up his bag and left resentfully.

Biyari rubbed his cheeks as he watched Luka's swaying backside. My face is not hot; I didn't get angry. The biggest taboo for a hunter is to let others find out he didn't have any luck hunting. I didn't do it on purpose—he was the only good person I met this morning. I hope I didn't hurt him. Maybe we can sit down and split a bottle of wine and sing about the forest and talk about the disgusting people on the flatlands, swear about those brown-skinned government workers and how unbending they have become.

"Hey, Luka, tell my woman that I'll bring back a big hunk of meat," shouted Biyari. But Luka didn't turn around.

Biyari stood there for a long time watching as Luka gradually disappeared in the thick brush. Biyari gathered up his things and went on his way, walking more slowly.

Through the brush, the firs, and the maples Biyari never noticed the bright red maple leaves or the sound of the fallen leaves underfoot. Not once did he turn to look back. The sun had already set by the time Biyari reached the cave. He took off his knapsack and sat down on a stone, panting.

"I'll forgive myself and—ha, ha—have some fun tonight." With both hands he pulled the corners of his mouth into a smile. He wished he had a mirror so he could adjust his smile. Night was falling in the forest. He stood up and took the things out of his knapsack and examined them. Seeing that everything was as it should be, he started polishing his previously hidden gun and removing the ants that had hibernated in the barrel during the winter. After checking his gun, he slipped on his cartridge belt and then got up to scout around the valley.

The scaly tailed squirrels were active in the evening, and the valley was their playground. After about an hour of crisscrossing the valley, Biyari heard the grunting of a wild boar at least a kilometer away. The flying squirrels barked vigorously and continuously as they skimmed low on the air. Biyari was never able to get off a shot.

Biyari was exhausted and his limbs felt heavy. He slowed his pace. His legs ached, his mind wandered, and his head hurt. Sometimes he stumbled backward; his stomach was cramped, and he felt like vomiting but automatically choked it back. His mouth was dry and he kept trying to moisten his lips with his tongue. A gust of cold wind seemed to penetrate his chest and his stomach contracted. Grasping his rifle angrily, he thought that even one flying squirrel would be enough.

He stopped on a two-square meter piece of flat ground and watched the waving fir limbs. He could see Pasula roasting sweet potatoes. He put down his rifle and thought that if he had only begged some sweet potatoes from her he could gather some wood and warm them himself and he wouldn't be suffering now.

"Yifan, let's not think of Pasula rolling hot sweet potatoes in her hands. I refuse to tell myself that it would have been better to stay at home," he said to his dog, clenching his teeth.

Biyari got up and continued to scout the forest, mumbling to himself, all stealth gone. Hungry, he lost control and swore, "Bastards, my God. Come out of your holes; don't hide. The forest is shamed by a hunter starving to death."

Somehow, Biyari reached the river. He strode to the river's edge, fell and thrust his mouth into the river to drink. The water was ice cold and hurt his rotten front teeth. Under the moonlight he found a small tributary stream. He cut some tree branches and with leaves and dirt blocked the flow of the water. In less than five minutes the slippery river stones began to appear amid puddles of water. Casually, Biyari caught ten palm-sized fish. He couldn't see clearly what kind, but all fish in the forest were edible.

Biyari no longer felt cold. Nearby was a cave with a hot spring that the hunters referred to as their "public bath". By the water he built a fire on which to roast the fish. The moon moved gradually overhead. Biyari ate his fill and not even the bones or heads of the fish remained.

Sabu'eryisi'ang birds cried continuously with a flurry of sharp, high-pitched notes that sometimes sounded like a truck horn. They started moving from the treetops down into the valley. Before the moonlight stopped shining brightly in the valley they had fled, one by one, back into the caves or holes in the trees. They liked to live in caves and like human beings they lacked a sense of security.

The sulfur vapors irritated Biyari's nose and the smoke from the fire bothered his eyes. With eyes tearing, Biyari extinguished the fire and quietly waited for the mountain deer to come down and drink. Suddenly a black shadow glided over his head and seemed about to land on him. He looked up to see the star-filled sky. It had been nothing but a cloud that had blocked the moon. He pulled in his chin and tried hard to recall if there had been a sign in his dream. He had been busy all day and hadn't given it any thought. He firmly believed that, without a dream to rely on, a person was like a blind man walking in the forest. He put down his rifle, set the safety, and threw on a blanket to keep the powder dry from the dew.

The steam from the hot spring formed a thin mist in the forest. The night wind blew, twisting the mist into a whirlpool in which the moon tossed and spun. The woods became ever more misty. Biyari took off his rain boots, coat, and pants. He weighted them down with some rocks then cupped some water in his hands and threw it on his chest and forehead. He patted his brown chest causing his whole body to tremble. His strong body pleased him and he quickly slipped into the hot spring.

"Come, Yifan! Let's soak away the bad luck of today. It's been a hard day and we can wash away the fatigue and the sweat," Biyari called. But the dog, having eaten its fill, was fast asleep.

Biyari made his way to the deepest spot, where the water came halfway up his back. He washed the smell of fish from his hands, scrubbed his neck and muscular chest, and rubbed his entire body. Then he found a boulder the size of a chair and sat down to gauge the time by the moon.

Biyari had been born in the twelfth month according to the Bunun calendar. It was the month of the Ear-shooting Festival when the adult men took the boys to practice archery by the light of the moon shooting at boar ears hung on a tree. Suddenly he recalled a story his father had told him here.

> A long time ago there was in the tribal village a man by the name of Tuobasi Tasikabinari. One day when he went off to work, he left his baby in the shade of a tree. Returning after work, he found that the baby had dried out and looked like a wild-grape raisin—its body all black and wrinkled. At that time there were two suns in the sky. He swore loudly to the suns that he would be revenged if it killed him. Before he set off to take his vengeance, he planted an orange tree in front of his house and left his young wife at home. He took his bow and set off for the mountaintop nearest the suns. Many winters passed and the village had no idea what had become of him, but his wife remained loyal to him. One morning

> the sky seemed softer—Tuobasi had shot down one of the suns, which became the moon of today. Before Tuobasi set off, the moon said to him: "Hence forward, human beings will mark time by the moon." When Tuobasi returned to the village, the orange tree bore fruit. He became a man of courage admired by his people; his wife became a woman who was praised by his people.

"What a dignified name!" Biyari thought. If Pasula hadn't miscarried, the baby, boy or girl, would have been named Tuobasi.

The moon was already going down the slope. Hunched over, Biyari no longer wished to think about the story. By this time the wild animals had had their fun and were heading back to their nests and caves to rest. Biyari hurriedly jumped out of the water, put on his clothes, and walked back to the cave and started a new fire. He warmed himself and bedded down very early.

In the morning Biyari woke up and brushed the dew—which the sun had not yet dried—from his hair. He gathered some dry leaves and twigs and placed them on the coals of the previous night's fire. He still had three fish. As he roasted the fish he wondered if Pasula was cold all alone under the covers. He wondered whether she thought of how he had slept. He was determined to get a boar or muntjac to make her happy.

A dry leaf floated down and fell into the fire. Before he could tell what kind of leaf it was, half of it had been consumed by the flames, the other half was unrecognizable. He looked up and saw a female monkey passing overhead. He didn't so much as move a muscle. The fish in hand lessened his desire for monkey meat. He continued roasting the fish.

He ate two fish and threw the heads to Yifan. Then he checked his knapsack and discovered that his sweat had dissolved half the salt he had wrapped in paper. He walked back to the cave and took a handful of salt he had stashed in the cave and, after packing his things, he picked up his gun and entered the forest.

It had been a dry winter, but it had been sleeting on the peak. Stones were poking through the surface of the river so Biyari didn't have to take off his pants. He hopped from one stone to the next to cross the river. Yifan, on the other hand, swam across to the other side. He and Yifan crossed another brushy area and a valley before they entered virgin forest. This was Biyari's hunting ground. It included three peaks, the source of a river, and a shared hot spring. There was a rule by gun that no one could enter another's hunting ground. Actually, the hunters had to obey this rule because each hunting ground was filled with various traps and anyone who entered risked being captured like an animal.

Yifan was sniffing fresh tracks. Biyari squatted to take a look and determined that it was a solitary muntjac about five kilos in weight that had passed the night before. He followed the tracks for only about five meters, after which the tracks had been erased by wild boars. The tracks apparently disappeared into a willow grove. Biyari went into the grove. The ground was covered with stones; farther on was a broad open space of blackish mud. There were even more footprints and the droppings of muntjacs and wild boars. In a hollowing that resembled a nest, Biyari found some brown fur and some droppings. He picked up some of the fur and smelled it.

"Yifan, hurry! A deer spent the night here. Look, you can see its tracks."

The scattered tracks sent Yifan around in circles and he couldn't decide which way to go. They had to leave the grove.

He was tired and thirsty. Stepping over a huge fallen tree trunk, he didn't know what kind of tree it was because the leaves and branches had long since rotted away. It was covered with yellowish brown *lingzhi* fungus. Biyari sat down on one and, just as he was lowering his gun, Yifan began barking in the grass.

Twenty meters away, Biyari readied his rifle, but the grass was still. He was poised to shoot, every nerve sharpened. He smelled a strange odor, but it wasn't the rotting tree. He hurried into the grass and discovered a dead fox, its mouth tightly closed. It probably didn't make a sound before it died, preferring to die in a trap rather than under the talons of a hawk.

He knew that the fox was filled with maggots. He skillfully slit its belly and without looking very closely, removed the animal's guts and tossed them in the grass. He put the cleaned fox into his knapsack. It was already high noon.

Farther on lay a plantation forest. He told Yifan not to enter because he knew there would be no tracks. He decided to continue his search for game on another peak.

It was gradually getting hot and the sunlight fell directly to the earth in vertical rays straight as fir trees. Biyari could no longer see the shadow of his own head. He took off his knapsack and rested in the shade of a zelkova tree. He had no lunch and no appetite. He picked up two small stones and rolled them in his hand.

He hadn't sighted a living animal all day and blamed the scarcity on the shrinking forest. In the not-to-distant future he could see the forest filled with the sound of people and vehicles; there wouldn't be a trace of any animals and hunters would disappear. The forest had been his refuge, his consolation. Biyari felt lonely and uneasy about the future of the forest. Well-off government employees should be brought to the forest to probe its secrets. Perhaps they were afraid of its mysteries the way a boss fears his employees growing healthy, wealthy, and wise. They should come and listen to the birds and beasts and the wind and falling leaves; they should go to the valley to see the magnificent cliffs; they should take off their shoes and put their feet in the water and watch the fish swimming in unpolluted water, unafraid of people. They would unravel the enigma of the forest and, like sinners condemned to hell, they would regret their previous lack of understanding in seeing the forest as nothing but a source of timber.

He gradually entered a state beyond himself, the way he did after drinking a bottle of rice wine. If a bear came, he wouldn't have realized his difficult situation until he found himself down the bear's gullet. He made an effort to focus, but, engulfed as he was by the silence of the place, the warmth of the sunlight, and the relaxing shade, he was soon hypnotized by the magic of the forest.

The sun quickly passed over the big trees, moving from the soles of his feet to his face. The strong light woke him; he mistook the sun's rays for ants walking on his eyelashes. Standing up, he felt weak; then he remembered that medicine to cure fatigue, depression, and other ailments: rice wine. He gulped down what was left of the previous day's wine.

He felt strengthened, his pulse quickened, and his eyes were sharper. The wine had made him feel younger, leaving him happy and satisfied.

The valley became bleak and desolate in the afternoon. The wind soughed through the trees. The falling leaves and breaking branches made it hard for him to hear. He stepped lightly so as not to add to the noise. But he was disappointed because the wind whipped up even stronger. He made his way over an escarpment and a grassy meadow but still saw no game.

He entered the forest that was all one green blur. It was so dark that Biyari slowed his pace. He thought about Pasula as he walked; her beauty as she slept and her plump figure filled his mind, but even more beautiful was how she called him to bed each night and nearly crushed him beneath her.

The sun was going down as images of Pasula continued to fill Biyari's mind. Suddenly a goat scurried out of the forest and stood staring at him from a distance of thirty meters. He was startled by the appearance of the big animal. Yifan also was startled and paused. The goat took advantage of the situation and lit out and disappeared in the grass.

"Go get it, Yifan. What are you waiting for?"

Biyari shook his head and mumbled to himself: "What a pity, Pasula loves the small intestines of goats. I must bag something or Pasula will not love me and Luka might be waiting to make fun of me."

He returned with undivided attention. All he wanted was a goat to take home.

The wind blew through the valley, dispelling the heat. Dusk was approaching and he grew anxious. Down in the valley he followed the river upstream. Suddenly, at a distance of about fifty meters, he saw a long and narrow brown shape beyond some rocks. It had to be an animal because the speed and direction it was moving was different from the surrounding grass. He figured it was the tail of some animal. He fell to the ground and crawled forward. He released the safety on his gun. Yifan saw it too and was about to rush at it when Biyari commanded the dog to be still.

"Easy, easy. I don't want to miss this time," he said in a whisper.

He crept for about twenty meters. The animal started for the precipice, but, before it came fully into view, Biyari fired. The bullet struck the animal's forequarters. Its right leg hit the ground as if it were going to run off. Before it hit the ground Yifan had already rushed to grab it by the neck. Its four legs thrashed about and its eyes stared widely. It grew weaker and soon stopped struggling. It was a buck muntjac.

Biyari lifted his head proudly as he stroked his rifle. Great hunters don't rely on luck, he thought. He tugged the muntjac away from Yifan. He felt its weight and was proud to have bagged such a large, fat animal. He placed the muntjac in his bag and then began to sing a song about hunting muntjac as he hopped and skipped back to the cave.

Returning to the cave, he put a paper plug in the barrel, wrapped his rifle in a cloth bag, and buried it to keep the monkeys from messing with it. After taking stock of the contents of his knapsack, he started for home, happy and lighthearted.

That evening he camped under an old pine tree. His legs were tired, but he was in high spirits. He thought about how good the muntjac venison would be for Pasula's health. Since her miscarriage, she had lost a lot of weight and hadn't had any good food from the mountains. The muntjac would put some meat back on her bones. He cut some branches off the pine tree; by the light of the moon he could see the dripping resin. He lit a fire and curled up and went to sleep.

He slept very well, as if dead to the world. After he awoke he realized that he was in the mountains around the two thousand meter elevation.

He picked up his knapsack, urinated on the fire, extinguishing all embers, and then headed for the industrial road. The road was covered with a layer of ice, and he had to keep slowing his pace. His chest felt constricted and he felt dizzy, as if his brain wasn't getting enough oxygen. Sweat poured from his temples. His underwear and pants were soaked. It took him twenty minutes to go the last three hundred meters to where he had parked his motorcycle.

Biyari happily pulled his motorbike from the grass. The other bikes he saw when he arrived were gone. He tried unsuccessfully kick-starting the bike several times, but it was no use. He wiped the frost from the accelerator.

Then he began to suspect that Luka, who wasn't very happy when the met, might have done something. He tried three more times before the engine started. He picked up Yifan and placed him on the gas tank.

As he approached the checkpoint, an immaculately dressed policeman rushed out and lowered the roadblock.

Seeing the short policeman, Biyari trembled with fear. What did he want? Before he could figure out how to elude the policeman's questions, he reached the roadblock.

The policeman was about sixty years old. His white hair grew over his ears. He had small mean eyes, though the left one looked handsome. His eyebrows were fine and short and he had a surprisingly round nose. When the policeman breathed, he looked like a wild boar in search of something to eat. Biyari found this very amusing. He discovered that the policeman's skin was very white and so was in all likelihood not Taiwanese. The low bridge of his nose terrified Biyari.

"Hey, savage, What are you looking at? What are you up to? Are you a hunter or an arsonist?"

"I'm from Renlun settlement," said Biyari, raising his voice while suppressing his fear and clasping his two hands tightly together.

"What did you say? Your Mandarin stinks."

"I came to pick orchids and then had some fun in the forest. Why not open the roadblock? Please believe me."

"OK Mr. Brave Hunter. Come in and register. I'm not going to let a liar go."

The policeman's fat face took on a deprecatory air. He moved closer to let Biyari get a good look at his badge. He was a high-ranking bar-and-star guy in a new black and pressed uniform. He appeared to be a patrolman or of even higher rank. Casually he removed the key from Biyari's motorcycle and entered the low, dark building.

Biyari saw there was no escape. Shaking his head, he helplessly got off his bike and followed him in, nearly hitting his head on the low doorway.

There was no light on in the building, but there was an old-fashioned black police phone. It looked as if he had just eaten breakfast. On his desk were some notebooks and comic books. The four walls were bare save for a religious picture with an incense burner in front of it. Farther inside was his bedroom and a smoky kitchen.

"What are you looking at? Come in. What's your name?"

"Biyari."

"I'm warning you—don't fool around. I want your Chinese name."

"Oh. Quan Guosheng. I live in the Renlun settlement."

The policeman took down everything in a notebook.

"You know there are laws against hunting and they've been around a long time. And you, motherfucker, here you come bold as can be breaking the law," cursed the policeman as he approached his telephone.

"If you don't confess and try to hide anything, one call and you'll go straight to jail and you can sort it out there."

"Yeah, I went hunting, but I set a trap—I don't have a gun," said Biyari, his sweat giving way to a cold sweat down his back.

"You motherfucker, Did you ever go to school? Have you no shame? Tell the truth, what did you shoot with your rifle?" he asked raising his voice at seeing Biyari's bloodstained knapsack.

"How do you know I have a rifle? Did you hear it?"

"Of course I did. I could also tell from the sound that it was an unlicensed gun. Am I right?"

Biyari was scared to death. Recently, the head of the settlement had told them that there were gun control laws. He happened to notice some meat on a plate and figured it was probably Luka's flying squirrel. He wondered if Luka had told on him, but then he thought that Luka had been in the same boat and had bought his freedom with the flying squirrel. Biyari imagined he would break Luka's legs if he had played a trick on him.

"Hey, you mountain people are cruel by nature. The government takes care of you people so that you don't have a care. But you people are lazy and dirty and break the law. Don't you know what the law is? It would be better to lock all you hunters up to teach you a lesson."

Biyari yielded to fate—he was a hunter and couldn't tell a lie, so he simply kept his mouth shut. He just wanted to go home as soon as possible.

"I'm a nice guy. I can't bear to see the animals overhunted by you so I have to arrest you. It doesn't matter if you have a gun or not—you still stole from the forest. You might be just a thief, but the law does not allow thieves."

The cloud-mist gradually seeped into the room and the snow mounted outside. Seeing that he was silent, the policeman looked him over from head to foot. He was big and tall, at least a head taller than the policeman. He had long black hair and carried a knife at his waist. Looking at him, the policeman felt nervous and softened his tone.

"What was your motive for coming to the forest to hunt? You must have trouble. Down out of the mountains there is plenty of meat. But everyday I have to wait for the truck to come up the mountain to get fresh meat and fish," he said, pointing to the dry pork hanging outside.

"I'm not greedy. I had a fight with my wife. She looks down on me and laughs because I can't find work. That's why I came."

"OK. Now tell me what you've got in your bag."

"A fox and a muntjac and some other things. The muntjac is for my wife who had a miscarriage not long ago," said Biyari. He saw that he wasn't giving him a hard time any longer so he told him everything.

"I'd feel bad if I had to send you to jail. Let's do it this way: leave the game here, that way I can make a report to my superiors and you can leave without any trouble."

Seeing that the policeman wasn't going to pursue the matter and that he wanted to get home as soon as possible so that Pasula wouldn't go back to her father's, and because the silence of jail terrified him, Biyari had to hand the muntjac over to the policeman. He would keep the fox for himself.

"Take it, *duhui* (bandit)," Biyari cursed him in Bunun. He knew he would be back even without a gun. He took his keys and left quickly.

"Hey, Old Boy. Take it easy and turn over a new leaf. Don't call yourself a hunter . . . "

Tears of a Fledgling

KOWAN TALALL

THE SOMBER LIGHT of the waning moon shone coldly on the dark mountain ridge. The sad otherworldly light was as weak and dim as the light from a ten-watt bulb.

A strong mountain wind shook the bamboo grove, setting the dense stalks to grating against one another. It was as if the hair-raising spectacle of countless ravenous spirits threatened in the long shadows under the moonlight.

Bendi quickly crossed the deserted path overgrown with weeds and entered the dense forest. He was one of the *fulalisen* (a young man being trained in the *palakuwan* or lodge) of Dazhu Village, a young man who had just left home to enter the *palakuwan* to receive rigorous training. At fourteen or fifteen he was dark-complexioned, short and small and thin. His deep-set eyes were larger than usual because of the excessive fear he felt! An owl up in the branches hooted desolately. As the echo broke the profound silence of the night sky in all directions, Bendi felt an inexpressible fear and trembled all over.

"What am I afraid of? I'm a *fulalisen*."

Although he said this to reassure himself, he had an unusually firm grip on the haft of his knife. Unable to walk anymore, he wanted to cry.

"Now remember, to be a Paiwan *fulalisen* is not as easy as you imagine. You have to be able to take the responsibility upon yourself to transmit orders and fight at any moment. For that reason you must, from this day forward, get used to walking alone at night. This is basic training for your courage. Otherwise, oh, you've seen what can happen!"

The words of the *lamale* (head of the *palakuwan*) weighed like a heavy stone on his breast. No, that impression was too deep for him ever to forget.

He remembered how on the third day after the youngsters had entered the *palakuwan*, a *fulalisen*, who was a year older, had disobeyed the orders of a *makazhufeng*, a higher-ranking member of the *pallkuwan*. The *lamale* had sentence him to *feinaiyoule*, a punishment reserved by the Paiwan people for the most serious crimes. Without the approval of the *maisaisaijilang*, it wasn't something to be carried out lightly. The youngsters had never seen such a harsh penalty (in most cases, to protect the name of the accused, the punishment was carried out in secret). Thus when they were assembled in the *kalasuotang*, or auditorium, to observe the punishment, they were filled with fear and dread.

It wasn't long before their brother who was to be punished was stripped naked save for a t-shaped cloth to cover his private parts. A thick "carpet" of broad, hairy *feiyoule* or nettle leaves was spread on the ground. It was so awful looking that it raised goose bumps. The *lamale* entered, his face solemn, and was led by the *makazhufeng* to sit in a high seat that had been prepared.

"Listen, all of you. The *palakuwan* teaches discipline, stressing obedience among ranks. Reasonable or not, the words of someone of higher rank are the same as an order. You are not allowed to disobey. If you have a legitimate gripe, fulfill your duty, then lodge a complaint with those in charge, otherwise disobedience will become the norm. Kabi!"

"Present!"

"Administer the punishment!"

"Yes, *Lamale*!"

After receiving his orders, Kabi in turn ordered the one who had been sentenced to lie down on the "carpet". He suffered the stings in silence, his eyes tightly shut, but his tears streaming out of the corners of his eyes. He writhed continuously and couldn't scratch himself because both his hands had been tied behind his back limiting his movements. His face twisted, all he could do was look at the ceiling.

Bendi stood to one side and watched, stupefied. He looked upon the fellow with compassion but was prohibited by the rules from helping him. Bendi realized that this strange and painful *feinaiyoule* punishment was not the sort of thing most people could take. Someone as thin and weak as himself, for example, would collapse at once. He began to worry about his future.

"Croooooak!"

Suddenly a loud roar brought him back from memory to reality. Bendi retreated several steps and pulled out the knife at his waist. A huge eagle flapped its heavy wings and flew over his head.

"That was close."

He rubbed his chest as he spoke, still fearful. Then he lean against a tree and panted. Then he thought he saw something moving vaguely on the tree opposite to where he was standing.

"Now what could that be?"

"Is it a bird, or what?"

"Could it be a ghost?"

"A ghost!"

"Wa—mazhziyagen, Yina—"

Wa! Help! Help! Mom!

At that moment he imagined the twisted face of a person who had hanged himself, his tongue hanging out and his protruding eyes. He seemed to see that vague shape approach. Staring straight ahead, Bendi looked on frightened and helpless. He wanted to shout but couldn't. His head felt as big as a dipper, his heart weak and his legs without strength. He felt dizzy and swayed. He felt like he was going to fall.

"Don't worry, child. Don't be afraid. This *bafuluogemen* can drive away ghosts and hail spirits. Hang on to it and keep it close at all times. Now go!"

He didn't know how long it took to overcome the fear in his heart. He recalled his mother's kind exhortations and the *bafuluogemen* she had given him right before he left, which consisted of a small bag commonly called *aliyuan*, meaning "friend" by the Paiwan, in which was placed two sliced-open betel nuts. Inserted between the betel nuts were pieces of steel and a string of pearls. For all these objects the *fuligao*, or shamaness, had sought the blessings of *adawucimasi*, the god of the sun. They were capable of protecting a person and warding off evil.

He carefully took the bag out of his undershirt where it hung at his chest. Then he mumbled words asking it to give him courage. It was very effective; in a matter of minutes his fear had utterly disappeared.

"*Chaye* . . . " (an expletive meaning "shit").

He carefully reexamined the moving shadowy form and, when he saw that it wasn't a ghost but rather some dry grass, he couldn't help swearing. He sighed softly, wiped his tears away, and sheathed his knife. Then filled with what was left of his courage he set off cautiously with his *bafuluogemen* firmly in hand.

He passed through the forest and over a small hill and walked south for about fifteen minutes before he arrived at a *linaiwule*, a solitary tree or stone for comforting those who died accidental deaths and for marking the grave of the deceased. The feeling of fear was more palpable at this place than in the forest. But the land around the *linaiwule* had all been given over to cultivation, which also lessened the ill feelings. So he boldly stepped forward to the boulder and in accordance with the instructions of the *lamale*, he picked up the proof—a block of wood—that had been prepared that day by the *malakazhufeng* and started to turn back.

"Good! You are very brave!"

"Biya!"

"Here!"

"Take our little brother here to the back to rest."

"Yes, *Lamale.*

Such was the praise he received from the *lamale* upon his return. Bendi was thinking, "Thank you, beloved *lamale*, for your praise and for the rare smile on your face. But I beg you don't torture me again this way." Of course that was only what he was thinking—he would never dare open his mouth and say such a thing.

Ginger Road

BADAI

"GENTLY, GENTLY!"

"Looks like you had a serious fall!"

"The last time I fell down the slope it wasn't so serious!"

"It's age. You should act your age!"

"What do you mean age? I can still shoulder a hundred *jin*. How many young people in the village can do that?" muttered Luben hunched over on a bench.

Yidai, his wife, helped him apply a capsicum plaster that had been purchased a few days before in the pharmacy at the base of the mountain to his lower back. She also scolded Luben for not being more careful.

Actually there are things for which no one is to blame, especially when age is involved.

Luben was close to sixty, and he went up the mountain all year round to do odd jobs for his employer. When there was no work, he looked after the fields of ginger and chayotes in the mountains.

He had four sons. The oldest had done his two years of military service and was now unemployed. He said he was going to go west to make a living, but there had been no news. He had had little education and couldn't hope for more than learning a handicraft of some sort, and he would never expect his oldest son to make a lot of money to support the family.

His second son was doing his military service on Quemoy. Recently, when the village song and dance troupe had visited the island, he entrusted two bottles of Gaoliang wine and some cash to a troupe member to give to his father to satisfy a craving for good food and drink. Luben had brooded.

Three and four were not planned for. One was in junior high school and one in primary school. Besides eating and spending money and working occasionally during vacations, they weren't much help. Fortunately, heaven had given him a strong body and over the years he had relied on odd jobs and mountain crops to support his family. Just a few days earlier, when he was taking the mountain path to the ginger field with his wife Yidai, he had slipped on some loose stones and fallen and twisted his back. The feeling that age was catching up with him left him sad.

"The ginger should be dug up!" said Luben as if speaking to himself, looking at the yellowing leaves in the field.

"Has Ni'en been here?"

"Everyday I go up and down the mountain with you. How should I know if Ni'en has been here?" said Yidai angrily.

"Should've been here." Luben took no notice of Yidai's protests and bent over the withered leaves, both cheeks in his hands.

March was a beautiful month, especially in the big 869 Puyuma Tribal Region in eastern Taiwan. Patches of light green were mixed in the jade green vista. It looked as if someone had carelessly let some water drip on a watercolor painting, then picked it up off the table and blown on it to dry it, leaving pale stains. One need only walk into the mountains amid the jade green to discover that those patches were actually flowers that had lain dormant through the winter and were now blossoming as if there were no tomorrow. There was a yellowish patch and a bluish one and one where red was mixed with white. Bees and butterflies buzzed and flitted all around. The entire mountainous region was an incomparable display of vitality at the awakening of spring.

Ginger is a mountain crop that is harvested in March. Normally, farmers in the mountains plant ginger in March and cultivate it for one year. In October the leaves and stems begin to yellow and stay that way until March, when the plants start to sprout. Only the fat, firm rhizomes wait just below the surface. It is at this time that the farmers dig up the ginger and sell it and plant the new sprouts. The buyers take charge of the whole show, allocating work, and reselling it for a profit similar to what the farmers made. During the harvest season the villagers do odd jobs to make extra money.

That night Ni'en arrived.

"Have you eaten?" asked Ni'en in his broken Puyuma, stepping into their house. He brought his wife with him and they are greeted by the barking of the family's big black dog Guluo.

"I must trouble you!" he says before sitting down. "Will you let me take your ginger off your hands this year? It must be very nice. How about it?" asked Ni'en very politely in Mandarin interspersed with Taiwanese to get an answer from Luben.

"Fine. The ginger this year looks really nice. You can take a look," said

Luben in his Puyuma-accented Mandarin so that the conversation was not monopolized totally by Ni'en in his Taiwan-Manadarin.

"Where do you want to dig first?"

"The same as last year—on the back side of the mountain," said Ni'en decisively, as if he had practiced many times.

Luben grumbled to himself. He had two plots of ginger, both about the same size—one on his side of the mountain and one on the back side that actually belonged to his sister's overweight husband. Because he could no longer cultivate it, he had turned it over to Luben in exchange for thirty days of work. The soil on the other side of the mountain was ideal for growing ginger—every year the ginger grown there was large, plump, and firm and brought an especially good price. The only problem was that the plot was far from the collection point, the path winding with a lot of ups and downs. Normally it didn't bother him, but since he had twisted his back, the mere thought of it made him wince.

"We can pay a little more in wages this year," added Ni'en's wife when she saw him hesitate.

"Heck, I'm not worried about that!" replied Luben, feeling insulted and peeved.

"You'd best find some people to help," interposed Ni'en, "the price of fresh ginger this year is pretty good. The factory has promised you a good price and higher wages. Twelve hundred for a male digger, nine hundred for a female picker, and eleven hundred for a transporter to carry it down the mountain. The work is hard, and, though I don't have a lot of money, I want to give you a little extra."

"Such a great favor," he said, scarcely able to get a word in edgewise amid Ni'en's Taiwan-Mandarin.

Luben calculated for a moment and saw that the wages were indeed better than last year's. If he worked a little harder, he could buy some more bullets and other things. It had been a long time since he hunted flying squirrel with his fellow villagers. Ni'en hadn't said exactly how much the factory was going to pay, but he knew Ni'en would shortchange him. Spoken or unspoken, the result was always the same.

"How many would be best?" asked Luben politely.

"Oh, there's no need to be polite. You decide. I'll spring for lunch tomorrow when you repair the path."

They chatted for a while, and Ni'en departed after he left the money for lunch the following day.

Luben stood and watched Ni'en and his wife depart. He was thankful to them for providing a few opportunities each year so that they could improve their lives.

"Stop looking. If you want a mistress, you'd have to have his long neck too," said Yidai behind him.

"What nonsense are you talking now?"

Ni'en was a Taiwanese. He was tall and thin and had a really long neck. He had married two sisters and lived in a village at the foot of the mountain. In addition to the crops he planted on the slopes of the mountain, he also handled the selling of the crops of the tribespeople. All the men of the village found his having two wives interesting. As a result, the women of the village used his "long neck" to taunt the men.

"Ni'en" meant "neck" in Puyuma.

Luben really had no opinion of him, but some people in the village regarded him as a little stingy. He liked to shortchange people and would haggle over a few cents. But there was no winning because he was the only outsider to handle the sale of the villager's crops and offer them odd jobs.

Luben's third son, Budan, who was in junior high, really disliked him. Every time he worked for him he was shortchanged. So, whenever he was out of school, he would steal the fruit planted around Ni'en's house as payback. Or else he would steal Ni'en's wives' panties that were drying on the fence and put them on the head of Ni'en's big yellow dog, making it into a batman he could play with. Strangely, Ni'en's big yellow dog also had a long neck. It was good-tempered and let the kids fool around. When his big yellow dog would run barking into his house, Ni'en would immediately come storming out, swearing a blue streak:

"Fuck your mother, you rotten little shit. Fuck your father . . . "

Only then would Budan be sufficiently satisfied to run home on the sly. But he could never figure out which pair of flowery panties, so different from the ones his mother sewed, belonged to which wife.

After eating, Luben went from house to house to arrange for workers and get a commitment on who would be there to fix the path. As usual there would be be drinking and singing all over the village afterward.

Lying in the bed of boards nailed together, Yidai calculated how much they would make from both the ginger and their wages combined. She had her heart set on a sewing machine. The year before she had watched as one shopkeeper in the secondhand market had demonstrated a foot-pedal machine. Sewn together, the two scraps of cloth looked like finished clothing. Yidai figured she'd be able to get the hang of it very quickly and make her own clothes for little or nothing and not have to worry about what to wear shopping, nor would she have to worry about hand-stitching the uniforms for the two kids still in school. She might even be able to make a little extra money. Thinking, she turned her head and looked happily at Luben, but discovered that his eyes were wide open as if he had something on his mind.

"Still thinking about a mistress?"

"Ha! As if there were nothing else to think about?" snorted Luben, pulling up his blanket and farting resolutely.

"It stinks! You're like a mountain boar!" shouted Yidai.

The rats running over the ceiling, hearing the happy implications in her words, stopped to listen.

Every year, Ni'en would make it a priority to buy, dig, and sell the ginger from the back side of the mountain. The ginger field was three kilometers from the exit for the cliff on the front side of the mountain. There was no industrial road and not only was it steep and precipitous but also, along the way, scree-covered stretches had to be traversed. Two places in particular were enough to make one very cautious, and, after the rains, they were even in a worse state and more difficult to cross. Every year, before Luben dug up the ginger, he would first see to it that the path used for transporting the ginger was repaired and safe.

In the past his oldest son dramatically called it Ginger Road, comparing it to the Silk Road of mainland China. He had no idea what the Silk Road was like, if it went up and down or whether the slightest misstep would land you in a ravine, but it must have been similar if people used it to make a living.

Before the sky was light a single file of people followed Luben on the newly repaired path to the back side of the mountain: four men, five women, and four children.

Strictly speaking, the scenery was pretty special, especially on the back side of the mountain. The small path sloped gently upward along the mountain streams and cliffs. The seventy-degree slope made the people look like ants climbing on a ball. Traversing a stretch of scree, Budan looked right to avoid looking down at the river below. His heart raced, and with each step he felt unsteady. Last year's fright when he nearly slipped and fell into the valley was still fresh in his mind. But because of his school expenses and for spending money, he was still willing to come along. And he didn't come alone—he convinced his brother and two of the Ximai brothers who lived at the end of the village as well.

"Where do we start?"

"Start down on the lower left side!" Luben liked to do it the same way every year.

"The ginger clumps are really big this year. Dig carefully. Try not to break them up," warned Luben after he dug up one half the size of a washbasin.

The old ginger skin was shiny and the brown, the plump rhizomes crisscrossed, each stretched out, strong and solid with moist black soil between each fork. Luben was comforted and hopeful.

"After we sell the fresh ginger, the house should get a new roof."

"Right, fix the house and get the oldest a wife. Shalong, Gushan's daughter, is eighteen, a match for your oldest. Wouldn't they be a perfect match?"

"There's no hurry. Take the money from the ginger and buy a plot closer to home and save yourself the trouble of having to travel so far."

"You're hopeless. This plot is worth three on the other side. Only a fool would make such a suggestion."

"Hey, Why do you have to belittle someone?"

"You don't believe me? Ask Luben."

With all the chatter among the male workers, one would think that the fresh ginger was theirs to sell.

Luben was silent and then he said to Gushan, who was also silent, "How is your son doing in the army school?"

"Not bad. Got a letter the other day saying that he was doing fine."

"What'll he do after graduation?"

"Don't know. We'll see what the government arranges."

"And what kind of salary?"

"No idea, but he should be able to line up a job before getting out of the army. I don't understand it, so I don't know what to tell him. Better let him take care of it. I'm just afraid he won't finish."

"You're right. Anyway, kids these days can't take any hardship. I don't know what to do after Budan graduates from junior high."

"Let him decide. They won't wait around to listen to our opinions anyway."

Luben was most worried about his third son, Budan and what he would do after junior high. He couldn't pay for him to continue school, and Budan would not be willing to go to work in a factory.

But how could one support a family on two plots of ginger? Could he study at the military academy?

Luben looked at the plot of ginger on the sixty-degree slope and the thick crop of ginger that took a year to grow. A plot one third of a *mu* in size, while it might provide a good deal of economic assistance, how could it be handed down and provide a living for his children? In another year his second son would be out of the army and his third son would graduate from junior high. He couldn't ask them to look after the fields, and, if he did, how many years would they be satisfied to do so? Luben had a lot of things on his mind.

The group of men worked from left to right and from bottom to top digging the ginger. Their wives collected the rhizomes, broke off the green sprouts, and separated the tender shoots into piles, after which they reburied the green shoots to prevent them from withering before they were moved.

The women were always moving and hadn't stopped since they set out in the morning. They sang and gossiped. One woman complained that her man hadn't given her any peace that night—he was always groping her breasts or between her thighs and it really annoyed her. Another said that every night her old man wanted to "teach her a lesson," and, though she seemed to be complaining, it didn't really seem to bother her.

Although Budan kept his ears open, he didn't hear much of interest so stuck close to the Ximai brothers.

"Have you been up to see the beehives on top of Ni'en's house?"

"What about them?"

"Yesterday, when I passed by, I saw Ni'en adding sugar."

"Really?"

The children's eyes lit up. This was a big deal. They had to get permission from their mothers to spend the money they earned, and to get money for candy took a lot of pleading and a promise that they wouldn't buy any the next time. But the beehives were different. In secret they would lift off the cover, and reach in for a handful of white rock sugar. But they had to be sure about the time because the bees would consume most of the sugar in a matter of three or four days.

"When do you want to go?"

"Let's go tonight after we get back and the adults start drinking."

Budan had clearly thought it through, because he replied without hesitating. He'd even taken into account the adults and their activities. It appeared that his youthful rebelliousness had not entirely disappeared even though he was normally well behaved in front of his parents.

"Budan, bring me the bigger of the shovels," shouted Luben, seeing the kids whispering with their heads together.

"OK." Budan pulled a face, but dared not drag his feet in taking the shovel to his dad.

"Come and help me move this clump of ginger to one side."

"*Ahma* (father), How long does it take for ginger to grow this big?" he asked, scooping up the rhizomes that looked like a giant's hand.

"One year, usually."

"Would it be OK to leave it in the ground?"

"Sure it would and the rhizome would be the size of a wash basin the following year.

"Then wouldn't you make more money digging it up every two years?"

"Fool, you think we could do without any money for a year?" Luben said, laughing.

Budan was embarrassed by his stupid question, but then he suddenly thought of something: "*Ahma*, can I ride a bike to school?" He paused for a moment before continuing, "taking the crowded bus I am often late to class and the teacher has scolded me many times." He looked a bit frightened as he spoke.

"That's a long way. Aren't you afraid you'll get tired?" Luben was curious because originally Budan had refused to ride his bike no matter what and now he had changed his mind. It was OK with Luben, because the boy could even get some exercise.

"No way!" insisted Budan.

"OK, you can ride my bike to school."

Luben had a twenty-year old bicycle with a big heavy frame and a big rack on the back. He bought it from a flatlander with the money he made the first year growing ginger on the back side of the mountain. He clearly remembered that in order to earn a little extra money that year he had carried some heavy loads. He fell several times nearly breaking a leg. After settling accounts, he had Yidai made up the difference and bought the bicycle.

"Can I buy my own?" asked Budan, not really daring to look his father in the eye.

"How much?"

"A classmate just bought one for a little over two thousand, I think."

"A little over two thousand?" said Luben returning to reality. They'd make several tens of thousands from the ginger and their wages, but it wasn't clear if that would be enough for a year. He wanted some things too.

"OK, work a little harder and see if you can buy one."

"You mean you'll let me use all the wages?"

"No, not spend all the wages yourself, but to buy a bicycle."

"Great!"

"OK for now. If there isn't enough money, there's nothing we can do."

"OK!"

Budan couldn't suppress his joy and immediately began working even harder moving the clumps of ginger his father dug up. He resembled an egret moving quickly in the wake of an old plowing ox. It seemed he could see a bike greeting him in the clouds above the Pacific.

Luben smiled, seeing himself years earlier working hard for a bike of his own.

Luben worked his shovel up and down along the plot, digging up the ginger as he went. But the pain in his back caused him to move in an exaggerated fashion. He was thinking of how the wages would be spent, but the pain kept pulling him back to reality.

The ginger field was filled with the sound of men and women talking and an occasional song. It was as noisy as a garden party and alleviated the sweaty fatigue.

"Hey, How's it going?" called out Ni'en in his broken Puyuma, breaking up the talk. He appeared at the head of the path followed by his two wives.

"Hey, Ni'en, Why are you so late in getting here?" asked one woman, first rising to the attack.

"Probably exerted himself too much last night so he doesn't have any energy left today," fired another woman.

"Right! Better have a little to drink for more stamina like me," added one of the men, not to be left out.

"Bullshit! How come I didn't know you have more stamina?" replied a woman, apparently the man's wife, making everyone laugh.

It was true, how could a guy who was scarcely able to marry give advice to a guy with two wives about more stamina? All the banter achieved was to make the two sisters blush and smile foolishly.

"Time for a break. I've brought some ice water!" said Ni'en, as if nothing mattered.

Luben greeted them but continued digging. He hoped to work while the sun was overhead and knock off early and head home.

Budan stood up, wiped the sweat away, thinking to take a rest. Then he saw Ni'en's two wives bending over to examine the ginger, their two rear ends side by side. He was suddenly clear about one thing: the smaller panties belonged to the second wife.

He nearly ran over to the Ximai brothers to announce his big discovery, but when his father saw the dust he raised he scolded, "Hey! Why so wild?"

Startled, Budan nearly stumbled.

After the short break, the sun gradually grew hotter. The men quickened their pace as they sang. The women chattered as they stacked the fresh ginger in piles. Ni'en and his two wives left after they had lunch.

By three in the afternoon a good part of the third of a *mu* plot had been dug, and there was enough to provide a load for each person to carry. Luben looked and calculated and decided to call it a day.

"I think that is enough digging for today. If we go on we won't have any energy left to sing tonight!" said Luben casually, but how could he be so casual the way his back was hurting?

Each one of the men took a large fertilizer bag, filled it with ginger, and carefully sewed up the opening with a big needle. They also put a layer in the bottom of their baskets on top of which they stowed the bags. After arranging everything, they hoisted the baskets on their backs one by one. The baskets, which weighed close to seventy kilos, didn't seem to trouble the men too much. The women adjusted the straps on their baskets and positioned their heads before hoisting them on their backs and setting off for home.

Yidai noticed that Budan, his younger brother, and the Ximai brothers all shouldered full baskets and was curious why they were so gung-ho to carry more than usual.

"Hey, Budan! Aren't you guys carrying too much? It's a long way."

"No."

"This won't do. What's wrong? Why are you carrying so much?" Yidai asked anxiously. It wasn't that far but it wasn't exactly close. Carrying some weight on the way usually was too much so adding weight on the way back would most likely be a problem. "What are you up to? All of you get over here and remove some of that ginger," ordered Yidai.

The Ximai brothers and Budan's younger brother all obeyed and immediately removed about half the ginger while tattling that it was Budan who wanted them to carry more. But Budan refused to unload any, while appearing dubious.

"Hey, Budan! Have you gone nuts? Asked Yidai, curiously setting down her basket. She was determined to get to the bottom of the matter.

"I . . . " stammered Budan.

"Speak up."

"*Ahma* said I could buy a bike with the wages."

"What? No wonder, and here I thought the sun would be coming over the mountains tomorrow!" When she heard Budan say he wanted to buy a bicycle, she immediately thought of the sewing machine she wanted to buy in Taidong.

"OK, but it won't be easy and the road is far."

Yidai muttered, but she was secretly happy that her son had the gumption to work hard. She urged them to go on while she quickly loaded the ginger from the children's baskets into her own. She was so filled with hope that it was as if she had loaded the sewing machine into her basket. After adjusting the straps on the basket, she set off after them. But all the women who had originally decided to walk together had already left.

Over the eastern foothills of the Central Mountain Range, the sun seemed to hesitate between resting and continuing to struggle with the cloud-mist to occupy the green peaks. Occasionally the mist would dominate, then the sun. Suddenly sunlight would spread over a part of the mountain, and then suddenly it would shine on the forest over there. The hot afternoon gradually cooled. The winding path on the back side of the mountain lay over the mountain like a beautiful hundred-pacer snake.

A group of people, each carrying fresh ginger and their individual hopes, followed the path down the mountain. Sometimes a distance would open between them, and at other times they were close, one upon the other. On the vast green slope they looked like bugs moving along a brown thread, so quiet and resigned to their fate, so firm and industrious.

Luben panted, suppressing the pain in his back. He seemed to hobble under the seventy kilos of fresh ginger. Gushan was close behind him. They panted, and not a single word was exchanged. The young men ahead of them had already disappeared around a bend.

"Shall we rest a spell?" asked Gushan, concerned about Luben's condition.

"Not yet. Let's stick with our plan and rest on the boulders before we cross that stretch of scree.

Luben panted and replied with a great deal of effort. He wanted to cover the distance remaining before the scree and then have a good rest. But the pain in his back made him huff and puff, and the sweat poured down.

"Getting old?"

The sadness of an aging hero seemed to settle in his heart.

"What was a hundred kilos back in the old days?"

"Perhaps it's because my back hurts."

The unwillingness to admit defeat was just another sign of age.

It was difficult to get to the rest stop. The other men had been there for a while and were chatting and smoking. The women arrived right on the heels of Luben and Gushan.

Yidai and the four kids trooped in last. Although their burdens were a little heavier, and their shirts soaked with sweat, they didn't feel that tired. Their happy expressions made Luben wonder, and he momentarily forgot the pain in his back. Just as he was about to open his mouth and ask, one of the men spoke:

""Is Ni'en really that strong?" It appeared that his wife's jibe that morning had been too much for him.

"You just won't give up and keep thinking about the same thing."

"No. Just look. He's so skinny and even walks funny. How can he be strong?"

"Only his wives know if he's strong. Did you ask them?"

"Why would I ask them?"

"Ask and see. Maybe they'll think you're stronger than Ni'en."

"Right. And your wife didn't say you were strong."

It looked like the vigorous males from the village would never tire of talking about "teaching the wife a lesson" at night. It was as if the sacks full of ginger and the awaiting stretch of scree were very distant matters.

Luben remembered how he had captured a wild goat alive the previous year. He didn't know how Ni'en came to hear about it, but, right when he was butchering it, he came to ask Luben to sell him a bowl of the blood. Luben, of course, knew why he wanted it but said nothing. He mixed the blood with onion flowers, medicinal herbs, and wine and gave it to Ni'en free of charge. But the following day his two wives came up the mountain and, when they came to Luben's door, they blushed and presented him with some fruit. They were very agreeable and since then Ni'en had kept an eye on what Luben is doing, especially when the farm work was slow and he went hunting.

There are two things under heaven that cannot be hidden from people: virility and money in the pocket. But was strength that important? He had two wives and a brood of children and didn't have to worry where the next meal was coming from or about his children's future. He was a boss and also handled the village crops. We're just his employees. So who was stronger?

A hawk that had been circling returned to its nest and the first wild cicada was heard. As he thought, Luben's eyes wandered to his wife and sons and his heart felt heavier.

"How's your back? Doing OK?" asked Yidai approaching him.

"Does that capsicum plaster really work?

"Why? Does your back hurt?"

"I've used it for two days and my back doesn't feel any better."

"What do you want to do? Maybe you should see the doctor tonight." Yidai was so worried she didn't even mention the sewing machine she had wanted to discuss.

Luben didn't reply. The mere mention of a doctor and Luben shrank. Several years before, he had become very ill and Yidai insisted on taking him to the hospital below the mountain. He lost his patience just waiting in line and demanded to go home. It took a long time before the doctor could see him and, when he did, he treated him like a child and asked a whole bunch of questions. There was not the slightest tone of respect in his voice and he got fed up, but didn't dare lose his temper in the hospital. He never dreamed that the doctor would insist he spend several days in the hospital so that they could observe him. In addition to staring at the white walls and gray ceiling all day, they also managed to draw his blood three times. A day was like several decades.

"Aborigines don't stay in hospitals! Luben angrily complained to his wife for several years.

Now that his wife had mentioned the hospital, he forgot all his other worries.

"Let's go. The sun is going down!" shouted Luben, without answering Yidai about seeing the doctor. Still laughing, everyone hoisted their baskets on their backs.

Between the stretch of scree and the front of the mountain lay a river and a cliff. Six switchbacks led up and down the mountain and through dangerous loose scree. The path across the scree was no more than a couple of feet wide. Anything that fell, fell all the way to the river below because there was nothing to cling to, root or clump of grass, nor any wide space. The public authorities saw no value in building an industrial road nor were they willing to invest the funds. But for Luben and his family this was an important part of their livelihood. They had to use the path and repair it every year.

No one talked as they formed a single file, three steps between each person. No one could pass anyone else. The men, who were quicker, went first, followed by the women, who were followed by Luben, his back in pain.

Yidai and the four kids she was leading made up a troop of their own at the very end. The heavy, solid basket pressed close to her back. She watched Luben's shadow hobble and struggle, and she became extremely anxious as they approached the first switchback.

"Is he going to make it?" she asked herself, while wondering how she was going to get him to see the doctor.

"Stubborn, proud man," she complained in her heart.

They soon found themselves shrouded in the falling mist, which made the sky darker. Yidai focused once again on the four kids she was shepherding, especially the overburdened Budan.

"Careful! Watch each step!"

"Keep your eyes on the road and don't think of anything else."

"We'll be able to rest soon."

"Be brave. Boys must be brave!"

"Keep steady and support both sides of the basket with your hands."

"Don't be in a hurry. Take your time."

Yidai, who sounded like a farmer urging his plowing oxen on with a whip, one word after another spurring them on, keping the kids focused on walking.

By the second switchback Budan realized how hard it was. He had been over the path many times, but never with such a heavy burden. His initial sense of excitement and expectation cooled soon after their first break. Entering the stretch of scree, the head strap of the basket slipped, mercilessly throwing the weight on his back, which made straightening it impossible. The sweat from his forehead ran into his eyes and down the tip of nose to fall on his legs. He felt a bit dizzy and dazed. He remained focused only because of Yidai's exhortations.

"Isn't there an easier way to make money?"

"Is it like this all the way down?"

"Why doesn't *Ahma* sell the land?"

Budan couldn't help thinking so much. Continuing down the slope, his legs started to feel weak. His attention lapsed and his left foot slipped nearly causing him to fall. Frightened, he screamed as a stone beneath his left foot went rolling down the mountain, causing the men below to shout:

"Watch the rocks!" shouted Luben.

"Watch your step. Don't knock the rocks loose!" shouted several men.

"Watch . . . rocks . . . " echoed through the valley.

Kerplunk, the rock hit the riverbed below.

"How's it going? Be careful!" reminded Yidai.

The kids were so frightened that they nearly cried. Budan, who was covered with cold sweat and had nearly wet himself, was now thoroughly awake. He kept his mind focused solely on descending the mist-shrouded path.

Yidai's words prodded the children on. The six switchbacks of the trail through the scree seemed to go on with no end in sight.

Nearly limping, Luben passed the cliff and arrived at the rest spot on the front of the mountain. He hurt from head to toe as if his whole body were being torn apart. Those who had arrived earlier stopped talking, surprised and concerned, when they saw him.

"Is it serious?"

"No. You go on ahead. Come to my place at seven."

Putting down his basket, Luben appeared exhausted. His voice was weak too.

"You guys go first. I'll stay with him and wait for the kids," said Gushan.

The group set off chattering. The next stretch was relatively flat, though longer than the previous winding portion. But it was the final stretch of the day. Coming out at the front of the mountain, they would arrive at the collection point, and then the weighing and the day would be done. That evening Ni'en would come to Luben's house to pay the wages and invite everyone to drink. It was always a happy occasion. For that reason everyone's steps grew lighter.

Luben felt better after drinking some water that Gushan handed him. He turned and removed the newspaper he had wrapped his sweet potato in from out of a crevice and fanned himself with it.

"You're getting older. Are you thinking of selling the land?" asked Gushan.

Luben didn't reply immediately. He wasn't clear. Even if he hadn't hurt himself, it was still a difficult path for a man of sixty.

"How will I live if I sell the land?" asked Luben."My land on the front side of the mountain doesn't produce as much as the land on the back side and, after all these years, how could I part with it?"

"You might not be able to part with it but you ought to think about it.

Every year the path has to be repaired and walked. Each year it deteriorates more, and it might not even survive the typhoons this year," said Gushan, worried for Luben.

Luben understood this, but one less piece of land meant less income. Even if it were on the front of the mountain, it wouldn't make his life that much easier. Despite the dangers and difficulties associated with the path through the scree to the back side of the mountain, he had grown attached to it. How could he bear to part with the land? Luben pondered as he fanned himself absentmindedly with the newspaper.

Yidai and the kids finally arrived. Budan appeared first, followed by the Ximai brothers and his little brother.

The kids didn't have to be told twice to put down their baskets and rest. The fatigue on their faces and their sweaty clothes told how difficult the path had been.

Gushan helped Yidai off with her basket. He saw Budan standing apart and alone. Enduring the pain all the way down the mountain, his body was so stiff that he couldn't even bend over. As soon as he got to the rest stop and could relax, he forgot his pain and what he wanted to do. Yidai, who felt sorry for him, helped him off with his basket, rubbed his head, told him to take a drink of water and rest. Without getting up, Luben tossed the paper to Budan so he could fan himself.

"Rest a little longer; this is the last stretch."

Luben spoke without intentionally trying to comfort Budan, and his words sounded strange. He didn't really know how to say something encouraging and had always lacked the custom. Perhaps, as a Puyuma male, he had been brought up that way.

"Sell the land and find another field on the front side to start with," insisted Luben to himself.

"But then won't the Ginger Road fall to waste?"

"Who cares? Didn't the Silk Road used by the Chinese for thousands of years fall to waste?"

Luben couldn't forget the comparison of his Ginger Road to the Silk Road. Perhaps it was because that's how he made his living or perhaps it was the only real link he had with the Chinese from the mainland.

"Yidai, we'll go first and take it slow." Luben had rested enough and wanted to leave first with Gushan.

"I'll go too. I still have to get home and cook," answered Yidai.

"Budan, you rest awhile and then leave with your brother," said Yidai to Budan.

"OK!"

Budan had more or less recovered. He recalled how he had nearly fallen last year and again today. He felt a sense of relief. As he fanned himself with the newspaper, he didn't know how to reply at first, but his fatigue made him want to rest a bit longer so he replied to Yidai with a single word.

He opened up the newspaper. It was all the business and financial news.

". . . trading on the stock market was hot. At mid-session the market was at 11 thousand and by the close of trading it was up another 235 points. 1.5 million shares were traded, delighting investors."

He didn't understand a word. Bored, he flipped to the back page and read:

". . . in high-tech, *Forbes* listed four new tycoons with an average age of 36 who had joined the ranks of billionaires, with respective fortunes of $25 billion, $22 billion . . . "

He still didn't understand. How many zeros were there in a billion? How many years would he have to grow ginger? How many baskets would he have to carry on his back?

"With so much money, how many bikes could they buy?" he asked himself, puzzled.

How could Budan, who was in his second year of junior high, ever understand the problems in his math book dealing with money and how to arrive at a dividend or minuend? How could he, living in a mountainous village where they slaved planting ginger and carrying baskets for a year's income far from the modern world, understand that a rise of a couple of points in the stock market meant pockets of cash? He didn't understand. His father didn't understand. The men and women workers who were planning on drinking, chatting, and singing that night didn't understand either.

A bird returning to its roost flew over his head. A blot of droppings fell, punctuating the end of the section of the newspaper. He simply shoved the newspaper back in the crevice, woke his brother and the Ximai brothers who were sleeping against their baskets, and started to worry if they'd get home before nightfall . . .

They didn't stagger home until after seven, tired and red-eyed from crying.

The following two days only Budan accompanied the adults.

That year Yidai bought her sewing machine as planned, and Budan joyfully rode his new bike to school.

The following year Luben, as usual, repaired the path and dug ginger . . .

In July the part of Ginger Road that ran through the stretches of scree collapsed because of a typhoon; nothing remained of the six switchbacks save a bare slope.

And the Zhongtou and Zhongzhang Highways on the western side of the island would be open to traffic by the end of the year.

Out of the Brush

YUBAS NAOGIH

IN THIS WORLD I was known as Bayan Hayong. My name, like that of my brave father, Hayong Gumao, was famous in the Japanese police files and registry at Nihonmatsu Station.

But in a matter of just a few decades my name has nearly been forgotten among the mountain tribes in the Da'an Basin. That saddens me.

This is particularly true of my descendants who seem to want to avoid talking about my exploits, which naturally fills me with anger.

Oh, people of this world! You might think that I have vanished completely from this earth. Wrong! You've got it all wrong! Even to this day I am lying stretched out in a hidden crevice in a cliff east of the defensive perimeter. There are two piles of bones at my feet. Ha! The skulls of the two Japs rolled to the bottom of the valley a long time ago. But I hold an ideal position—my dead bones are undisturbed and intact as ever.

Fifty or sixty years ago there was a landslide. A boulder slid to a place not far above us and stopped. Since then it has prevented the falling rock and soil from covering us. It also cuts us off completely from the path four or five hundred meters above. That's why we have never been discovered.

I really am grateful to this boulder for allowing us to guard this castle of ours and to live in solitude and peace for decades and to enjoy the warmth of the sun during the day and the cool breezes and bright moon of the night.

On the battlefield my ancestors measured success in battle and a warrior's bravery by the number of heads he cut off. Returning home after battle, the warriors first congregated at the men's lodge or in the headman's house to drink in revelry. After nightfall they would hold a ceremony for the enemy heads to appease the souls. As part of the ritual, rice cake and pork would be stuffed into the mouths of the enemy heads and then sprinkled with wine. The chief sacrificer would intone:

"Yesterday we were enemies, today we are friends. Our warriors defeated you today. We want to absorb your spirit of bravery and your strong wills, transforming them into our own strength of spirit to be ever victorious over our enemies and successful in our exploits. Having benefited us, we will definitely treat you well and continue to look after you. We hope that you will be at ease here and attract some others like yourselves to keep you company and relieve you of your loneliness . . . "

After the ceremony was over, all those present joined hands and sang and danced around the heads of the enemy.

When we three skulls were lonely we would respond to the ritual words "yesterday we were enemies, today we are friends" and chat.

Everything is very strange in the world of the dead. In the world of men I couldn't understand a word of the a-i-u-e-o of Japanese, but among the shades we learned one another's languages very quickly. After we were able to converse freely, the three of us would often chat and gossip in the crevice of the precipice.

But of course that was before their skulls rolled down the slope. I haven't spoken to anyone since that typhoon blew away their skulls.

I've lain so damn long in this crevice that I'm about to go crazy from the dullness and loneliness.

I remember it was a night of a bright moon and few stars. Three skulls occupied a torturous and lofty crag. At first the thin upright bones of the two Japanese faced northeast—the direction of their home—for a long time and then bowed deeply.

They repeated the same movement several times a day.

After going through these motions they would sing the Ironha dirge together. The lyrics went something like this:

Though the fragrance of flowers must fade
This world will exist for ages to come
Today we surmount the mysterious mountain of karma
That shallow dream unseen and us not drunk

Once they finished singing they embraced and wept. That extremely aggrieved song echoed in the valley for a long time.

Oh, yeah. I forgot to introduce you to these two buddies of mine. The big set of bones is Miyagawa Seibe and the short one is Oyama Kotaro. They were both around forty when they died and both were police officers of the utmost scrupulousness in their duties.

When they interrogated me in the police station, they asked me very practical questions such as why I wanted to kill people; why I wanted to kill an unarmed old man; what kind of courage was it to murder an old policeman who had come to fix the water pipe; and after mercilessly killing him why did I have to cut off his head and take it away, thus making him into a headless zombie.

It's cool like water tonight. A pale yellow waning moon yellows several clouds on the horizon. The mountain peaks across the Dahu Creek are sometimes visible and sometimes obscured. Now I'm in the mood. Between turns interrogating me, I make my skeleton comfortable in the rocky crevice to prepare for a night's conversation with my two buddies:

"I had to kill," I begin, "because this is the one right my people have bestowed on me—the opportunity to offer an explanation and the right to clear my name. I had to kill because it was so important; otherwise I couldn't show my face in the village. You know? This is to say that even if I didn't kill, I couldn't survive, I couldn't go on living. You know what I mean! There's no way I could go on living . . . "

"That's strange. Hattori Jiro received his own salary from the emperor and ate his own hard-earned rice. What harm could he have done you? If you didn't kill him, what kind of harm could he really do to you? That wouldn't let you go on living?"

Oyama Kotaro shook his dry skull vigorously. He waved his hand, his wrist bones clattering against the stone.

I imagined that if any flesh had clung to his face it would have twitched without stopping. His eyes would also have flashed with an evil look.

"Don't interrupt me," I roared. "It is a sort of an occult ceremony of the village. You know? It is a kind of rule, a kind of custom, a ritual of sorts . . . anyway, it is a custom that has developed through history—a long, long tradition. You get me? This custom existed long before you Japanese occupied our lands. You should understand that we indigenous people are a fighting race of warriors. Having lived in this tropical mountain rain forest for thousands of years, tribes have had no choice but to look upon each other with hostility and hatred if they are to strive for territory. That is why we have always looked upon everyone as an enemy except for our people and our friends. And naturally enemies must be annihilated. Our ancestors established all sorts of sound strategies for killing and repulsing our enemies. Headhunting is just one such strategy. You'll never understand this custom. I tell you that all men count the taking of the greatest number of heads as the greatest glory because it makes them heroes and real men of the mountains. After headhunting, the people will hold a hero's banquet to celebrate the success and to display one's acheivements. The heads are kept in a special place as a sign to glorify our ancestors.

There are two forms of headhunting: collective and individual. The collective form involves a tribe and usually is carried out in years of epidemics and natural disasters. Heads are taken and offered as sacrifices on the altar to ask our ancestral spirits' help in overcoming difficulties. Sometimes it is for revenge, and heads are taken to console the ancestral spirits. These rituals are collective in nature. As to the individual form, among the reasons for coming out of the brush to hunt heads are revenge, self-vindication, and to rectify a wrong. Sometimes it is purely a form of expressing one's individual heroism."

"I don't care why you kill so many people and cut off so many heads," hastily replied Miyagawa Seibe. "I don't care if you kill off all the enemies among your people, but killing one of our Japanese policemen is a heinous crime. Does a guy like you understand that killing a Japanese policeman is a heinous crime of the first order? He was a noncombatant who, after retirement, decided to stay at the police station temporarily to help out because he couldn't get a date to sail and get home as quickly as he'd like. He hadn't used a gun in ages and, aside from a knife he carried for show, he was basically unarmed, and the knife was for cutting grass. So aren't you ashamed of yourself?"

"Ashamed? What's there to be ashamed of? At the very least we were evenly matched to be a victor and loser. Let me explain the whole thing again to you." The following is what I told him:

"And me! I waited for him at the hollow where the water pipe for the police station originates. I waited a whole day and a night. I waited patiently because I knew he'd come. You need water, don't you? When I got there I pulled the bamboo pipe out of the water so that not one drop would make it to your place. And me! I just kicked back on top of a boulder and soaked up the sun. I lay there until the waxing moon rose above the treetops. I rolled over excitedly, my body burning, my mouth twisted with a strange feeling, my mind filled with images of what would happen the following day. I was certain someone would come to fix the pipe because you're not like camels that can go for months without a drop of water.

And, sure enough, at around noon on the following day I suddenly heard an unusual noise amid the rustling leaves and the sound of the cicadas, birds, water, and wind. It was the sound of someone cutting brush down the slope. I rolled off the boulder and assumed a squatting position. Then I heard the sound of metal striking stone. I nodded.

"Hey, Bayan. So the quarry finally arrives. You'd better be careful." I immediately leapt behind a large tree beside the river. I muttered to myself: "The guy has brought a long samurai sword in a cherrywood scabbard. That'll make great spoils, but he had better get ready to defend himself."

Before I had finished speaking, Mr. Hattori was standing by the water looking all around. You say that he is old and retired, but in fact he was as strong as a bull and stood straight, his chest thrust forward and his eyes bright and piercing. He didn't have to guess what the problem was because he plainly could see that someone had intentionally ripped up the pipe he had set in the rocky crevice and thrown it to one side. He stood there for a while before agilely crouching like a leopard cunningly examining the primeval forest around him. I was afraid he'd flee out of fear, so I was there at his back quick as a flash to first cut off his retreat. I crouched in the brush behind him to ascertain what sort of weapons he was armed with. After a while I determined he had only a long-handled sickle. I couldn't help but smile.

He was wearing a black kimono, the lower hem of which was rolled up and tucked into his pants. He wore black trousers bound tightly with khaki leggings worn by soldiers. His shoes were black rubber—the kind that look like mittens for the foot. He was dressed for mountain climbing and had an overweening air about him.

"Hey!" I hooted at him

He was a real man. Anyone else would have given up the ghost hearing my gloomy call behind them. But not him. He just slowly turned half around, raising the broad straw hat with his left hand as he fixed his narrow eyes on me from under the brim of his hat. Then he slowly stood up, standing steady, his two feet planted firmly on the ground. He slowly grasped the handle of his sickle and pointed the pointed blade to his right foot.

Wow! You should have seen him move! It was like seeing Musashi Miyamoto and Kojiro Sasaki fighting on the beach.

And, although he moved a lot, he never took his eyes off me for one second. I couldn't stand his stare, so I smiled scornfully at him.

"Prepare to die, you dirty swine!" He shouted.

As angry as he was, I figured he couldn't stand the way I smirked at him.

But how could I explain to him my motives and attitude? I couldn't think of anything else but smiling wryly or grimacing to eliminate all the embarrassment produced by the surprise at our chance encounter.

You can just imagine our discomfort at that odd chance encounter.

I continued to stand there grimacing. The situation was so uncomfortable that my scalp itched so badly I had to scratch. For a moment I wished I could peel off my scalp and cover my face with it because of his intolerable expression.

I felt like telling him that I didn't want to kill anyone, especially old men in whiskers. I also figured he had an old woman anxiously waiting for him as well as a passel of adorable kids waiting for him.

"Hey! Tell me, guys, did he have any kids?"

"Of course he did!" Miyagawa Seibe mumbled. "He told us he had two boys and two girls. His oldest son joined the army before finishing college and was a second lieutenant in the Kanto Army in Manchuria. He was a radical young soldier. The second son joined the army shortly after graduating from high school and immediately went to fight in the South Pacific. He was proud of those two boys. His two daughters were still quite young, but since he hadn't been home in a long time he didn't know that much about them."

"I knew it. I knew by that the two upturned curls of his mustache that he had a bunch of kids," I shouted. But what choice did I have? I had to kill him. I had to lop off his head, take it home, and place it on the wooden mortar that had been prepared. I had to in order to prove that I wasn't guilty, that I was innocent, and to clear my name. Do you understand? I'll explain it to you. All I did was catch a few brown trout with bamboo fish traps in the upper reaches of Dahu Creek. It was just a few. But, unfortunately, I was seen by several guys from Madu'an tribe. They actually pulled out their knives and chased me with the intention of killing me. They kept shouting that they were going to kill the thief who had been poaching in their hunting territory. If I weren't so fast on my feet, I'd have been a goner. It was a close call.

I knew that the creek had been divided by the village headmen: the upper reaches belonged to our Tiangou tribe; the middle reaches were for Madu'an tribe; and the lower reaches for Xidaobang tribe. The territories of the tribes were clearly marked, but how was I to know how they were marked? Was it that tree? Or was it that stone? It wasn't clear to me. As a result, I must have set some of the traps beyond our boundaries. But ignorance is not guilt. If they had any understanding they should have forgiven me on account of my youth and ignorance. There was no need to try and chase me down and kill me just because I simply didn't know.

I was like some mangy cur, chased and beaten. Panting and out of breath, I climbed to the defensive perimeter in the saddle of the mountain where fortunately I ran into Kagei Naobasi, the chief of the Tiangou tribe, and Yougeihe Wadan, a tribal elder, and some others. They were returning home from working in the dry upland fields and were resting in the saddle of the mountain. The moment I saw them I knew I was safe. I immediately hid behind them and, despite their questions, I was panting and unable to say a word, my mouth gaping like that of a yawning hippo.

"Ghost touch your head? What's wrong, Bayan?" shouted Youming Wadan. I just pointed down the mountain. I was covered with sweat and pale as a corpse.

Shortly, a group of warriors from Madu'an tribe in a towering rage charged to the saddle of the mountain. As soon as they saw the head of Tiangou tribe and several elders sitting there, they sheathed their knives. Still agitated, they stood there in a furious rage, unable to calm down. I knew the matter was coming to a head. I huddled behind the village head, scarcely able to breathe for fear of making a sound. I hung my head as if the only thing supporting it was the thin skin of my neck.

"Young men of Madu'an tribe, why are you trying to harm this youngster?" shouted Kagei Naobasi coldly. "By whose authority are you here? Dulai Fuyong, your tribal chief's, or Gainu Bawan, your village elder's?"

"He was poaching in our hunting and fishing territory. We want to take him to be tried by our village court . . . "

"I asked you under whose authority are you here?" roared Kagei Naobasi, the village head.

"We came on our own. We wanted to catch the suspect first then report to our superiors!"

"What's your name? Speak up," shouted Kagei Naobasi pointing at the guy who had replied.

He was big and tall and glared fiercely. He had a square face and brick-red skin and was probably dull as a brick. He never took his despising eyes off me.

"My name is Dagen Gulasi, the eldest son of Gulasi Kainuo . . . "

"Well then, Dagen Gulasi, hurry up and tell your village head to come and discuss this. I'll wait for him here."

"Why bother the village head over something so insignificant? All we want to do is take this suspected thief away for his just punishment."

Clearly it was turning into a standoff. I decided it was the moment to step forward and defend myself. So I hurriedly protested, "Who says I'm a thief? I didn't steal anything. All I did was . . . "

"You set three fish traps in our river," said one of them cutting me off mid-sentence. "We saw your traps and they all had fish in them. Isn't that stealing?"

I shouted for a while, but I didn't know how to explain things to them.

"Now, Bayan, tell me the truthfully," said the village head as he fixed his eyes on me. His eyes were like daggers. "Did you really set fish traps in their river? Hurry and speak up."

"I didn't see any mark. I didn't know if it was a tree on the banks or a . . . "

"We piled ten stones on top of a huge boulder on the side of the river. A pile, small on top and large on the bottom like a tower. Didn't you see it?"

"No!" I answered, my eyes wide because I hadn't seen a pile of stones.

"You young people are like that. You have eyes but can't see. Everything you do is reckless and a mess. I'm telling you, Bayan, that if you did what they say and set three traps in their river and caught their fish, you've broken the law of our people. Trespassing is a crime. If that's the way things are, there's nothing we can do about it. I'd like to help you, but I'm powerless . . . "

"No, no, this is not right! I demand justice," I shouted in a panic before the Madu'an warriors could grab me. "I'm telling the truth. I didn't see your pile of stones. Really. I'm willing to swear an oath that I didn't see it. There was a typhoon a few days ago, right? Maybe the wind blew over the pile of stones. How could I have seen it? I demand justice. I hope you will give me the chance to prove my innocence. I'm willing to take my chances and gamble on my luck with the men from Madu'an by coming out of the brush. At the appointed time I'm sure the gods will judge fairly. Please, all of you be my witnesses so that I can at least die content."

"OK, you will gamble for justice by coming out of the brush. That is fair," mumbled the one called Dagen Gulasi. "At Madu'an community we have taken so many heads that we haven't been able to arrange them. They're just piled there stinking. And you? How many heads have you at Taingou community taken? If when the time comes you cowards don't take a single head, you'll be sorry. Not only will this little bastard accept our punishment, but you at Tiangou community also will have to cede your hunting and fishing territory to us permanently for our use. You will have nothing to say because these are the rules established by our ancestors. Hopefully tradition will not be broken . . . "

Normally a person would be very careful about behaving in an unbridled fashion in front of Kagei Naobasi, head of the Da'an River Basin, and mock or call the warriors of Tiangou bastards or cowards. Such an insult could be immediately repaid with a few thrusts of a knife.

But, at that moment, the village head and the elders just stood there with their heads lowered and their faces red. Not a single one of them dared look Dagen Gulasi or his fellow villagers in the eye. Even Youming Wadan just clutched his hair and vigorously shook his head, looking as if he wished he could find a hole to crawl into.

"The sun has nearly set." He sighed hopelessly and then spoke in an odd tone of voice, "Old Kagei, we still have to hurry down the mountain. We're leaving. Let little Bayan take care of things here. Anyway this mess is his own doing, right?"

"OK, Listen to me, Dagen Gulasi," said the village head, pronouncing each syllable clearly as he slowly got to his feet. "I'll take the prisoner back with me. Go home and report to Dulai Fuyong and Gainu Bawan. Tell them that one of Kagei Naobasi's youngsters might have trespassed into your territory. But, out of good conscience and the fact that Bayan Hayong really might not have seen the marker as he suggests, we will give him a chance to clear himself. Our ancestral spirits have eyes, and they will give him a fair judgement. Let's set the time for the night of the next full moon. At that time both sides will meet again to resolve the matter. I don't think it's impossible for us to resolve such a small matter as a few fish; otherwise we'll be the laughing-stocks of all the other villages. We will certainly have plenty of opportunities in the coming days to meet, whether it be on a bright mountain slopes in the full light of day or in a forested valley under the moonlight, or by a rushing torrent or by the side of a placid stream. There's no reason for us to come to blows today over such a small matter. That's no good, right?"

"Enough nonsense," replied Dagen Gulasi coldly. "Madu'an has taken so many heads that we have run out places to keep them. They are just piled there, giving off a stinking. Since this little thief from your village has elected to seek justice by coming out of the brush, we'll keep our mouths shut for the time being and wait to see if you win or lose next full moon."

"Dagen Gulasi, you keep telling us how many heads you have taken, but what kind of heads?" asked Kagei Naobasi, who was about to leave, upon hearing the other's venomous attack. He fixed his angry gaze on him and, with a malignant laugh, said, "If we were like you and took the heads of women and children every time we came out of the brush, we could have piled them to the sky by now. We don't murder women and children. That's despicable, you know? I believe that Bayan Hayong would disdain . . . anyway, at the next full moon he'll bring you the head of an adult, the head of a brave and fierce warrior."

"Ha! Easier said. We'll wait and see!" said Dagen Gulasi, grimacing hideously. Then he gave a sharp order for his fellow villagers to head down the mountain.

A few days later I sent my tearful wife and kids home to her mother, while I made preparations for battle. As a result of the nightmares provoked by thinking about the cruelty of battle, I awoke several times each night in a cold sweat. Once awake, I'd hear my aunt who knew something about shamanism saying prayers for my victory. Her deep chanting in the middle of the night was gloomy enough to wake the demons resting in the ground. I couldn't figure out if she was trying to scare me or curse me.

That day, facing the towering presence of the Mr. Hattori, I was actually frightened. Standing there, cold and sticky with sweat, and there was a bitter taste in my mouth and my breath was foul. Something was wrong; I didn't feel right.

He just stood there calmly without moving. His face a steely blue, his lips sunken, his wrathful eyes glared at me, immobilized me, and I didn't know what to do. I just kept smiling wryly, tweaking my ears and scratching my cheeks, making a face.

I eagerly looked forward to him attacking me without mercy or anything else. In that case I could act and not feel so embarrassed and stupid.

Damn, the guy really was ignoring me. He stood there calmly without moving. But I was growing impatient. Standing there, my legs and back were getting sore. I moved my eyes to look around me. Everything was still save for a few butterflies fluttering by the river. Their dancing only increased my feeling of impatience. Even the sound of the flowing water and the autumn cicadas calling in the trees made me feel more ill at ease. My ears roared and my head felt like it was going to split open. I reached up to adjust my rattan helmet covered with black bear fur, which was made so hot by the noon sun that I thought my forehead was on fire. I quickly removed it.

But when he saw me take off my hat he moved.

He quickly raised his left hand and undid the hat string at his chin. Then he took hold of his strange bamboo hat by the brim and took it off, revealing his bald head.

"What a round bald head!" I shouted.

He quickly placed his hat on a large boulder next to him. Grasping his sickle, he once again pointed it to his right. I could see that his two hands had a good firm grip.

In that time he never once took his eyes from mine, but he stood there calmly. His patience was really starting to get to me.

I slid my loincloth to one side and tightened the knot of my scabbard. Because I hadn't eaten anything since the previous day, I was so hungry that my scabbard was loose. It would be terrible if I couldn't get to my knife, so I tightened the knot. I then grasped the haft and adjusted it so that it was easier to pull out.

I never expected that, as I touched the haft of my knife, he would roar and raise his sickle above his head.

Looking at him, I was sure he meant to leap and cut off my head.

"What do you want?" I shouted at him anxiously in Atayal.

"I want to chop off your head, take it home, and use it for an ashtray . . . you know what an ashtray is, right? Animal! And, ha, ha, I also want to cut off your penis and feed it to the crows. You understand, feed the crows? You animal!" His reply stunned me. His Atayal was actually better than mine. I stood there dazed for some time. Slowly I came to myself and realized that he was just a Japanese and not an Atayal.

"Hey! Can either of you tell me how Mr. Hattori was able to speak fluent Atayal? Where did he learn to speak it? How could he speak so well, as good as a native?"

"Oh, him! Before he came here," replied Oyama Kotaro, "he had served for seven or eight years as a police officer in the Jianshi District of Xinzhu. He always talked to us about the Atayal language group and how your language was identical along the Takejin River in the Jianshi Distict, the Xiuluan River Basin, and the Da'an River Basin. He knew a lot about linguistics and was naturally gifted. If there was a native language competition in Taipei, he would always represent Xinzhu and would invariably return with all the prizes and certificates. After a while he became our Atayal teacher here . . . "

Oh! No wonder he was so fluent and his language so pure. I thought he was playing a nasty joke on me at first—make an ashtray out of my head? That was just too much, right? But that he also wanted to cut off my penis and feed it to the crows was really going too far. Most of us guys don't wear underwear so I immediately reached down to touch that piece of cloth hanging there. I was worried that in the fray it might fall off, and that would be really embarrassing.

I relaxed after I touched it. It was still hanging there and hadn't fallen off.

I figured he was making fun of me, so I smiled wryly at him again. But, looking at his cold, impassive face, he seemed like a piece of granite; he flexed his sinewy sweat-covered arms, which shone under the afternoon sun.

He pursed his lips in an extremely disdainful way, and he had a strange look in his eyes. He stood there lofty and awe-inspiring as a small mountain.

"Hey, savage! Come and meet your death. What are you, an idiot? How long are you going to stand there like a fool?" he shouted, breaking the silence with his piercing voice, shaking his left index finger above his nose.

I guess he wanted me to come and fight with him.

But I wasn't going to fall afoul of his evil plan. I was clear that if we were going to fight I was at a disadvantage because his sickle was twice as long as my knife (one arm long as opposed to his, which was two arms in length). He was also in a broad open space by the river, which gave him plenty of room to wield his weapon.

My shorter knife put me at a disadvantage so I had to stick to close combat amid the brush and entangling vines.

I was impatient, so I imitated him and pointed my index finger at my nose. Wow! I shook my finger a couple of times and he roared with anger, scaring the heck out of me. I had just regained my calm when I saw a dark object hurtling at me like a cannon ball.

Something was wrong and I had no time to respond. "Wait, you have to let me pull out my knife," I shouted.

But he had already rushed to within three or four steps away from me. In a flash, a curved shadow fell toward my neck with a whoosh. For a moment my neck felt cold, and I shuddered.

"What's going on?" I shouted, leaping up off the ground as if I were an onion being pulled up. I raced behind a monkey slips tree and, as I was pulling out my knife, a curved black shadow like a rainbow fell out of the sky with a whoosh. I dodged to one side and the blade loudly lopped over a tree as thick as a man's upper arm.

My neck felt cold and I trembled. My spine stiffened as if I had been plunged into a tub of ice and every hair on my body stood on end. The skin on my head tightened and my hair shot up. But it was sobering, and I realized that I was involved at that very moment in a life and death struggle.

"That's not fair," I shouted as I leaped over some mossy stones and ran to a relatively open area covered with ferns.

With a rattling clang, I unsheathed my knife and held it firmly in my right hand. Before I had my footing, with a horrendous shout like fabric being rent, he charged me. That guy leaped over the trunk of a fallen monkey slips tree, and as he was trying to step over a pile of stones his sickle got tangled up in a vine. He lost his balance and slipped on the mossy stones and he came crashing down to the ground like a bundle of firewood.

He just lay on the ground without moving. But Atayal warriors will not kill a man when he is down. So I just stood there looking at his moss-covered legs and his dirty shoes.

I coldly mumbled to myself, "Huh! How can people in shoes like you tread this land?"

Lying on the ground in the mottled light, he looked like a poisonous hundred-pacer snake. He slowly got to his feet. Getting his balance he cast an angry gaze at the sky and muttered that incomprehensible Japanese of his. Then he roared as he raise his sickle and started wildly slashing at the vine above him, chopping off branches and tangled vines. He uttered murderous shouts and, as if expected, the tangles mess of branches fell.

"Hey! I'm over here!" I shouted.

He paused, stunned for a moment, then he slowly turned and looked at the knife in my hand. Sneering disdainfully, he slowly leaned the sickle against his right side, spat in his hands and rubbed them together and then gripped his sickle and raised it above to his right. His eyes flashed red.

He continued to sneer disdainfully and laughed fiercely.

I too slowly raised my knife, and it glinted in the afternoon sun with cold piercing gleam.

"Come on over here," I said through my teeth. Before I had finished speaking he had already charged. He squatted and swung with his sickle, attacking my calves; in no time I watched as the brush was mowed down toward me. I had no choice but to leap again. In the nick of time I grasped a vine and swung to his right.

His sickle plowed into a pile of rocks, sending up a bunch of bright sparks. He immediately rolled away as I swiped close to his head with my knife, putting fear into him.

I swore that if he was still wearing that strange hat I would smash his head.

Standing there, he was breathing rapidly as he repeatedly rubbed his head with his left hand. He eyed my legs treacherously. I guessed that he had decided attacking my lower body was too difficult, so he raised his sickle high above his head. His face was green, his eyes shone fiercely, his nostrils flared, and his mouth twisted in a funny sneer. From his twisted mouth emerged the following words: "You wait, I'm going to cut you in half, you animal . . ."

As he spoke, he brought the sickle down with all his might. Like a speeding shadow, I dodged his blade and, as he was pulling it out of the ground, I knocked the handle out of his hands with my knife. He stooped down to pick up his only weapon, but my blade had reached his neck. Just as he was about to stand up and struggle to get free, it was too late as my cold knife cut through his warm throat. Stunned, his legs trembled and he fell in a pool of his own blood and breathed his last.

The land became quiet once again. And he showed scarcely no trace of having struggled. He lay calmly as I took his head.

When I stood up, I could almost taste the stench of blood; bluebottle flies buzzed all around me. As the blood spurted, my hair seemed to stand on end and heat seemed to rise from the soles of my feet to the crown of my head. An evil flame seemed to leap up in my heart.

I was confused. All I wanted to do was ascend to the summit and shout to inform the people of my village that I had been successful.

With that thought in mind, I picked up the enemy head, leaped the stream, crossed the valley, and pulled myself up the cliff by the vines. Near sunset, I shouted from the summit.

The rivers and mountains stretched off in all directions. The bright red sun hung over Ahwani Mountain. The afterglow from the sunset made the forest look as if it were on fire and turned the Atayal village a blood red.

I stood on a jutting rock, knife held above me in my right hand, the enemy's head in my left. Facing the village below me I loudly sang the song of triumph so often sung by our warriors after battle:

Listen! My fellow villagers!
Look! My people!
Bayan Hayong is a warrior unto death,
Today I return from battle!
Under an ancient pine at the foot of the mountain,
After a fierce battle,
I hold a bunch of pine needles in my left hand,
I hold a pinecone in my right hand.
Towering like a peak, my clothes shake,
Fervently I sing,

I return home triumphant.
Listen! My fellow villagers!
Look! My people!

My song echoed on and on throughout the valley. As I finished singing, I felt a few more words were required to let everyone know. So I beat my chest and shouted: "The Atayal hero, Bayan Hayong, today took one enemy head to clear his name and console the ancestral spirits. I also warn the cowards of Madu'an that they are not to take lightly Tiangou Village led by Kagei Naobasi. It's not so easy to bully us! Nor is it any easier to trespass on our territory. The gods of heaven and earth have eyes and that is why they have decided fairly in my favor."

After I finished shouting, I could hear faint shouting from below. I figured it was the warriors of my village coming out to meet me. My mind was in turmoil. To tell the truth, I was drunk with the thrill of victory.

I strode directly down the path, whistling. Halfway down the mountain, as I was about to head off into the dense forest to avoid the government road, I was spotted and surrounded by more than a dozen of you policemen. Your guns were all aimed at my chest. Even if I could sprout wings, there was no escape.

So I was captured without a struggle.

At the police station at Nihonmatsu, you told me to kneel. A piece of wood pressed to the backs of my legs. After a while I could no longer stand the pain nor could I stand being beaten and kicked by so many of you, beaten with wooden clubs and cut by bushido blades. You accused and I confessed.

"OK," the police officer in charge hit his desk and ordered, "murderers will be put to death. This animal will be executed tomorrow morning at Dahu. His head will be cut off as a warning to the public.

I was not afraid of death, but I at least had to die in my own territory; nothing else would do.

So when the two of you were escorting me to that cliff I looked at the mountains, the rivers, the trees, and the brush before me. In what way were they like those of home? They weren't. Everything was wrong. I felt the air had lost its freshness, the sunlight its brightness, the soil its fragrance, the flowers their beauty, the trees their green. Looking, I realized that I no longer walked in the same country.

"This will never do!" I shouted. And when you were not paying attention, I used all my strength and leaped off the cliff to kill myself, and you chained to me.

That's why we are still here below the cliff.

"You wanted to die in your own land, so why didn't you think about the two of us?" Miyagawa Seibe shouted angrily. "We too wanted so much to die in our own homeland."

"Who told you to invade this land of ours? Who told you not to stay at home? Who told you to come all this way to meet your death?"

I asked them one question after another. Silenced, they couldn't answer me.

Elegy

LEKAL

UNDER AN OPPRESSIVELY bright blue sky a number of children, naked above the waist, rising and falling with the swells. They swam in the vast Pacific Ocean under the scorching afternoon sun. Nothing but the crashing waves could be heard.

"Mayaw, quit playing. Come and help me pick seaweed," shouted Lekal toward that group of children bobbing in the waves. His voice drowned in the sound of the waves. Mayaw, his older brother, paid no attention, and continued playing energetically with the other kids. Lekal shouted several more times and then gave up. Carrying a basket, he lowered his head and concentrated on picking seaweed. If his father were a carpenter or a fisherman, they would have been better off . . . anything was better than being a pastor. It was really hot. Lekal put down his basket and leaped into the cold ocean water; he then set off, swimming toward that group of children his own age, rising and falling with the swells.

Changguang was a village, neither large nor small, located near Changbin. If you stood in the street and looked south you could see the Changbin market grounds. No one could say why, but for some reason the wild herbs had grown especially well that year. They were like manna from heaven—there was plenty to eat, but it couldn't be stored. Lekal actually didn't stand out among the kids in the village—he wasn't especially bright or well built. Compared to Mayaw, his older brother, the only thing he had going for him was that he was praised for being warmhearted and considerate. Although Lekal was in the fourth grade, he still couldn't add, subtract, multiply, or divide without using his fingers. He was always behind in his homework and occasionally he simply stayed at home to help out with looking after the water buffaloes, catching fish, or picking wild herbs. He much preferred rowing the boat out to sea and catching fish with his father than going to school to study those incomprehensible Chinese characters.

Night, as warm and strong as Grandmother's hands, led the brave Ami people into the darkest time before dawn; night, like the little bag given to maternal uncle by his lover, waiting for that enveloping affectionate warmth.

"Is there any money in the house?" Ina asked Papa Halu, raising her voice. "Don't just sit there and say nothing. Think of a way to make some money!" Almost everyday the children watched the same performance staged in their bamboo house; everyday the same dialogue ended in the sound of snoring. Was he content with his lot, or was he helpless in the face of the situation? No one knew for sure.

"Lekal, get up!" Called and shaken, Lekal woke up. His father was going fishing. While the rest of the village slept, Lekal and his father groped through the darkness and with a flashlight made their way down to the seashore. This was the first time Lekal had gone fishing before daybreak. Unable to see on account of the darkness, Lekal stepped in the water and gave a startled cry. The seawater he was so accustomed to immediately covered his feet. Swaying, Lekal boarded the raft rocking on the waves and untied it. The sound of rowing oars broke the serenity of the night over the undulating, unbroken surface of the sea. In the rhythmic sound of the oars, Lekal accompanied his father to the other side of the sea. Once he was certain they had reached the open ocean, Halu pulled in his oars and sat on the raft as it rose and fell on the swells. Lekal feared the vastness of the night and the sea.

"Lekal, sit down and listen to the sea."

Lekal was so frightened that all he could hear was the beat of his heart. Gradually, he came to hear the water as it lapped against the side of the raft, lapped it gently, swaying him softly. The sound of the water lapping against the raft and the way the boat seemed to dance gently on the seaweedlike waves reminded him of how Ina patted a *wawa* on the back and sang the tunes of life but, even more, resembled the village shaman chanting to the moon. Through the hazy fog the east coast loomed in the golden rays of the sun . . .

"Lin Zhenming, have you done your work?" sternly asked the teacher in his heavily mainland-accented Mandarin as he stood behind the daydreaming Lekal. The teacher picked up the notebook in which the boy practiced writing new words and flipped through it. It was blank. "You have to finish before you can go home," said the teacher coldly.

"Teacher, I can't—I have to go home and help pick herbs," said Lekal as he stood up.

"You 'mountain people' don't study, you just pick herbs," said the teacher as he struck Lekal over the head with the notebook.

After school had let out, the classroom was empty save for a single grade-school student who, with his head down, practiced his writing. Lekal lifted his head and looked around the classroom—the teacher had already gone home. He put his homework in his drawer and, barefoot as he was everyday, ran home down the road to the village. From a distance he saw Manu putting flying fish his father and uncle had caught the night before out to dry.

"Why are you so late?" asked Manu as she moved among the racks to hang the flying fish.

"The teacher made me stay after class," replied Lekal as he squatted and put a string through the head of a flying fish.

Manu looked at the grandson she had raised and smiled as she took the flying fish he handed to her. With the arrival of flying fish season, all the families were busy catching, drying, and smoking the fish. Every family stored up the gifts of the sea.

The teacher rode up to Lekal's house on his bicycle and stopped in front of the flying fish drying racks. When he saw Lekal, he said, "I told you to stay after school and practice writing your characters, but you sneaked home. I want to talk to your parents." The teacher's accent was as heavy as the smell of flying fish in the air.

"My Ina and Mama are not here; only my Manu is home," said Lekal in a low voice.

The teacher turned to the boy's grandmother and said, "Lin Zhengming often misses class and doesn't do his work or concentrate on his studies. You must discipline him.

"*Maan*?" Lekal's grandmother asked the teacher in Ami.

The teacher pressed Lekal to repeat what he had just said in Ami. The teacher's eyes were as angry as those of the wild boar the village warriors killed during the Harvest Festival. Lekal looked at his grandmother and hesitated before haltingly repeating what the teacher had just said in a near whisper.

"Lekal is the best boy in the village, and the most helpful when it comes to picking herbs, watching the water buffaloes, and raising pigs," Manu said, raising her voice and smiling.

"What did she say?" the teacher asked Lekal.

Somewhat embarrassed, Lekal lowered his head and said, "She said that I'm the best boy in the village and the most helpful when it comes to picking herbs, watching the water buffaloes, and raising pigs."

"Ask your grandma what good does it do to pick herbs if you mountain people don't study? Do you want to raise pigs your whole life? The government spends a lot of money to educate you. Why don't you take advantage of it? Why pick herbs and raise pigs? Will raising pigs put food on the table?"

Lekal lowered his head, unsure of how to convey to his grandma what the teacher had just said.

"Tell her what I said," pressed the teacher, his heavy accent once again mixing with the fishy smell in the air. Stunned by the angry and excited tone of his voice, Lekal stared at his teacher, that molder and shaper of young people.

"Tell her."

Panic-stricken, Lekal recalled himself and timidly conveyed to his grandma what his teacher had said.

Displeased by the teacher's shouting, his grandmother raised her voice and scolded, "No one in this village would dare to raise their voice to an older person. It is you who needs to be educated." So saying, she turned and went inside.

The teacher sensed that the old woman's attitude was not friendly so he asked Lekal to repeat in Mandarin what the old woman had said. Lekal squatted and picked up the strings used to bind the flying fish and softly repeated what Manu had said. The moment he finished, he saw his teacher go blue in the face, grab his bicycle, and in a very strange, heavily accented Taiwanese, swear, "Savage." He then got on his bike and rode off, leaving Lekal arranging the string with his head down.

The sea breeze blew along the rising ground to the mountains by the village, while the wind from the mountains blew toward the sea. Two chimerical winds met and mixed in Changguang Village: no wonder the people there breathed both sea and mountain air. The old shaman A Fan was walking from the lower village to the upper village.

"*Nga'ayho*," said Manu, greeting the old shaman from beneath the betel palm beside the bamboo house. The old shaman A Fan and Manu had grown up together. Manu was already a grandmother and A Fan was still an unmarried old woman who respected and worshipped the ancestral spirits. While most of the villagers had converted to Christianity or Catholicism, only she steadfastly believed that it was the ancestral spirits who protected the village. Her aged footsteps, like the tattered old shaman's bag she carried, gradually vanished in the fragrance of the land.

"You're drying flying fish," said the old shaman, stopping to look at the flying fish drying on Manu's racks.

"Where are you going?" asked Manu, handing her a betel nut.

"To Kacaw's house to cure his *wawa*," said the old shaman as she chewed the betel nut.

Sunk in thought, Manu remained silent. Her daughter had married a pastor and they were all pious Christians who looked upon shamanistic healing as the devil's work. If she blessed her it would be a greater heresy. Seeing that Manu wasn't speaking, the old shaman said good-bye and set off toward the mountains to the upper village.

"Kacaw, if the pastor finds out that we sent for the shaman to cure the child, we will be punished," said Kacaw's wife as she walked into the house carrying the child.

"The Public Health Clinic couldn't do anything for the child—we must have been cursed by our ancestors. If we don't ask the shaman for help, the child will die." Kacaw took the child and walked to the door. "I didn't tell anyone that we had asked the shaman to come so the pastor won't know." In the doorway, Kacaw looked at his only *wawa*. The shaman was standing by the doorway and Kacaw realized that she must have heard the conversation between him and his wife. Embarrassed, Kacaw greeted her and invited her inside.

Kacaw placed his *wawa* on the bed. The old shaman opened her tattered old bag and took out a betel nut and a small rusty knife that she wiped on herself. She then knelt and cut the betel nut in half. She waved a banana leaf with one hand as she murmured a spell. She focused her spirit on each heavy breath of the child.

Exhausted, the old shaman set off from Kawcaw's house for the lower village. She deeply believed that the ancestral spirits would heal their descendants and allow them to multiply in this world. With the setting sun behind her, the shadow of the old shaman was stretched out a long way over the ground. Coming in the opposite direction was Tamih, the pastor of Changguang Village.

"*Nga'ayho*," said the pastor as he respectfully greeted the old woman.

"*Nga'ayho*," said the old shaman, politely returning his greeting.

"I heard that Kacaw asked you to cure his *wawa*," said the pastor, handing her a betel nut.

"That *wawa* needed to be healed by the ancestral spirits, so I had to go and cure the child," said the old shaman, chewing the betel nut as she sat on a log by the roadside.

"I was just on my way there to pray to God for the child's recovery and to break Satan's curse."

The old shaman didn't reply and just chewed the betel nut. Seeing that the shaman didn't say anything, the pastor sat down.

"Old woman, everyone believes in Jesus. Why do you persist in not believing in the true God?"

"Because my ancestral spirits chose me when I was still young to be a shaman. I will always be a shaman in order to protect our village. Recently, the ancestral spirits indicated to me through signs that I should find a successor. I will instruct them in the shaman's way so that I can give an account of myself to the ancestral spirits."

The pastor sat quietly looking at the old woman in front of him. "Shamanism is superstition. Protecting children is the work of God, not the spirits. You will be judged if you don't repent," said the pastor somewhat excitedly.

The old shaman slowly stood up and, after patting the dust from the seat of her pants, walked away toward the lower village.

Sunday morning Lekal's Mama and Ina got ready to go to a pastoral meeting in Jingpu. A Lik, his little sister, raised a ruckus because she wanted to go with them. "You go to church with Manu, not with us." Ina put A Lik's hand in her older brother Maywa's and gestured that he should take her in the house. A Lik thrust aside Maywa's hand and sat down on the ground where she began crying loudly.

"I can't take this," said Ina as she picked up A Lik and placed her on the gas tank of the Wild Wolf motorcycle. She then sat down sidesaddle on the back of the motorcycle. They set off for Jingpu church where Mama Halu was in charge of the pastoral meeting.

"OK, wash your faces and after you finish eating *hakhak*, I'll take you to Sunday school," said Manu as she walked into the house.

Sunday morning and a cool breeze rustled the breadfruit tree on which the fruit had just set. Several children were playing with rubber bands under the tree. Lekal stood in the door of the church looking in as he wiped his feet that had never worn shoes on the threshold. The children were not allowed to enter the church lest they play with the piano or cause some commotion to disturb the solemn atmosphere. Lekal suddenly noticed the pastor looking in his direction so he quickly ran and joined the children playing with rubber bands.

In the afternoon a lot of people congregated on the seashore. The old people sat under the bamboo awnings to stay cool. The chief had called the elders together to discuss the matter of *Kilum'an*.

"The priest said that the Church will contribute three cases of rice wine and, with the five cases provided by the Village Hall, that makes eight cases . . . " The chief looked at the young fishermen and sighed. "There are fewer and fewer young people."

"It's possible that only half of the villagers will attend the *Kiluma'an* this year," said one of the elders as he took a sip of rice wine, "I hear that the Protestants over there can't attend."

"Hurry and take the fish over there," shouted Mama No Kapa at the young people as she pointed to a woman who was starting a fire.

"That's impossible. Though we are Christians, we are also *Pangcah*!" said another elder as he chewed betel nut.

"What do you think?" the chief asked the old shaman.

"We must pass our traditions on to the next generation," replied the old shaman as she chewed betel nut. "We don't want to make distinctions between Catholics and Protestants because we are all one tribe."

The chief nodded and toasted the old shaman with rice wine. The old shaman first dipped her finger in the wine and made an offering to heaven and earth before drinking.

It was time to eat fish. The young people served fish in sections of bamboo to the old people. The children ran up and looked at the fish and fish soup spread over the ground. A little girl by the name of Panay touched the head of a fish, and her Ina quickly pulled her hand back.

"What are you doing? That's bad manners. The old people have not eaten yet." She quickly picked up the girl and took her to where the women were.

The sea breeze mixed with the drunken singing, the melody changed magically into dancing bubbles only to disappear as the waves hit the pebbled beach. At dusk on the beach, the sound of their singing and dancing as if by magic seemed to scatter a layer of celestial golden powder that floated on ever wave that came and went.

At the hot end of June Halu sat under a thatched awning weaving bamboo. He was humming his favorite Ami love song. His nephew Kusin also sat under the thatched awning. Kusin picked up a betel nut that he had smeared with lime and then popped it between his thick lips and chewed it vigorously.

"Uncle, I'm thinking about leaving here to get a job. What do you think?" asked Kusin as he watched Halu who concentrated on his weaving.

"Why do you want to leave?" asked Halu putting down the half-finished basket. He too picked up a betel nut and, after smearing it with lime, put it in his mouth.

"I gotta make some money. My woman is pregnant again and I can't feed a family by farming."

"What do you want to do?" asked Halu as he picked up the basket and continued weaving.

"They're looking for fishermen at a fishing port in Taidong. I'm thinking of signing on." Kusin spat the betel nut juice on the ground and then drank some water. He felt cool.

Halu lowered his head to think for a moment and then said, "You'd better think it over and ask around some more."

"Actually, there are lots of job opportunities in Taidong. I don't have to be a fisherman. I could be a carpenter," continued Kusin. He had grown up in Changguang and had been no farther than Chenggong. For someone who grew up in Changguang, Taidong was prosperous city.

On summer nights the heat of the day disappeared. Manu, the old shaman, and the other old people sat around the square, braiding the hair of the children for *Kiluma'an* and watching the young girls practice dancing.

"The dances of the girls these days are really awful," said Manu, watching them.

"You're right! Their hands have no strength, their feet don't move, and they don't know how to swing their butts," said Kazu's manu, laughing.

"Girls who don't swing will never attract the boys," Manu shouted at the group of dancing girls. The advent of *Kiluma'an* seemed to take all the old folks back to their vigorous youth with that kind of hope for an evening visit from a lover. The dancing and the singing gave rise to all of their expectations.

The chief called together the village elders to discuss the details of the coming *Kiluma'an*.

"Are you sure that the Protestants from over there are not coming?" he asked the elder in charge of contacting them.

"They say they're not coming, but on *Kiluma'an* they'll come running to dance," said the elder confidently as he took a swig of Whisbih energy drink.

"That's fine. Then this year each class will take care of the things they usually handle. Hurry and go pick up the wine that the Village Hall is providing. We have to test everything first. The day after tomorrow, the young people will go to the mountain and cut down some bamboo . . . "

The beautiful *Kiluma'an* came with a bumper harvest, the days mixed with the salty smell of the sea. Memories would be revived amid the singing and dancing under the thatched awning.

The old shaman sat in her house carefully examining the ritual implements she would use the following day. Her tattered shaman's bag stood in stark contrast to the shiny banana leaves on the ground.

"*Nga'ayho*," Lekal softly greeted her, carrying a bag of *hakhak* and three flying fish.

"*Nya'ayho*," replied the old shaman as she paused from sharpening her small rusty knife to look up at Lekal.

"Manu told me to bring this to you," said Lekal, placing the *hakhak* and flying fish on the table, after which he squatted. "Are you getting your things ready for tomorrow?" Lekal softly asked.

"Yes. I have to perform the ritual tomorrow and I don't want to spoil our *Kiluma'an* by using broken things. I also have to get my shaman's clothes ready!" The old shaman laughed as she continued sharpening her knife.

"But at Sunday School our teacher's wife told us that if we don't believe in God we'll go to hell," said Lekal, watching the shaman as she was bent over sharpening her knife.

The old shaman paused, looked up and smiled at Lekal. Then she lowered her head and resumed sharpening her knife.

At night the old shaman examined her old shaman's clothes as if she examined her whole life and all her memories that were fading with time. She touched each tarnished piece of silver on her headdress. They were no longer shiny. Had the efficacy of the ancestral spirits become tarnished and dim like the once shiny pieces of silver? Under the brightly shining moon the old shaman repeated the words of the first prayer she had ever said for the spirits when she was a young girl. Her voice was as soft as the footsteps of time on her face, where it had deeply etched eternal memories on her once radiant skin. The old shaman walked over to the already erected bamboo awning and examined every part of it. The previous year two other shamans had joined her in warding off the evil spirits at the *Kiluma'an*; this year she was the only one left to insist that the mountains and the ocean protect the people of the mountain and the ocean. The next morning she would display betel nut at the four corners of the tribal village and recite the incantation to protect the people of Changguang. She walked barefoot to the shore, where the moonlight turned the water into a shimmering sea of silver. Only where the waves crashed against the shore was the calm broken. The waves lined up one after another in the boundless darkness on the calm silver sea, only to break with a roar for the sufferings of which no one was aware. Before the beginning of the fun, she had to be alone and calm. Were the beliefs of others right? Or was she right to maintain hers? Was she the only one sober in a drunken world? Or did she alone persist in error? Lekal's innocent words were like a small boat that started ripples on the sea of her faith. At that moment even a wise old woman like herself was confused.

In the morning, the old shaman put on her ceremonious black robe and went to the square. She opened the rice wine, recited an incantation, and performed her ritual. She assumed that the chief and the elders would soon join her in the square and assist in the ritual as she visited the four corners of the village. The beautiful golden rays of the sun shone over every inch of the land being harvested. The chief and the elders arrived in the square accompanied by the priest. The shaman didn't look twice and concentrated on performing her ritual.

"A Fan, you don't have to perform the ritual . . . " said the chief to the old shaman, "we have asked the priest to come and offer a prayer before the *Kiluma'an*."

The old shaman looked at them with surprise. She had just spit out the rice wine and some of it trickled down the wrinkles around her mouth. "Why?"

The elders bowed their heads, and the silence thickened in the warm air.

"Protecting the people is God's work and his blessing," replied the priest in Ami with a foreign accent.

"It is our ancestral spirits who protect the Ami," said the old shaman, standing to face the priest.

The priest looked at the chief, unsure how to speak to the old woman.

The chief stepped forward with his cane, lowered his head, and patted the old shaman on the shoulders without uttering a word.

The old shaman slowly gathered up the banana leaves, rice wine, and betel nuts from the ground and placed her bright and polished little knife in her tattered shaman's bag. Stoop shouldered and barefoot, the old shaman slowly walked out of the square.

No one saw the old shaman until the Sunday morning after the *Kiluma'an*. As the congregation sang a hymn, murmurs arose. The old shaman entered the church barefoot. She saw the two other shamans, who had already been baptized, nod to her. Those nods pierced her heart with sadness . . .

One cool evening the old shaman took out her black shaman's robe, touched every thread, pearl, and piece of silver. She softly sang every ritual song she knew, the words of which fell on every thread, pearl, and piece of silver. The small bells tinkled bespeaking the trust of the ancestral spirits in the shaman. The old shaman carefully placed all of her robe in a box and, with the moon as a witness, put it in a hole she had dug earlier beneath a betel nut palm. One scoop of earth followed the next . . . the ritual songs sung by the old shaman and the tinkling bells bespeaking the trust of the ancestral spirits broke with the waves, spraying over the sea where the ancestors lived.

The Last Days of Ikafaduan

SIYAPENJIPEAYA

IN ANCIENT TIMES there were nine tribes scattered around Orchid Island. Originally there were two tribes in Langdao: a big tribe of more than one hundred households and a small tribe of more than thirty households. The larger tribe was dispersed by a natural disaster with the remnants joining the smaller tribe, which gradually grew to become today's Iraralay. The Yeyou also consisted of two groups: today's Yeyou Yaya, which consists of fifty households, and the Ivaeas, which consisted of more than one hundred households and, for unseen circumstances, joined the Yeyou tribe. By the same token, the Dongqing tribe also included a group of more than ten households called the Straolo-did that had joined the Dongqing tribe for unseen circumstances. The Yeyin, Yuren, and Hongtou tribes experienced no changes. The ninth tribe was the Ikafaduan tribe.

The Ikafaduan tribe was the evilest on Orchid Island. When members of other tribes passed through their village on the way to visit family elsewhere, they would be robbed of their luggage. All the other tribes knew how overbearing they were, so they began taking their boats to visit their relatives. But they too would board ship and rob them. The other tribes did not wish to fight because the Ikafuduan had a giant headman who wielded a wooden club the size of a rudder with which he savagely beat people.

When the gods saw how overbearing they were, they sent a deluge that was down a mountain that blocked a small stream that turned into a small lake that contained small fish, shrimp, crabs, and other creatures. The people of the tribe never once imagined that the small lake could be the source of disaster and so went on with their rapacious lives as usual. The gods saw that they did not change their ways, so they performed a divine miracle: under the shining sun, while the people sat in front of their houses chatting, a huge purple flying fish emerged from the sea and flew over the village to the small lake above. As the villagers discussed the occurrence, someone even said that it was proof positive that they were the strongest tribe on Orchid Island. Unfortunately, they didn't know that a great catastrophe was approaching.

Naturally, there were a few good households in the tribe. At night the gods spoke to them in a dream, saying: "Oh, good people! In the coming days you must sleep on your porches. If you notice anything the least bit amiss, you must flee quickly." After several days another deluge fell, filling the little lake above the village. Late at night the good people recalled the dream of the previous day and immediately fled. But the bad people slept soundly. After a short while the gods removed the mountain damming the river and the water flew toward the village. In a matter of seconds the whole village was drowned.

The following day members of the other tribes came to look, and the village really was under water. From then on no one tyrannized over others and everyone was allowed to visit their relatives in peace.

The Legend of Gubachae

LIGLAVE A-WU

THE BAWULAI WERE an important family in Old Wushan Village. Lidage, the eldest son, married Hesi, a girl from the Northern Yaner Village. The couple loved each other very much. They often went down to the stream to catch fish and shrimp, especially among the boulders around Gubachae, Zhoubulili, and Shaleqima, which they were often reluctant to leave.

During the busy farming season the couple worked with everyone in the family. Hesi was in charge of cooking and fetching water, but she had a habit of not eating with the family. In those days an oven was no more than a hole dug in the ground covered by a slab of stone. A wood fire was lit beneath the stone slab. When the stone became hot, it was removed and taro and yams placed in the coals and then the stone was replaced and thirty minutes later everyone could enjoy the deliciously cooked taro and yams.

Whenever Hesi cooked, the family always found that the food had a funny taste to it. After one month everyone in the family was noticeably thinner. The old man of the family thought to himself: "We're still eating the same amount of food and the same kind as always. Why are we getting thinner? Something is wrong." So he started keeping an eye on his daughter-in-law's activities.

One day when the family went down to the fields to work, the old man made an excuse to return home. He hid nearby so as to watch his daughter-in-law. At first there was nothing out of the ordinary. As usual, she put the taro and yams into the oven. But then something strange happened. His daughter-in-law whistled twice and at once several different kinds of snakes appeared. She casually picked up two hundred-pacer snakes and placed them in the oven, covered the hole with the stone slab and earth. She then took up a bamboo bucket and set off to the stream to fetch water. The remaining snakes slithered away. The old man was nearly overcome with fear. Stumbling, he hurried back to the fields. He led the entire family back to the oven and anxiously scraped away the earth, removed the stone cover, and took out the two hundred-pacer snakes. Everyone was horrified. The hundred-pacer snake was a god to the people. How could they be cooked and eaten? At that moment Hesi returned carrying the bamboo bucket of water on her back. Seeing that the family had uncovered her secret she froze.

Finally the old man spoke. Though he sounded unhappy, he was still polite. "The hundred-pacer snake is sacred to us. We worship it. How could you cook them for us to eat? You are not welcome here." The old man sighed and continued: "No wonder we have grown thin."

Hesi knew she was wrong and said sadly, "I am sorry. I should leave." So saying, she picked up the hundred-pacer snakes, placed them in her skirt, and left without looking back. She ate the snake meat and spit out the bones as she walked. But strangely, when the snake bones fell to the ground, they turned into living, squirming hundred-pacer snakes. She made her way in this fashion to Shanaqinao. She thought of how much her husband loved her and that he would definitely come for her. She waited and waited, very bored. She sang to pass the time and, as she passed, she drew on the rocks. Strangely, whenever she touched a rock, it became as soft as New Year's cake. She drew patterns on the rocks, waiting for Lidage, her husband, to come, but he never showed up.

Later, she went to Gubachae, where, on the largest rock, she drew hundred-pacer snakes, human heads, lover's hearts, human bodies, and clouds. Only she knew what the pictures meant. Hesi covered the rock with drawings, but Lidage still did not show up. Then she thought that perhaps he was waiting for her at Zhoulibuli, so she crossed the stream and went to Zhoulibuli. Hesi leaned against a boulder and cried bitterly. Finally she decided to go back to her home at Yaner Village. Strangely, the boulder she had leaned against retained the image of her sad figure.

She crossed the stream, ascended the mountain slope, up over the mountain crest, and then over one mountain after another. Hesi slowly walked home. When she reached Saimao, she once again traced hundred-pacer snakes and human heads on the rocks by the roadside. She was disappointed, sad, and angry that her husband had not come for her so the snakes and heads she drew all looked fierce and brutal. When children pass these rocks, they cover their eyes and hurry by, not daring to look. After Hesi returned to Yaner Village, the people felt they had been greatly shamed, and the two villages, which had once been on friendly terms, began an endless, bloody feud.

Afterward

Today there are a number of petroglyphs of human heads, clouds, and snakes in the mountains of Maolin Township in Gaoxiong County. This legend had its origins in this area. There are lots of petroglyphs around Gubachae (Old Wanshan Village), Zhoubulili (today's Wanshan Village in Maolin), and Gubachae (the mountainous area near today's Wanshan Village in Maolin). The legend has it that Hesi, the sad Bunun girl who waited for her husband, drew the pictures.

The Hunter

HUSLUMA VAVA

1

Every life and spirit lives in its own niche in the dense, vast forest. Growing in the deep silence, even the old withered leaves lie thick on the ground, returning to the bosom of the earth in silence.

"I have to get to *mai-batu* (cave) before it gets dark, otherwise it will be a disaster." Banidun quickened his pace as he looked up at the small patches of sky that flashed through the tree leaves. What change was he expecting to see in the sky?

From the oral teachings of his father and brothers as well as years of experience in the mountains, Banidun understood the significance of all the expressions of the sky. It was the only channel open to his people to understand the joy and anger, happiness and sadness of *Dihaning* (the god of Heaven and the highest spirit of the Bunun). When he was very small, a village elder told him that the god of heaven was an immense god and that only his face was visible to the people on account of their insignificant abilities. The sky was the face of the god of heaven and its blinding light forced them to shade their eyes or squint to look upon it.

Or perhaps it was because people did so many bad things that, whenever they looked up to gauge the sky's mood, they had to partially conceal their faces out of a sense of shame as well as squint humbly.

"The god of heaven leaves people in awe!" Banidun believed the words of the elder.

Banidun paused beneath a huge tree and rested while he caught his breath.

He looked up at the peak ahead of him and stretched out his right hand as if to measure the distance between two objects.

"Still two fingers to Stone House," said Banidun to himself. From the corner of his eye, he could see the sky was growing darker. He frowned until his face ached.

Stone House was not a house or a worker's hut built by his people but rather a large boulder that jutted out from the slope of the mountain that formed a cave. From a distance it looked like a house without walls. It served as a *kanadan*, or landmark, for the smarter hunters and a shelter from the weather. For this reason it was called *mai-batu*. Normally, all sorts of animals sought shelter there to rest and sharpen their teeth. But as soon as a human being arrived, the animals fled to the dangerous forest because they knew if they didn't they would end up being hurt and ravenously gulped down. So when Banidun arrived at Stone House, alone and solitary, all he could do was stoop inside and with his hands identify the various droppings.

"There have been wild goats here the last few days." The piles of droppings on the ground were enough to tell Banidun what sorts of animals were active in the area.

Banidun cast aside the handful of droppings and pushing aside the droppings covering the ground, he could see that the moist earth was covered with even-toed hoof prints. He squatted to see what information the hoof prints might have for him. Among the disorderly prints, some looked as if they had been made by the middle and index fingers of a small child. The edges of the prints were dry.

"A herd of muntjac was here early yesterday morning. The hind leg of one had been caught in a trap and it probably wouldn't live out the winter," thought Banidun as he touched the prints that seemed to float on the surface of the earth.

Other of the sunken tracks looked like they had been made by the middle and index fingers of an adult. They were still moist. He picked up some of the larger pellets to examine them. They were still moist. Happily, Banidun affirmed that a long-haired goat had been there early in the morning. Not only that, but it had to be nearby watching his every move or was resting before foraging in the evening.

Banidun stood up and, after examining the entire interior of Stone House, proceeded toward the open area to his right and slowly placed his rifle and net bag on the ground while simultaneously sweeping the sparse droppings away with his foot. He sat on the ground next to his bag and patted the ground with his hands as if happy with the clean spot of ground.

"The iron pan goes on the ground, the millet goes into the pan, the wood and powder go into the crevice." Banidun always liked to talk to himself to dispel the uneasy solitude. All hunters were the same: whenever they were out hunting alone in the forest, they always talked to themselves to increase their courage and drive away solitary demons.

There was a loud booming sound and a flash of blue light that made Banidun pause in organizing his things. As he turned to look outside Stone House, he discovered that the stones, trees, and bushes had all become black, and the increasing darkness frightened him.

"These thick *iisav* (treetops) like nothing better to than to make the earth dark." He had not yet organized his things and before he could get comfortable it had become dark making it difficult to do anything. He was also annoyed looking at the big trees that blocked out the sky.

"I'll get a fire going first! And let the solitary demons know that Banidun of the Bunun is staying here." He raced off into the forest to gather some dry wood.

As he parted the brush he looked around him and slowly entered the dark forest. On the slope to his left he saw a fallen tree, its bark gone and its golden branches resembling deer antlers.

"This tree—it looks like it has been dead a long time—should keep me warm all night."

Banidun broke off some of the smaller limbs toward the top of the tree then, with the veins standing out on his face, forcefully squeezed and pressed them together as if he wanted to reduce them to dust.

"This is great kindling." Satisfied, he took the knife at his waist and began to chop the wood into suitable lengths to make it easier to carry back to Stone House.

The muggy weather quickly made him feel tired. He cut a vine and tied the dry wood together into a tight bundle and then squatted to hoist it on his back. He saw some small tree seedlings that had been pressed into the ground for a long time by the dead tree. Feeling sorry for them, he reached out and propped them upright. In all seriousness he spoke to the trees one by one:

"You have to grow upright if you are ever going to become big trees. I'm taking the old wood away, now you hurry up and grow. Someday when my people come here to hunt you'll have to supply them with some dry branches so they can start a fire and stay warm and not catch cold."

Banidun believed that with this sort of pious worship of the little seedlings the tree spirits would provide his people out hunting with lots of dry branches after they grew up and would keep them warm on cold and lonely nights.

The blazing fire gave off a lot of warmth and the flickering firelight made the Stone House move with living force. Banidun lowered his dark-complected face and concentrated on making an *ahu-mushut*, or neck snare, out of tough, strong cord, using the skills passed down by his ancestors. It was a wisdom obtained by long-term observation of the habits of the prey. The cord would be cleverly camouflaged on the paths frequently used by the animals so that, suspecting nothing, they would enter the trap head and neck and then the force with which they ran would tighten the cord, holding them fast.

2

The neck snare was one of the traps used by Banidun's clan, the *taki-banuw* (one of the six large communities). The Hepisi tribe of *isbubukun* (Jun community), on the back side of the mountain, excelled at using the *ahu-bantas* (foot snare). But they buried their snares on the frequently used trails. Passing animals would step into the snare and be held fast, unable to flee.

"A snare buried in the ground could be further concealed with dead leaves or soil, but a neck snare had to set in the air at the same height as the animal for which it was intended. As such, only a skilled hunter was able cleverly camouflage the trap to make it invisible to sharp eyes of the prey. Banidun stood proudly upright, satisfied at being a member of Luan Village.

"Year after year the wild animals ran in the wind and rain through the forest, the strength and speed of their legs outstripped the imaginations of the people, so it was easy to imagine an animal breaking a foot snare cord." If the hunters of Jun community failed to trap anything, they usually blamed it on the snare rope being broken. Banidun slumped a bit into a more comfortable position and quickened the making of the snare.

One year, the year he received the blessings of the god of heaven, he used a neck snare to snare a lot of animals. On a particularly productive hunting trip, Banidun had shouldered a wild boar and was on his way home when he ran into Salilang of the Hepisi tribe. He discovered that Salilang walked lightly and quietly greeted him and offered his blessings. Banidun lowered the heavy boar from his back and slowly placed it on a large boulder by the road. After wiping the sweat from his face, he looked at the unencumbered hunter and said:

"How's it going? Have there been any animals foraging in the hunting ground lately? Are there many tracks?"

"Perhaps the god of heaven is dissatisfied with us? Or perhaps the animals have found a better place to forage? Aside from the sound of ants moving in the leaves, our hunting ground is as silent as a grave. A lifeless hunting ground is frightening." Other than in war, the only way for the Bunun to show their courage and agility was by struggling directly with animals. Ordinarily they were reserved and shy. And Salilang was actually showing fear!

"Perhaps the kids are overly active at home or the women gossiped, transgressing the *samo* (taboos) established by the ancestors." Banidun believed that often a hunter's immediate family was to blame for the shame he had to bear.

"Maybe it's because I'm so lazy that I don't even dream when I sleep," said Salilang, embarrassed.

Game was the gift of the god of heaven bestowed on his favored hunters. If the god of heaven were dissatisfied, even the most diligent hunter would come up empty-handed, since even the most capable of hunters couldn't necessarily bag the noblest of beasts as they wished.

"The animals are not born just for us," said Banidun squinting up at the sky.

"The blessings of the god of heaven will eventually descend upon your people," said Banidun to comfort him while removing the boar from his net so as to place it on the boulder.

"Look at the size of that boar! Its tusks must be four or five fingers long, right?" After being removed from the constricting net, the boar seemed even fatter. No wonder Salilang had shouted in amazement. He immediately measured the boar's tusks with his fingers, and they were indeed four fingers long.

"Tusks this big could rip a hunting dog's belly open." Salilang could imagine how a cornered boar would charge madly, skinning the hunting dogs and leaving blood everywhere the way a hunter used his knife on his prey.

"This wild boar was probably feeding little ones with these teats not long ago," said Banidun, lightly touching its teats. This was how a hunter handled the spoils of war, the way a man caressed the breasts of a woman.

"Hunting is not easy and it requires a lot of luck. You take it home for your people to enjoy," said Salilang, as he watched Banidun take out the knife at his waist. He knew what was about to happen and he was embarrassed.

The Bunun believed that game was bestowed by the god of heaven. For this reason it could be shared with others who saw it; it is the duty, then, of a successful hunter to share his game with those around him.

"This is the oldest of traditions. What power do we have to change it?" Banidun waved his shining knife in his right hand while pinching the flesh of the boar's foreleg with his left hand and eyeing the meat on its hind legs. Then he turned and said to Salilang:

"How many kids do you have under your roof? How many old people?" Although Banidun knew Salilang was a member of the Hepisi tribe of the Jun community, he had never been to his house so had no idea of how many people were in his family.

"Seven or eight kids and old people," said Salilang, roughly calculating how many people he had living with him.

"Hold the boar's head. I'll cut off a hind leg and you can take that home!" Banidun spread the big, fat hind leg to cut it off.

"No! A foreleg is OK—just enough to make soup is fine." There wasn't as much meat on the foreleg as on the hind leg. As a hunter, Salilang was embarrassed to take the meaty hind leg.

Banidun's movements were precise and rapid. He quickly had the hind leg in his hands and was pushing it on Salilang. "Take it home for the kids. They've been waiting at home for a long time." Banidun recalled how he stood in the doorway gazing at the distant green mountains when his father went hunting.

"Don't worry about it! Take it! The next time when the god of heaven looks after you and we meet on the road, you'll have to give me a hind leg." Banidun was the older hunter so no one would really object to what he said.

So that's the way it was. That time he had trapped a "three-legged" boar. The village and his relatives as always would admire and praise him. That was because the hunters in the area often caught "three-legged" boars and even four-legged ones, if they managed not to run into anyone on the road.

The thunder was growing louder. The flash of bluish light was so bright he could clearly make out the mountain rats climbing the walls of Stone House.

"It's going to be a big storm tonight." Banidun finally had finished the snare he was going to use the next day.

The water quickly came to a boil and the millet was soon cooked. Cooking was a simple matter in the mountains. He selected a relatively flat piece of dry wood from the pile of firewood and using his knife fashioned a simple spoon and began filling his hungry belly. After several bites he pulled a small leather bag out of his net bag. He took out a pinch of salt and sprinkled it on the millet. This would make the millet even more flavorful for the hungry hunter. Millet with a little salt was the best food for the ever-changing forest and for following the tracks of the quickly moving beasts. As the old saying put it, "Don't carry too much stuff because it will only slow the tracker's steps."

To determine the force of the rain outside, Banidun stopped chewing so that the sound of his teeth wouldn't interfere with his acute hearing. He could hear the rain beating on the tree leaves. It fell hard and heavy, knocking old and sick leaves to the ground, giving them no chance to resist. Illuminated by the lightning, the falling rain looked like dense shafts of *husau* (wooden pestles) falling from above to pound the earth. Sometimes the wind would blow the rain into larger columns. The earth looked like a stone standing under a waterfall, struck and battered by the water.

"This is an evil storm." Banidun pressed the millet into small balls that he then stuck on the end of a stick. He held the stick and turned it over the flames, roasting the ball of millet until it was very dark. Watching the millet darken by the fire, his expression became increasingly serious.

Banidun then stuck the end of the stick firmly into the ground and squatted and fixed his eyes on the blackened millet on the end of the stick. Piously he prayed:

"*Hu*! (a shout to call the spirits) Let all the wild animals in this mountainous area come tonight and eat this millet on which I have cast a spell. Let the animals that eat the blackened millet not see the trap I set and lose all strength to run away or resist. Let them lie down on the ground and welcome my arrival. Let capturing plump and lovely wild beasts be as easy as plucking millet." Looking at the wild storm outside of Stone House, he realized that the sound of rain drowned out his prayers. He began to have doubts about the efficacy of his prayers. This was a ritual to appeal to *mailan-tangus* (ancestral spirits) for help in catching game. This is the way his people had piously prayed since the earth began.

3

Sleeping soundly on the ground, Banidun was awakened by the urgent squeaking of a rat in addition to the sudden sound of thunder. His longing for sleep was hurled into the darkest part of the valley. Instinctively he kicked both feet. The gray haired, white-breasted rat fell from his thick, strong legs to the ground. Seeing the rats scamper off in all directions, Banidun, now fully awake, pondered his present situation.

"What scared these 'lazy women'?" Banidun was afraid the animal that frightened the rats might also harm him. After all, people were the same as any other animal in the forest—they had to protect themselves from bigger, stronger, and greedy animals. Human beings possessed guns and were bloodthirsty by nature and that is why the animals in the mountain forests avoided them.

Banidun instinctively picked up a wooden stick and carefully turned over, his sharp eyes—like those of an owl seeking its prey—swept over every corner of Stone House.

"Is there no other animal other than me that can scare the rats?" Banidun felt there was enough room in the small Stone House for himself as well as for the rats to find a quiet place out of the rain. He had no intention of harming such weak animals. Satisfied, he watched as the rats scampered about for a safe place and then threw the stick at a large rat glancing all around. For an animal to stay calm in his presence was always enough to aggravate a hunter, and Banidun was no exception.

"Were these rats really once women?" Watching as the rats bumped into each other as they scampered all over for safety, Banidun recalled the following story:

> In ancient times a young woman by the name of Tanifu lived in the Jun community. She was extremely lazy and liked to sleep. She often slept from morning till night and did no chores around the house.
>
> One evening, after her family had finished working for the day, they returned home very tired. They assumed Tanifu would prepare dinner and they would be able to enjoy a piping hot meal upon returning home. But there she was asleep in bed. Impatiently, her mother shook her awake. She opened her eyes and, seeing that her parents had returned, she nervously jumped out of bed and, half asleep, put the unhulled millet in the pot to cook. Shortly thereafter she brought the food out for everyone to eat. But how could they eat unhulled millet? Unable to control himself, her father began to berate her for her numerous shortcomings. Ashamed, Tanifu grabbed the millet and ran into a hole where she became a shy rat.

"If you had acquired the habit of diligence in those days, you wouldn't have been punished by the god of heaven and forced to wander about destitute in the forest. We're not going to lose any millet on your account." Banidun felt sorry for these "lazy women" who were found all over the forest and who had no one to depend on.

The striking of the wooden stick increased the agitation of the rats. Some of the braver rats began to flee outside and the remaining ones, like obedient children, quickly followed suit, disregarding wind and rain. Unnatural occurrences always make one feel uncomfortable, and Banidun began to feel as frightened as the rats, his mind was filled with inauspicious thoughts.

"Don't underestimate the reason for their fear." With the old saying in mind, Banidun wanted to get to the bottom of the rats' flight despite his own fear.

The fleeing rats that remained inside Stone House were soaked to the bone. Occasionally they would pause and use their forepaws to wipe themselves and bow their backs and shake the water from their fur.

Banidun looked at the water seeping into the cave, running like small waterfalls through the crevices. There were as many waterfalls as there were crevices. Then he recalled the things he had placed in the crevice and immediately removed them. Actually, the only things he could get to were soft and soggy matches and gunpowder.

"Damn! The water is even going through stone tonight."

"I'm getting out of here with the rats!" In such a dangerous situation efforts had to be made to escape, to find a way to go on living. Banidun hurriedly put all the things he had brought with him into his net bag and, somewhat hunched over, took off in the same direction as the rats, putting some distance between himself and Stone House. The Bunun people know that forays into the forest were made to plunder the lives of other creatures to ensure their own. The animals lived off the forest. For that reason the animals knew how to survive better in the dangerous forest than men.

The rain striking his face forced him to squint; amid the storm sky and earth were so dark that they seemed not to exist. Banidun paused, and, as the lightning flashed, he clearly saw the placement of the trees and listened to hear which way the rats were headed. The brush above swayed more vigorously than that close at hand and he frequently heard the urgent squeaks of the rats.

"The rats are fleeing to the peak!" Banidun pushed through the brush without hesitating. A hunter's road could be anywhere except a sheer rock face.

The Bunun were not painstaking builders of roads. For them a road could be taken easily at any place or any time. In the early days when the various peoples of Taiwan did not trust one another, outsiders were unable to attack Bunun, because no telltale roads marked the location of their villages. This custom and ability allowed the Bunun to live free and at ease for a long time.

Besides making use of the flashing lightning, Banidun relied on his sense of hearing to follow the intermittent squeaks of the rats to the peak. Occasionally, he would toss a stone into the bushes to raise a sound from the rats when they grew quiet.

The thunder cracked and echoed through the forest. The entire earth seemed to shake with the rhythm of the thunder. Banidun fell frightened in the bushes.

"Was that lightning? Was that thunder?" Banidun huddled in the bushes like a sick old man. A loud roar of falling trees and sliding mud and rocks rose from below.

"The rain pushed the whole Stone House down into the valley!" Banidun stumbled and climbed to his feet and ran for the slope. Being just above the Stone House, he figured the ground would soon give way and follow. He could vaguely hear the faint sound of the rats moving across the slope. The rain slowed his steps, but fortunately everything was clearer amid the flashes of lightning. In his flight Banidun left a twisted chaotic trail like a python. The plants in his path suffered the same evil fate at the hands of the disaster as Banidun.

4

Banidun touched the dry wall of rock at the foot of the cliff, which seemed to fall out of the sky. He closed his eyes to catch his breath as if he were confident that the cliff could protect him.

He looked over the right side of the cliff to where the water formed a roaring torrent. He believed that old saying, "The greatest force is the most yielding and the gentlest." Water was yielding enough that it could be drunk and could cool, but it could also push the Stone House into the valley and completely change the face of the forest.

"Water is like the breast of a woman." Banidun smiled a lone smile amid such trouble.

On days when they were not busy farming or hunting, the men of the village were accustomed to gathering in the houses of the best hunters, mostly to exchange hunting stories, but they always ended up on the subject of women. When they talked about women they were as excited as if they were facing their prey. Dama Darumu had once said, "Even the most able of hunters can be overcome by the breasts of a woman." In addition to smiling foolishly, everyone lowered their heads to conceal their shame. Like the other hunters, Banidun, upon hearing his children sleeping soundly beside him, would softly caress his woman's breasts and peacefully go to sleep.

Caressing a woman's breasts also rid a man of his fears that she might leave for no reason as well as to comfort him in his solitude with no one to rely on. Banidun looked for an open place as he put down his net bag.

"I'll have to sleep standing up tonight." He twisted his body in an effort to find a depression in the cliff to lean against. Disasters cause by a storm could come at any time and any place. Sleeping sitting up, one could quickly stand to confront any danger. In this calamitous situation he trusted only the cliff because it was bare and therefore could not produce a disaster. Banidun admired the cliff to no end. Only in the embrace of the mountain range did the hunter appear brave and the mountain range inspire awe.

"Bravery and majesty arise from this naked cliff." Having made up his mind, Banidun closed his eyes. Spending the night in flight left him exhausted and without much desire to check his traps. His many years of hunting experience told him that his traps had probably been lost, buried under the sliding earth in the valley or destroyed by falling trees.

"If I live until tomorrow, I'll find my way home." Banidun closed his eyes, thinking about his future. "I hope the big tree that shows the way is still alive; otherwise who else can show me the way home?" Entering the forest, all hunters take note of the large trees to serve as landmarks so as to avoid getting lost. Banidun was no exception. The forest is no place for people to live, so if a hunter loses sight of his landmarks or his way, he becomes the weakest and most vulnerable of animals in the forest.

It was deep in the darkest part of the forest, and Banidun couldn't spot his landmarks. He had to keep moving. Rushing ahead, he was like a bit of dandelion fluff blown ahead by the wind. Then he seemed about to fall into a deep valley, the bottom of which couldn't be seen. He vigorously thrust his hands into the sky, pleading for the god of heaven to help him, to reach forth and grab his two hands. After a sharp pain, his shout caught him below the cliff. A chill in his right hand told him his hand was bleeding. Looking at the blood stains on the rock wall, he said helplessly, "The unfortunate ones are those able twins." He was referring to a tribal legend. After speaking, he lowered his head in shame, a shame for being at wit's end. After the change in the face of the sky and earth, Banidun, like a hunted animal, had fled in the rain. He had relied on the rats to find his way and had even been injured in his sleep. He was ashamed of his own uselessness. He really was at a loss.

"The *taisah* (dream) of a moment ago was not very auspicious." The god of heaven told the future in dreams. Banidun was frozen with fear.

"Does the spirit of heaven wish me to perish in this valley of death?" Banidun piously tried to find an answer.

He saw a beetle clamber out of the dry leaves at his feet. Excitedly, he stood up and said, "It's daybreak and the rain has stopped. If I'm going to die I'm going to die in the village; otherwise, I'll become an evil spirit and be unable to protect my people."

Those who die of old age or illness in the village have the right to be buried in their houses. Because they died in peace, their souls become good spirits, and good spirits can return to the "eternal abode of the ancestral spirit" as well as obtain greater power to protect their descendants. By contrast, those who die outside the village die an evil death and must be buried in the open country. Their souls become evil spirits and as such they not only cannot return to the eternal abode of the ancestral spiritsbut also do their people harm. Their people will also view them as *pakpak* (malicious spirits).

After using the wet gunpowder to stanch the blood flowing from his hand, he quickly shouldered his net bag and set off for the peak. He hoped to find a wide, open space from which he could spot a large tree or the location of the village. Like a squirrel, Banidun scrambled up a snapped-off tree and squinting, gazed over the distant mountains.

"Aha! Dama-fafa, which lay in the direction of the village, is still standing after that night of rain." His joyful face beamed with admiration.

Dama-fafa was, in fact, a huge old pine tree. The people liked to name the huge old trees after deceased ancestors. In addition to showing respect, the giant trees served as directional markers for the village. Banidun had chosen the name Dama-fafa, the name of his grandfather, for the tree.

In the opposite direction the trees on the mountain had disappeared, leaving nothing but golden mud that shone fiercely under the sun. Disappointed, Banidun figured the traps had disappeared with the trees.

Looking at the silent sky, Banidun decided not to patrol his trap line but rather to head in the direction of Dama-fafa, because that was the way to the village and hope.

"Was I scared out of my wits or am I just getting old? The tree is clearly there in front of me, but why haven't I come to it yet?" Amid the snapped-off tree, Banidun sought an appropriate route as he gazed in the direction of the old pine.

"Did I go the wrong way?" He seriously considered the situation before him.

Suddenly a chilling cry was heard, a cry of death. Banidun ran in the direction of the cry: "Is someone hurt?"

The cry stopped and Banidun paused and then walked cautiously on the dry leaves lest the sound affect his keen sense of hearing.

Again he heard the high-pitched, chilling cry. The sound came from a huge fallen tree directly ahead of him, but the dense foliage prevented him from seeing what was crying. He approached the tree in an attempt to find out. Under the shaking leaves he saw a black animal rocking back and forth. He quickly and instinctively raised his rifle, but just as quickly set it down on the ground because he saw that his powder was wet, making the gun nothing more than a metal tube. His eyes wide, he slowly bent forward like the *dunath* (black bear) catching a glimpse of his prey. He saw an old monkey struggling to pull something from under the tree. He took a closer look and realized it was another monkey about half the size of the old one.

"Her baby was caught under the tree. No wonder she is making so much noise." Banidun stepped forward confidently. The brush around the tree trunk had all been trampled into the soft muddy ground, a sign of the monkey's anxiety. Had she struggled so fiercely to rescue her baby? Half of the small monkey could be seen sticking out from under the tree, but, in attempting to pull it out, the mother had pulled out most of its fur and its bluish skin was clearly visible in the light of day. One moment the mother would pull the baby by its arms or head, the next moment she would sit quietly beside it, her head down touching the baby's fur as if she hoped to awaken her baby with her tender gestures and forget what had happened.

The mother suddenly charged at Banidun, leaving him dumbstruck. She puffed herself up and bared her teeth, her face so filled with rage that Banidun retreated a few steps.

"Animals really won't allow anyone to encroach upon them." Banidun clutched his rifle and prepared to defend himself. The female monkey angrily eyed the invading enemy. She swayed constantly as if trying to shake the earth to demonstrate her strength. Banidun stared at her without flinching and waited for her all-out attack. After watching him for a minute, she squinted and raised her tail in the air, displaying her fire-red rump to Banidun. Then she slowly walked back to her baby and brushed its sparse fur while crying softly. Occasionally she would lift her baby's cold body, as if she hoped it would sit or stand up. As she turned and walked away, Banidun breathed a sigh of relief. He could not distinguish between fear and insult and just wanted to come out unharmed.

The mother charged once again. Banidun was on his feet at once, running to a higher piece of ground and assuming a defensive posture. Once again the monkey swayed, gazing at him angrily. Then once again she raised her tail in the air and displayed her fire-red rump and returned to brush the fur of her baby. After seeing her repeat the same movements, Banidun was less frightened and sat down as firm as a rock on the ground. He wasn't the least bit angry at the insult.

"Her baby is dead so why is she still treating it with so much tenderness?" Death was a frightening thing. For ages life had always fled from death.

"How stupid," scolded Banidun, seeing that the monkey didn't understand the rationale for life and death.

Watching her repeat the same movements, Banidun started to feel sorry for the monkey that had lost her baby. The anger in her face was familiar, and Banidun felt he had encountered such an expression before. Once again the mother ran at Banidun, baring teeth and claws. Seeing her face, which looked like it was going to explode, he felt that it resembled his own dead woman's. The angry eyes, the trembling with rage, and the angry face were exactly the same.

He was saddened by his memories. This sadness combined with his utter exhaustion nearly reduced him to tears.

5

That year like the previous night seemed to have been cursed by evil spirits. Rain fell day after day and the land seemed to dissolve like wood ash. The old stream was swollen and new rivulets had been carved out of the soft fields by the rain. The crops that had been tended with such difficulty were washed down the river. Amid the rain, heaven and earth seemed weak and aged, with little life left.

To survive, the people braved the rain and ran along the water's edge plucking wood and wild herbs from the flood. Banidun, his wife Tanifu, and their only son were among them.

"Look at that bunch of *sanlavhudu* (black nightshade) floating this way," said Tanifu, pointing at a black mass floating downstream.

"I'll swim over; you two wait here on shore." The current was strong and he didn't want his family taking risks.

Banidun, who was very strong, quickly pulled the black nightshade to the shore so that they could pluck the tender leaves with which to make soup. The smiles of mother and son seemed to blot out all the rain and wind.

"These are hard days. Take whatever can be eaten." Women were generally more careful and didn't want to waste any food provided by the land.

Banidun gazed at the river as he plucked the leaves hoping to spot something of use. Suddenly he heard a noise upstream where the people were scavenging. The noise continued but was indistinct in the wind and rain.

"Tempers flare up in difficult times." Banidun figured they were fighting over wild herbs or some other thing of use.

Then he heard the roaring sound of stones in water drawing closer and closer. He looked up and saw the bank being washed away by the surging water. He grabbed his woman by the hand and ran toward the slope. His woman fell and he pulled her to the mountain face.

"Wumasi is still in the water plucking wild herbs," she said breaking free of his grasp and running back to the water.

"It's too late, Tanifu!" Banidun pounced on her like a bear on a muntjac.

"I have to save my child! I want my child!" Tanifu struggled in his grasp, kicking and hitting him. He bore her blows, filled with regret for having forgotten their son. He held her tightly on the ground. Exhausted from striking him, she weakly embraced his shoulders. Holding one another on the muddy ground, they submitted to the blowing wind and rain.

The noisy earth emitted the sad cries of women.

Tanifu, who was normally quiet and withdrawn, passed each day in utter silence. She frequently ran down and gazed over the river, her eyes filled with rage. She would come home, filled with anger, only after night fell.

It was getting colder. In order to store more food to get through the harsh winter, Banidun went hunting alone in the mountains. After several days he returned happily to the village with lots of game, a bountiful hunt. The villagers did not praise him; instead, he heard how his wife had taken their son's clothes and run down to the river in search of him and had not returned.

After this, Banidun would dream of his wife looking for their son on the river, her eyes filled with rage, her face with hate.

The mother monkey stopped toying with the fur of her dead infant. She looked up and let out a chilling cry, a resounding cry, and then walked off into the dense forest the way his wife had walked to the deepest part of the river. Seeing this, Banidun couldn't help but think of his dead wife and son. He bit his lip, suppressed his tears, and approached the place where the little monkey had met its end.

As a hunter, Banidun calmly faced the animal crushed by nature. After looking at the tree, he squatted and began to dig the muddy earth from under the monkey with his hands. He extracted the baby monkey with ease. Looking at the crushed corpse, he wondered if his son's body had ended up as tragically after he drowned. Moved, Banidun knelt and hugged the body as he wept. But because his face was so wrinkled, the tears didn't fall, they pooled in the wrinkles. His dark face shone with tears.

The weeping of the old hunter could be heard coming from the forest, interspersed occasionally with the chilling cries of the monkey.

On and on, without end . . .

The Thunder Goddess

IT TA-OS

EARLY IN THE morning Dabajian Mountain, dark and awe-inspiring, looked down over the land below as it always did. A stream from high in the mountains cut diagonally across the land, sonorously irrigating the broad mountain valley. The many bamboo huts peeked out of the forest, indistinguishable from greenery as if they were trying to escape or hide.

Suddenly a ray of light shot to the ground. The silence was broken by a loud and frightful noise that shook the valley, knocking the morning dew from the leaves and sending the birds and beasts and dogs and chickens in a panicked flight. After a long while every inch of the village was filled with the sound of anguished lamentation and stifled tears.

Leaning against the wood fence, Dayin petted the three newborn pups he held against his chest. A whistle and the barking of dogs were faintly heard from the facing mountain. He hurriedly put down the puppies and shouted into the hut:

"Mom, they are leaving. I want . . ." Before he had finished speaking, Maya came running out of the hut and, deeply concerned, said:

"Look at you! You say you've got everything. You don't want to get hungry!" As she spoke, she slung a heavy woven hemp bag over her son's shoulder. Ahrou felt his way along the fence to open the gate.

"Don't come out, Dad!" Dayin shouted to his blind father. He bent down and picked up his wooden spear and disappeared in a flash into the shadows of the vast and dense forest. The three puppies played on a piece of heavy cloth spread at a corner of the fence. Maya sighed heavily:

"This child is always so forgetful. It's going to be cold the next few days." She looked uneasily toward the vast and lush green mountain forest.

The wild and intractable ridges of Xue Mountain, which seemed to block out all the sunlight, was circled in layers of thick mist. The elated hunters walking through the mist, unafraid of the dangerous mountain path, teased one another.

"Darou, wasn't it strange how that boar sow kept following you last time? Why do you think she was doing that?" The mocking tone of Wumao's innuendo set everyone to laughing.

"Wumao, you're good at climbing trees, right? How is it that you were pecked all over by that hawk, almost falling to your death and ending up with a bruised and swollen face?" said Darou countering sarcastically.

"Yiti was kissed on the lips by a tiger-headed bee, swollen duck lips. Ha, ha," said Da'ao, starting another battle of words. The column of hunters burst into laughter.

"And who's the idiot who pissed on the fire! His thing is so swollen . . . "

"OK, OK, that's enough," shouted Fa'ai, who was bringing up the rear. His bare chest was covered with glorious battle tattoos. The fun and games and the increasingly crude banter that had been going on amid the gradually changing scenery came to an abrupt halt.

"After we set up camp beside the waterhole on the other side of that cypress just ahead, let's each gather some food and prepare the night's meal." Fa'ai issued the order without a smile. It was so wild, dense, and dark that no one knew when night would stealthily fall on the boundless and hideous mountain forest, remote and quiet.

A short while later, the aroma of mushrooms, wild lettuce, rattan heart, wild fern shoots, and shrimp and crayfish from the river wafted from the campfire. To this was added the millet, taro, and sweet potatoes that each hunter had brought along, and right there on the spot, in their simple hunting camp, they consumed a nourishing meal.

"Keep your hunting gear with you at all times. Don't be in too much of a hurry when we corner prey; the hunter could become the hunted with the slightest misstep," ordered Fa'ai, after a loud belch. "And whatever you do, don't go alone," he continued. "Always stay in pairs at the least. Don't be like my little brother and get lost. We mobilized the entire village, only to find a pile of rotten flesh and white bones." Fa'ai frowned and angrily threw some wood on the fire, raising sparks along with tongues of fire into the air.

"Dayin, since this is your first time hunting, take some food out of camp and offer it to the spirit of the mountain. Wuming, you go with him." Fa'ai squinted as he exhorted him to obey the customs.

The frantic baying of the dogs commingled with the shouts of the hunters—a sambar deer had been surrounded on top of a big rock. Suddenly an arrow was heard whizzing by; it hit the deer in the neck. The deer fell on the spot.

"Hey, hey, hey, depart! Leave us the meat," shouted Biling as was necessary, whenever a large animal was killed, to comfort its spirit so that they wouldn't be possessed by an evil spirit.

"Look how strong I am! I can hardly carry it," laughed Bilig, his eyes full of mockery at Dayin, who had only managed to bag a flying squirrel, a civet cat, and a pheasant.

"So, Dayin. Do you see what I am carrying in my basket?" Troubled by his absence of luck, Dayin again had to take Youming's teasing.

Everyone returned to camp around sunset where they began butchering and salting the game. Once again saliva flew in a battle of words. Dayin frowned at his paltry catch. He had trouble sleeping that night because the snoring and the talking in sleep seemed to be mocking him.

Before dawn, on the third day of the hunt, a peal of thunder was heard and the sleeping land was shrouded with dark clouds. Soon the rain began to fall, sharp as arrows, extinguishing the campfire and sending up white smoke. With the fire out, the camp became active.

"Hurry, cover the food and the fire stone. Don't let them get wet . . . "

"Ah, Dao, you stepped on my sweet potatoes!"

"Hey, where did my serape get to?"

"Kalei, your arrows ended up in my ass. Ooh, they hurt . . . " As day broke, everyone was scurrying around madly. They ran to find shelter in a cave in a strange-looking rocky overhang.

"Get your gear together—it's at times like these the animals are most frightened. Daruo, you stay behind and look after the game. The rest of you to the hunt." Fa'ai, relying on a hunter's experience, refused to be cowed by the rain and roused the other hunters forward with his firm tone of voice.

The curtain of rain limited their vision. The dark sky and land looked vaster and gloomier, making the green treasure house resemble a forested hell. Suddenly the sound of whistling leaves was heard through the rain . . .

"Hurry! Find the game." Responding, everyone rushed toward a thicket of thorny devil's rattan. Inside were two wild boars, each as strong as a calf.

"Wumao and Youming cover the front. Ahdao, get several wooden spears ready. Kaleihei, pull the rattan aside," ordered Fa'ai in a low voice staying close to the ground.

The killing began. Ready for a battle, their hands trembled and their eyes were bloodshot, showing their fighting spirit. Hearing the commotion, Wubai and Da'ao joined the group, adding their strength. The wooden spears flew at the dark shapes from all directions. A brutal squealing brought the harsh atmosphere to a pitch.

"Careful, they'll charge," the men shouted, cautioning one another. The most frightening thing was a madly charging wounded boar. There was no telling how many hunters had met their end under the gnashing tusks. Quick reflexes combined with utmost patience and strength were essential to capturing such quarry.

"Ow, it hurts!" No one knew how Yiti's buttocks had been wounded, but the blood was pouring out.

"Daheshi and Youmao, hurry and bind his wounds," Wubai shouted as he stabbed the boar in the throat with his wooden spear. Squealing, the boar fell to the ground and died. The other boar died under the spears of the others.

Though the rain had not stopped, sweat or rain stood out on the hunters' faces. They had been cut by the rattan, scraped themselves on the rocks, and poked by branches, actually just too many things to enumerate. Just as they were about to butcher the game, something unexpected happened. Dayin was missing.

The people gathered in the wooden building by the square to generously share the abundant food the way they did every year. But the usual festive atmosphere was missing. None of the old people stood in a circle to sing; there was no vigorous dancing. Some people frowned and others wept.

"Spirit of the mountain! Ancestral spirits! Please protect the child!" Wudan, an elder, raised an offering of food as he mumbled a prayer.

"Dayin, my child, come home . . . " shouted a grief-stricken Maya for her beloved child as she swooned among the women folk.

"Well, is there any news? Do you suppose he has already . . . " asked the dejected Ahruo again of the shaman he sat next to.

The shaman fixed her eyes on the motionless diving pearl at the end of a stalk of silver grass. With both hands, she waved the smoke rising from a fire made of wood from an evil-repulsing tree. Beads of sweat on her face reflected the leaping tongues of flame. One moment she squinted, the next her eyes were wide open.

"The divining pearl does not move. I can't say for good or bad!" replied the shaman, discouraged. She felt alarmed, for, if the news were bad, it would be devastating for parents who had had a child so late.

"The weather in the mountains is bad. Wait till the rain stops then every family will send two men to search the mountains." Wadan the elder made this painful announcement to avoid any complications. The pitter-patter of the rain could be heard on the roof above and the wind could be heard passing over the square and through the bamboo grove. The village was shrouded in a sad mist . . .

"You guys go on ahead, I'm going to take a dump," said Dayin to his fellow hunters before going off into the dense bushes. As he answered the call of nature, he noticed through the bushes a huge tree that emitted a red light on the other side of the valley around which floated a misty form. His curiosity piqued, he decided he would investigate once he was finished.

He descended the slope clinging to vines then he crossed the already somewhat turbid stream. He climbed up a big rock and, looking up, saw a camphor tree. The strong-smelling tree had been hit by lightening—its trunk was split open and blackened and a number of broken branches were still smoldering. Disappointed, he was about to turn and depart. Standing at the edge of the precipice, he heard the sound of a woman's voice coming from below. He was scared out of his wits.

"Who's down there?" he asked, his voice trembling.

"Who's there? Speak up!" he asked, raising his voice to shout down the precipice while placing an arrow to his bowstring as he cautiously neared the place the voice was coming from. There was a noise and suddenly he found himself face to face with a woman. Startled, Dayin fell on the rock and lost the arrow he had readied, which shot past the woman in a parabolic arc and landed some distance away.

"Who are you? Are you a ghost?" Dayin quickly got to his feet and backed away, speaking incoherently.

"My name is Youwai. I lost my way and then it started raining, so I took shelter here."

"Jumping out so suddenly the way you did, I thought you were a monster. You scared me to . . . " shouted Dayin, still a bit startled. But he wondered how a woman could be out wandering around in the mountainous wilderness. Still suspicious, he couldn't help but look her over again, because she had scared him out of his wits.

She was of medium build with thick, black hair. Her eyes were not small, but she had long lashes and double-fold eyelids. She had an oval face and two dimples. Her clothes, which seemed to drape over her, were clean and spotless. This was the first time that the twenty-year-old Dayin had ever looked at a girl completely spellbound. Extremely beautiful, she set his heart to pounding and he blushed violently. He quickly lowered his eyes.

"Oh, no!" shouted Dayin when he saw how the stream had swollen.

"I wonder how much longer this heavy rain will last . . . " said Youwai, helplessly looking up at the sky.

"What am I going to do? We were hunting on the other side. If I don't get back, they'll be worried sick." Dayin paced anxiously. At that moment water began to fall over the cliff in several white falls. The dirty, roiling water roared, filled with woody debris. It looked as though Dayin's return route had been cut off.

Between the Mid-Autumn Festival and late autumn when the maple leaves turned red, a search party of around fifty people had set off three times full of hope to search the mountains but had returned three times in despair. Rumors gradually began to circulate like mountain fog in the village.

"Dayin fell into the swollen mountain river and was swept away."

"He was killed by the Atayal people at the foot of the north side of Dabajian Mountain."

"Dayin was eaten by a big black bear."

"He was carried off by a mountain monster."

The rumors multiplied and Dayin's poor parents were nearly prostrate with tears. They had gone from hope to disappointment to hopelessness. Both became ill because of their profound sadness. The old couple insisted, "Even if he is dead, we still want to see the body!"

In a cave filled with the aroma of camphor, Dayin, who was already given up for dead by his people, sat alone by the campfire doing nothing. He gazed at the swollen river that refused to subside. Helplessness and worry could be seen in his knit brows on his sharply chiseled face. He clenched his fists, angry at himself for having acted so willfully.

"Hey, have something to eat. There is no sense being upset. This kind of weather . . .," said Youwai, handing him a bunch of wild grapes.

"Where do you live? What's your name?" she continued.

"I'm Saisiyat. My name is Dayin. Our village is located at the south foot of Dabajian Mountain." When he finished, he suddenly realized that he was in Atayal hunting territory. Then the woman must certainly be Atayal. But she spoke Saisiyat. He was confused. Then he asked:

"Are you Atayal?"

"No, no I'm not . . . " She seemed to want to say more, but held her tongue. She lowered her head, her lips tightly shut. Deep in thought, she fanned the fire.

Actually Dayin felt like talking with her, but whenever he asked her about her background she became quiet. Being smart, Dayin realized that if he stayed away from the subject of her background, the talk flowed freely. They talked, asking and answering questions nonstop—the wind, rain, flowers, birds, white clouds, chickens, dogs, and one another's hair, eyes, noses, mouths, and feet. There wasn't a thing they didn't talk about and the distance began to disappear and a playfulness began to arise between them.

"Dayin, your eyebrows look like two wooly worms, the way they move."

"Youwai, there's a spider behind you, and a snake!"

"Dayin, spread your toes and place a stone between."

"Youwai, open your hand." Dayin put a cockroach in her palm and so scared her that she went pale. When Dayin was resting against the wall of the cave, she laughed, playfully drawing circles around his eyes with charcoal.

Time seemed absent from the mountains. Day and night followed one another but the sound of laughter never stopped. They seemed to have left the world of human concerns for a pure place for two innocents where there was no pride or disappointment, no degeneration nor evil. If he thought she was hungry, he would brave the rain and exert himself picking wild herbs and fruit; if he thought she had disappeared, he would fly with all speed back to the cave. Feelings of responsibility and happiness sprouted and grew. Love vaguely began to develop between them.

The village youth gathered up the wood washed down in the floodwaters and carried it to the square. In the light of the sun Fa'ai grit his teeth and used a needle to extract a thorn from the sole of his foot. Smoking a pipe, Wadan the elder wove a basket as he watched the children play, chasing one another under the watchtower. After the storm the village had returned to its normal peaceful way of life.

"Hey, hey," shouted the women, who were plucking lice from one another's hair as they patted their seats, when Dayin suddenly appeared outside the fence around the square with a woman.

"Dayin's back! Dayin's back!" The news spread like wildfire through the village. Everyone put aside what they were doing and surrounded Dayin, asking a hundred questions at once.

"Thanks be to the spirit of the mountain! At least you have returned," said Wadan weeping with joy as he squeezed his hands.

"Dayin, where were you? We turned the mountain upside down looking for you," said the villagers. Eyes red, Da'ao, who was closest to Dayin, made fun of him: "You said you were going to take a dump. What took you so long?"

Fa'ai limped along and pushed his way through the crowd and scolded him in a whisper: "You must have suffered. Running off like that, you're lucky to be alive."

"Hurry and go see your parents, they've been worried to death about you. Hurry up." This was the first time that Youwai had tasted such an emotional reunion. In tears, she followed everyone to Dayin's house.

The weeds had grown and the ground was littered with fallen leaves. A crowd had gathered at the weathered old bamboo hut for another touching reunion.

"My Dayin! Your mother has been worried sick about you," wailed Maya, grasping her son tightly, afraid that he might disappear again and tenderly caressing his face. Dayin approached his father's bed and spoke:

"Forgive me, Father, for worrying you and making you ill." Ahruo touched his son who had disappeared and now returned. He mumbled:

"At least you're back. It is a blessing from our ancestors." Dayin helped his father up and they sat side by side with the elder on the bamboo bench.

The hut was filled with people standing and sitting. Youwai pushed open the bamboo window and the sun shone in, filling the place with a soft golden light.

Dayin began to tell about what happened during the time he was missing. He pulled Youwai, who had stepped outside, before his parents and introduced her to everyone:

"This is the girl who was lost in the mountains."

"Who is she?"

"Where is she from?"

"She's so pretty."

Questions and compliments filled the air. Suddenly Ahruo covered his eyes with his hands and stood up. Slowly removing his hands, he trembled and shouted:

"My eyes, my eyes!" His strange manner caused a stir.

"I can see . . . ha, ha!" Ahruo laughed excitedly, and everyone was in a commotion. The miraculous cure without medicine was termed odd and astounding.

Ahruo threw aside his cane and walked unsteadily out the door. He looked at the green mountains, blue sky, and white clouds. His eyes longingly took in everything like a child who had received a desired toy. He leaped and shouted with joy.

A series of strange things occurred at Dayin's house, leaving everyone with different opinions.

"The spirit of the mountain has given Dayin strange powers."

"He has been possessed by a spirit."

"Perhaps that girl Youwai . . . "

Yes, Youwai and her mysterious background were suspicious. But everyone liked her for her affable down-home smile and her natural and graceful appearance. The old shaman especially treasured her and unstintingly gave her fine cloth garments and jewelry. Youwai felt very warm her first winter in the village.

But Dayin was the happiest—they were to be married come spring. As he dreamed at night, he laughed madly, waking the hunting dogs outdoors and setting them to barking, disturbing the tranquility of the hope-filled valley.

Butterflies danced in the air; drops of cold dew glittered on the sprouts; birds flitted among the branches and sang without stopping. Spring was coming to the village.

"Daheshi, slow down, my shoulder aches!"

"Change shoulders and it won't hurt, you fool," sighed Youmao as he slowed his pace.

"Daruo is very selfish. He runs ahead to the river and doesn't help carry it." Two men carried a boar on the small path to the stream, chatting as they walked.

"Biling, Youwai is very pretty. Strange, we've been hunting for a long time and never ran into her, and Dayin goes to take a dump and he walks away with her," Wumao chattered, still not able to resign himself.

"That's enough. My sister's nice, I'll introduce you."

"Oh, no. Her legs are so short and her head is so big. Give her to Ahdao, I don't want her," said the two following behind. Shortly the two groups arrived one after the other at the stream.

Neatly and skillfully the boars were butchered, roasted, and cut up at one go. Solemnly, Fa'ai faced east then west and made offerings and prayers. He thanked the spirit of the mountain and the ancestral spirits for their blessings. He also prayed that all would go smoothly with the sowing ceremony and invited the ancestral spirits to be present for Dayin's wedding. That night each household sent one person to take part in the sowing ceremony; each household supplied food that was shared by all. They spent the night chatting together and welcomed the new day. When the sky was barely light, the head of the ceremony walked alone to a previously chosen place of open ground where the grass had been pulled and the soil loosened. In his left hand he waved some silver grass and with his right hand he scattered some seed. As he did so he mumbled a prayer:

In accord with the teachings of our ancestors
We hold this Sowing Ritual, sowing seed
Shoo away the birds, pluck away the bad bugs
Please break up the stone, move away the old brush
Let these seeds sprout and grow

The Sowing Ritual was done and the sky was light. No one could work that day to avert breaking the tender shoots and violating the taboos. Strictly upholding the taboos, the villagers wove baskets and cloth or put their farm tools in order.

Dayin also sowed. All day and all through the night to the dawn they celebrated the wedding with song and dance. The village was sunk in warm and joyful merriment. The mountains were witness to the joining of two hearts and bodies after their strange chance meeting. A thin spring mist rose gracefully from the foot of the mountains to protect and envelop the bride.

"Youwai, you are my wife now. Don't leave me," he said smiling. She pinched his arm lightly and said angrily,

"Silly! We just got married and you mention leaving." She then pinched his nose and said,

"From today on you are not to ask about my background, OK? Or else . . . "

"OK, OK . . . Tomorrow we'll go look at the fields we have to open and sow."

Holding one another, they talked quietly. The wind blew through the branches. It seemed to whisper its blessings for an endless number of tomorrows as it waited for them to join together to perform a single piece of music.

This was a field? What a field! It was a wasteland full of weeds and a confusion of stones. She watched as he sweat pulling weeds half his height. Frowning, she said, "Dayin, don't bother with that now. Go fetch some water from the river . . . " He figured his beloved wife wanted water to wash with, so without a word he picked up two bamboo buckets and set off.

Youwai tossed aside his shovel, machete, and axe. Then she strung a hemp rope from tree to tree making a circle. She stood outside the circle and mumbled. With a wave of her right hand, the scene suddenly changed: the poor and barren land became a fine fertile field. The brush was turned to ashes, the soil turned and furrowed, the stones lined up at the edge of the field. Dayin returned carrying the water and panting like an ox. He scratched the back of his head and, glancing right and left, wondered.

"That's strange! How did I end up at someone else's field?"

Youwai said with a captivating smile, "This is the right place. This is our newly opened field."

Dayin's thick eyebrows rose as he opened his eyes wide and shouted, "That's impossible, impossible. I ran all the way to fetch the water and back!"

He nearly keeled over—it would still take him three or four days just to clear this much land, let alone make it into a field that could be sown.

"Dayin, don't just stand there, get me the seed."

As if in a dream, the blockhead handed her the basket. Another strange sight sent him deeper into his dream, leaving him amazed and speechless at the side of the field.

Youwai sowed handfuls of seed that fell like snow and immediately sank into the soil. With the same movements of her hands, she sprinkled the river water, forming a tight network of rain in the air that fell gradually over the ground. With only two buckets of water, she had soaked the earth.

"Come on, let's go home!" His wife startled him awake. He looked up and the sun was directly overhead.

On the way home, he thought to himself how since Youwai had entered his house his father's eyes had been cured without medicine, how the old house seemed to become new, and today he himself had witnessed her unimagined magical powers. Then he recalled something mysterious the shaman had said to him: "Dayin, Youwai is a strange girl. You have to look after her and whatever you do don't make her angry, otherwise our happiness will vanish."

Over the next few days she had him call the owners of the fields away. As usual, she did the same and in a moment all the fields of the village had been cultivated, sown, and weeded. With less time spent on farming, she taught them techniques of hunting more quickly and safely in their free time. Without exception, digging irrigation ditches, building fences, setting snares, clearing ground to prevent fires all reduced the injuries in the mountains. Strangely, all common illnesses seemed to vanish.

The strange magical powers that exceeded the imagination of the people continued to create prosperity. Youwai was esteemed and worshipped as a goddess. But she had her own secret worries. She had sown the seeds of intractable regrets among her in-laws because she found ways to avoid kitchen work.

As spring turned to summer, the mountains were newly adorned in green and the bamboo shoots were thrusting up through the soil. Through her husband, Youwai made another startling announcement: they would soon be harvesting.

"That's fast, it seems like we just sowed."

"Dayin is confused. He probably fell out of bed last night and banged his head."

"Let's go find out. His wife is really sharp. It might be true."

As the hunters and farmers made their way along the small path to the fields, they expressed their doubts. They all quickened their pace to get to their own fields.

"Hey, Daruo, what the heck's growing inside the gourds? They're broken open and laying all over the ground."

"Mine too. So many of them. Maybe they're rotten." Daruo and Wubai, whose fields lay side by side, had never seen the like of all the panicles of golden grain, which nearly touched the ground because they were so heavy. But the gourds all seemed to have cracked open and were filled with a yellow grain. No wonder the two of them gasped at the strange sight.

The grain was known as millet. It was round and tallow, easy to dry, easy to wash, and easy to cook. It was more flavorful than sorghum, sweet potato, or taro. Pounded, it could be stored for a long time and ground up to make sweet and pungent millet wine. More important, it was drought resistant, grew fast, and was easy to grow. Two or more harvests were possible in a single season. From then on, the people never lacked grain and their granaries bulged.

One evening when Ahruo was at his hut weaving a basket for the millet, the old shaman and Wudan the elder arrived.

"Ahruo, was your *yanai* (daughter-in-law) really lost in the mountains?" The elder sat down and began stroking his beard.

"That's what Dayin said. To tell the truth, I don't know."

"Is Dayin here?" the elder asked, peering in through the open door.

"He went with *yanai* to the other side of the mountain to train three hunting dogs. Strange, it's dark."

The topic was changed and they began talking about Youwai's miracles. The old shaman and Maya came out of the kitchen carrying food and stopped their talking. Maya put down the food and went to the door and glanced outside and sighed, "Lets go ahead and eat. I'm old and cooking wears me out."

"What? Doesn't your *yanai* help you?"

Maya shrugged her shoulders and, somewhat disgruntled, said, "This *yanai* of ours can do anything, but refuses to go into the kitchen and cook. At first she said her hands hurt and she had a headache, but that's impossible for a whole spring season. I scolded her several times. What kind of woman is she if she can't work in the kitchen?"

Maya got more upset as she spoke. Then she coughed and continued, "If she's at home when it's time to cook, she locks herself in her room and refuses to come out, otherwise she runs off to the bamboo grove with a bunch of men to talk about or teach something about hunting. She's been married to Dayin for a while now, but still her belly shows no signs." For all her resourcefulness, who cares if she cooks when she hasn't continued the family line? Is that proper?" Maya began to cry as she spoke. The two old men looked at each other in silence.

The old shaman dished up the millet and, controlling her excitement, tried to console her, "Maya, don't be that way. Your *yanai* has difficulties of her own. I tell you what, I'll come and help when you . . . " The shaman held her tongue and walked into the kitchen, somewhat embarrassed. She was angry with herself for making such an indiscreet remark. Helping with the cooking was fine, but how could she come and help deliver, and at her age?

After the harvest festival the village entered a period of eating and drinking and singing and dancing. It was a paradise in which there was everything in abundance. In late autumn a cold wind blew through the valley, chilling to the bone. A thick mist settled over the mountains. How many eyes, mouths, and voices were aimed at her, holding her without letting her go?

"Youwai can't have a baby, nor can she cook."

"Youwai is a demon who seduces men with evil magic."

"Youwai is a bastard . . . she's a tree spirit."

"Youwai is . . . "

The public clamor, confounding right and wrong, spread like wildfire in the simple village. The once-haloed goddess was ridiculed as a whore and feared as demon.

Dayin gave in under the flood of rumors and began to speak to his wife coldly. Youwai was a woman and her unhappy in-laws and her husband's rebukes left her sad and frustrated. Although at night she could cry the tears she saved up during the day, after months of being wronged and tormented she had no more tears left to cry and her heart was dry. Her husband went hunting without telling her. He left resolutely and categorically refused to ignore all exhortations from the heavenly spirits.

On the second day of the hunt, Dayin slept soundly under the bright moonlit sky. He smiled the smile of a hunter who has caught a big black bear. Suddenly he awoke with the sound of thunder. He sat up and looked around, only to see the bright moon in a clear sky and the chirping of some insects. As he was about to lie down and go to sleep again he heard a sound like a buzzing mosquito, a sad and sorrowful voice.

"Dayin. I am Youwai. I am the thunder goddess from heaven. The heavenly spirits ordered me to go down to earth and help you. They admonished me not to reveal my true identity or open a pot on the stove and I could stay on earth forever and be your wife. But given the indifference and the insults from your family and the vicious way I was treated by your people, I decided to return to heaven. I've come to say good-bye forever."

Surprise gave way to fear. Dayin suddenly realized that his whole body was shaking uncontrollably. He was off in a flash and shouted sadly, "Youwai, don't leave. Youwai, don't . . . " The other hunters, who had been startled awake, pursued him, only to see him inexplicably vanish in the darkness of the night.

At the break of day the rooster began to crow. Outside his daughter-in-law's room, Ahruo shouted:

"*Yanai*, please get up and cook. Your mother-in-law is not feeling well. Come out and cook."

"*Yanai*, *yanai*, come out and cook," said Ahruo, his voice becoming cold and stern.

"*Yanai*, please come out and cook this once."

Youwai opened her door and came out. Her steps were labored and she swayed. She fell to her knees in front of her father-in-law and sadly said, "I am sorry, I must leave. Dayin is on his way home now. Take care."

After she said a bitter good-bye, her eyes swollen and red, she got up and went to the kitchen where she lifted the lid from the pot. Suddenly there was a loud noise and a thick smoke billowed. When the smoke had cleared, Youwai was gone. A banana tree was rooted where she had just stood.

Cut and scraped and as dirty as if he had rolled in mud, Dayin charged helplessly into his room. Then he rushed out of the house and ran around like a headless fly, shouting madly, "Where's Youwai? Where's Youwai?"

Still terrified, Ahruo told his son everything he had witnessed with his own eyes. Dayin staggered to the kitchen where he hugged the banana tree and cried despondently:

"Youwai, come back! Please forgive us, come back, come back."

When the villagers learned the whole story of why the thunder goddess had descended into their midst, they all beat their breasts and stamped their feet; they were filled with regret and sadness and they all wept.

Gone forever, sadness unending. A cold wind rose in the valley, shaking the bamboo grove. A great wave of sadness engulfed the village.

Eternal Ka-balhivane (Home to Return To)

AUVINI KADRESENGAN

ON THE ROAD back from saying good-bye to his *ahma* at Tatukulu community, the road he had traveled before, every stone and step were saying, "Life is but a fleeting shadow, coming back again is not something that happened in the past."

He was nearly to Jiazhepangyan community, a place where he could rest. Several smooth, large flat stones had been placed in the shade of a tree. When he traveled between Jiazhepangyan and Tatukulu communities, he sat under this very tree, daydreaming and reluctant to leave, more times than he could count. On this day, the bottoms of his feet thick with *lisapasapa* (calluses) were saying, "Regardless of how one struggles in life, life is but a drop of morning dew."

Sitting there, he swept the area, near and far, with his keen eyes. Then he lay down, closed his eyes, and recalled that happy moment he had hunted and killed a black bear. A cool breeze blew and the dry leaves floated softly to the ground and onto his body. The purple morning glories blossomed. The scene brought back memories from the last two years. The trees and bushes beside him dripped with the past, and the *tabalhilu* (a type of thrush) sang of parting and blessings.

"I'll be back to see you." He kept softly repeating."

"Ancestors, please extend your helping hands and bestow your blessings on us!" As he softly prayed, a *lalay* and a *masasiang* to his left and right sang, echoing each other. He was convinced that this was the response sent by his ancestors. Hope and comfort, like a cool spring, filled his heart. He drifted off to sleep and dreamed he was standing in a strange and obscure place. A strange woman handed him a bundle of evenly cut bamboo and said, "This is for you." Then she suddenly vanished.

He woke from his dream and rubbed his bleary eyes. Confused and alarmed, he got up and set off on his way home. He busily gathered firewood on his way home, but he couldn't forget his dream.

He had been busy at Drekay (high elevation) for a long time. First it was the potato fields, then, after harvesting the taro, he had spent another year opening taro fields. Finally, he sowed a field of millet when the tender leaves of the *dauku* trees had just sprouted. Just after the sowing and before it was time to cut grass, he made a suggestion to his wife: "I want to go hunting east of Balhukuane but I need some gear first, so I think I'll go to Dalumake to get the things I need." He added, "I hear that some people from elsewhere are there and have brought all kinds of good things, especially new guns and iron tools."

"How many days will it take?" asked his wife.

"Seven days there and back."

"Do you have someone to go with you?"

"I'll go with Chiamare, the neighbor below us."

"It's winter so it won't rain. Don't worry." He spent several days gathering firewood for his wife and son while his wife prepared his bag and food for the journey.

Early one morning he shouldered his beloved Dutch rifle, threw his bag over his back, and received the blessings of his wife and son. The two friends said long good-byes to their families and then set off in the direction of the sunrise. But Esai hurried back after only a few steps to kiss his son Langepao and say, "I'm going to get a gun for you, a nice gun, so behave yourself while I'm gone." He repeated his words one more time, kissed his son again, and then left.

"*Ahma*! *Ahma*! I'll be waiting for you to return . . . " The echo of his son's voice reverberated behind him. They walked on and on, but he could still hear the blessings of his wife and son.

They walked eastward along the old road and, passing sacred Balhukuane, they veered right and headed south along the crest of the mountains and then east along the old Zhiben River road. It took them two and a half days to get to Zhiben community and another half day to get to Dalumake community.

They first went to locate the headman to let him know why they had come and to present him with gifts. The headman received them with *ikakes*, a sweet wine made from glutinous rice. The headman was a good host, and that night the fatigue of the journey vanished under the charms of the *ikakes*.

They bartered for goods—a mountain deer for an American rifle—one with a long barrel and small bore, making it extremely accurate—and his old rifle and some deer antlers were exchanged for a shell shoulder belt and a roll of steel wire. The trading proceeded smoothly amid excited smiles that would produce singing in a dream. The next morning they saw how small the headman's wooden mortar for pounding rice was. They spent most of the day going to the mountains, bringing back a log, and fashioning the headman a new mortar as an expression of thanks for his assistance. The following day they took a different road home out of Zhiben community. They walked upstream along Tabuali River, passed through the right side of the Vilaolaore community's tributary valley and up through the Tulhitulhiki community, veered right up the mountain slope and entered Madrekadrekare, the old hunting territory of Jiazhepangyan community.

"This primitive tableland is home to the animals," said Esai.

"The hunting hut of our ancestors is not far from here."

"After crossing the Zhiben River here, it's another half day to Dratane, another tableland that is the home of Cekele ki Lhikulao, Clouded Leopard, our hunting dog. As that is a sacred place, we should go with this place." They stopped every few steps to point at the animal tracks, whispering continuously. "We'll be hunting here in the near future, and we'll need certain gear . . . "

Esai was extremely satisfied with the outcome of their long journey, especially with obtaining a new rifle. Holding the gun, he tried to divine the luck he would have with it. But it was growing dark so they quickly set off for the hunting hut to spend the night. That night, he dreamed that he and his friend were in a vast and boundless village. They gazed over the village shining under the sun; the villagers were friendly. One of the villagers asked, "Where are you going?"

"We're just going to cross the road," he replied. "We are on our way back to Jiazhepangyan Village."

Suddenly, someone brought out a bag of something and handed it to them, saying, "You might get hungry on the road; this food is for you." So saying, he turned and vanished.

Esai woke early and started a fire. He kept wondering what the significance of his dream of the night before was.

After hurriedly making and eating breakfast, they couldn't stay and hunt because they only had one portion of food left. So they had to rush home. It had already been seven days since they left, and they missed their families. They shouldered their bags. Being strong and their bags light, they quickly made their way over the sacred peaks of the Central Mountain Range, homeward bound. Although it was difficult going up the mountain slope, the thoughts of the gifts they were taking home and their longing to see their families made them forget their fatigue. Along the way the *masasiang* accompanied them with song, and later the sacred *tukeke* (the rusty-cheeked scimitar-babbler, a bird sacred to the Rukai and one that tells the time) sang vigorously to their right. This startled them:

"We're going home, but this bird's words possess great significance for hunters."

"We're in the middle of our ancient hunting ground—it's hard to say what me might encounter," said Esai.

"This is the world of our ancestors. It would be easy for them to bestow something upon us," he added.

Mounting the peak, they leisurely and happily began their slow descent to Baluguan, the eternal abode of their ancestors.

Upon arriving, they put down their bags to rest a bit. Esai wanted to conduct a *nguaraisy* leaf ritual. He walked over to a large tree and took the ritual implements from his bag and arranged them in the usual four equal rows. Each row, according to the general arrangement, included, in addition to a fallen leaf, two arrows, one bow, and a *kaluluthu*, a piece of embroidery used only for the *nguaraisy* ritual. Then Esai piously intoned:

Kusu ka yia Babeleng ka ua bekacenaiyiane! Kusa ka mubalhithi!
Creator in heaven! Ancestors!
Ua lhibalhibatenay ka iki balhio ta, luiyiasi kai nay thingathingale.
We are crossing this sacred home of ours, if unknowingly.
Sii kulhangane nay ku drekase nmi, paceacepanga.
We transgress your sacred teachings, please forgive us.
Lavavalake ana nay aii pasingiaki dremdrem nay kai tikianeka ipakituvalane nay
We are still immature, but are hearts are pious, we offer this small heartfelt gift
Pelaelane kai satua kuciacingalhe si isaua kuludru nay numiane.
As an expression of our esteem and respect for you.
Pa tarumara nayiane ku pucacuganane nai thingale paudrua ka patarumara numi.
Give us the wisdom to know how to use the good fortune you give us.
Bulhua naiyiane ku kilibake la nai thingale paukalhete ki tuagagane numi.
Give us the love so that we know how to raise your descendants fairly
Pasa selebana naiyiane la nai pu lhingalhingau lu drekase numi ki aleceganeany.
Give us calm spirits so that we might understand your guidance and signs.

Pasa gathimana naiyiane, lu kaesaesai nay lu kaesaesai nay la nai thingalengulhingao numiane.
Give us grateful hearts so that in good times we can know how to think of our ancestors.

After completing the ritual, Esai slowly walked over to his friend. Jaimanle said, "Why are all the birds silent?"

"The birds should not be heard here. If they are heard, it indicates that one of our people has left this world and that his spirit has already arrived here," he softly explained.

They shouldered their bags and set off again. After a ways, they exited via the west side of the sacred city; just beyond the steps was a place where Rukai rested going east and west. Then they stopped, put down their bags, and relaxed their anxious minds. It was high noon.

They stood at the main gate of the abode of his ancestors. It was the highest place save Wutou Mountain on their right and Northern Dawu and Chabuyan mountains to their left. They looked down on the world of men, everything spread before them. A cold wind blew, sweeping Esai's mood into the eternal recesses of time. He could see two ancestors along with their beloved sacred dog Clouded Leopard from the low banyan grove, coming out of the sacred city to rest. They were gazing west over the vast sea of green that extended to the horizon. With his own eyes he witnessed how, five or six hundred years before, his people had fled from Dalumake comunity to Jiazhepangyan community under the incursions of outsiders. He even saw them when they heard the news from the people at Jiazhepangyan: "We are being harassed by the *su-ariv* (enemies)." The headman ordered that the main door of the *palhakuan*, or young men's house, be opened and all able-bodied men were sent as an army to help Jiazhepangyan. He also saw with his own eyes another time how Cegao-Druluane and Lavausu-Kadrangilane left home one after the other to marry into their wives' families in Kalatadrane and how they turned for one last look at their home and their people.

"Ancestors! All of our ancestors who live here. When they come here and look at all of us, their descendants, what do they think?" wondered Esai.

"Wumu, I'm sure you are thinking of me." Suddenly the cloud-mist thickened, a drizzle started to fall, and a cold wind to blow.

"Let's go," said Esai. His friend had dozed off and he had just come back from the eternal moment of a dream.

The dreamer rubbed his bleary eyes. Esai had already disappeared on the winding mountain path. He had just started walking when he heard a "ping." He quickened his pace to get to the bottom of the sound. A buck deer was twitching as it breathed its last.

"Friend, we've got a buck with young antlers," said Esai.

"This is the gift you dreamed about, that's why the birds were singing all the way."

"A lot of hard work and suffering went into getting this gun, and it has bespoken its destiny," Esai explained.

"Let's hurry up and take care of this. We have to at least get to Dumulane before sunset." They worked for a spell and then shouldered their burdens for the return trip, talking cheerfully. They gave it all they had and passed Dumulane and went on to the Taravaravadrane River where they prepared to camp for the night as dusk fell. Their families looked over the road they were traveling, waiting for their return.

The families of the two men were worried by their tardy return. The two families questioned each other as to why they hadn't returned. Their gazing eyes could not penetrate the deep mist covering the mountains and their anxious hearts could not get beyond the torture of time.

The following day the long shouts of a hunter were heard as they hung and broke through the heavy mist. Debolan stopped what she was doing and listened carefully, asking herself who it could be.

"They didn't go hunting, they went to Dalumake." Then she knew it for the voice she knew so well, but she couldn't believe it was her husband.

The neighbor came out and said, "It sounds like your husband."

"He went to Taidong to buy some things; he didn't go hunting," she replied.

"But that is clearly your husband's voice."

Her uncle came out and announced the good news: "It's him. He's either got a buck with young antlers or a wild boar, that's clear from his shouts." Half doubting, Debolan took up her broom and quickly swept the house.

Finally, the two men appeared through the dense mist and slowly made their way back to the homes they had been away from for so long. A little boy followed by a puppy ran to greet his *ahma*.

"*Ahma*! *Ahma*!" The child missed and wanted to hug his *ahma*. Esai took his hand and led him into the house while asking him, "Who gave you the puppy?"

"I don't know."

"Let's call him Lhingulu."

Happily the little boy repeatedly shouted the dog's name. Then he added: "*Yina* got it."

They entered the house. Members of both families came to greet them, followed by villagers who came to offer their congratulations. When they saw how much he had come back with from his trip east, they were amazed and said, "No one has ever come back from a journey with so many good things."

"Hey, why don't you tell us? What did you bring back?"

"A rifle, a shoulder belt, young deer antlers, and a roll of wire."

Esai placed the deer with young antlers before the ancestor column. From its face they could see that it was a deer among deer. The new rifle was leaned against the ancestor column like a one-eyed, cold-blooded killer. The belt was hung from the ancestor column. Judging from the spiral purple patterns etched in the shells, it was clear that a lot of time had gone into making it. Pointing at the most attractive shell, Esai explained to Debolan, "This is a *balabalare*, or purple shell, it's what gives the bag its value." He continued, "If by chance our son should marry lesser nobility, this shell is sufficient for a betrothal gift; if she's a headman's daughter, then this shell plus a ceramic vessel is enough." Listening to his explanation, Debolan could already envision the most glorious day in little Langepao's life twenty years later when he married the daughter of a headman. A new strength infused her heart and a new spring burgeoned. The roll of wire was placed to the left and resembled a dog curled in sleep. Esai still wanted to give them shape, but he had already given them life and soul and had even named them. Seeing how wonderful it was, Debolan stepped forward and, patting the deer, said with great satisfaction:

Maelanenga su ka Mubalhithi nay! Ani taku alalai kai sipi miyia ki acilai besai mia kao ngotokadre.

Thanks to our ancestral spirits for blessing us! And wishing us this luck that flows like water and falls like a landslide.

Kusukayia beleng! Ani takua lalalai mia ki minu elebane ku asasipianane, I sii ku akir agathane.

Ancestral spirits! The happiness you have bestowed has opened the door of fortune for this family, allowing prosperity to enter uninterrupted.

Then she spoke to the deer:

Ililuka ki la lhitudrane su pakaredede le.

Bring in the members of your family without end.

Kusu ka kuange nai amani su ka tharange nay lhaili nay sa malhamalhane nay sa malhamalhane nay ki aki ragaragathane.

Oh, gun! You are our spirit, and our arrows are the fishhook for our happiness.

Kusu ka lingase! Lhiikainga su ruthuruthuku kai apa piayiayia sana nguapapalha.

Oh, steel wire! Don't miss any chance and hold tight and never come lose.

She then removed the shoulder belt from the ancestor column and let Lanbao, her little boy, try it on and said, "Now you have a gun and a beautiful shoulder belt." She patted her son on the shoulders with both hands and said, "You're so handsome. Hurry up and say thank you to *ahma*!" She then turned and moved over to where her husband was eating and told him how much she missed him. The people there were working on the deer and preparing for a banquet. Cangale-Aruladeng, a great deer hunter who invented the wire snare, came late to offer his congratulations to Esai: "I'm a little late because I just got back from the fields." Touching everything Esai had returned with, he continued, "Esai's ancestors were all heroes and great hunters and it would be inappropriate for their descendants to surpass them."

He turned and spoke to Esai: "We are comforted that the fire of Kalesian's family is rekindled. All I can offer are my boundless, heartfelt blessings to his children and encourage you to keep that fire burning bright." Debolan took out Esai's wooden cup and filled it to brimming with new millet wine and handed it to her husband. Esai took the cup in both hands and toasted the old man.

Esai and his friend busied themselves making snares out of the wire they had purchased to begin their hunt east of the Central Mountain Range. He had been a hunter for almost thirty years, including the time he hunted with Ahmakalawan, and he had 120 deer, more than 70 boars, and 3 black bears to his name. But he had not got many small animals, immature deer, boars, goats, and muntjac. On this matter his hunting friend asked him, "You always get big animals. Is it luck or your technique?"

"The most important thing is that the strength of the cross pieces under the treadle of the snare. That is the key to how big or small," he replied.

A number of young people had studied the practice, theory, and spirit of hunting with him, but some failed because they lacked the innate ability and some threw themselves into it and paid for it because their ancestral spirits did not live up to their diligent efforts and their sweat and blood. There were as many as ten of this sort. At the end of every year the hunters celebrated by wearing lilies. The young people he took had worn at least a hundred lilies and, respectfully holding their hunter's cups, they had sought out their *ahma* Esai to share a hunter's honor and glory. He would always just drink half a cup and return the other half cup to be drunk to his honor and glory.

That afternoon all the hunters of the village congregated there. After a few cups of millet wine, everyone was a bit tipsy and the mood soared like a hawk in the blue sky of the sea. Their buoyant spirits seemed to travel in a mystical realm of eternity, as if each one of them were the king. Excited, they sang:

Pala-I—lay! Runangili rudalapay pacegese tagarausu ini-pala-I—lay.
Oh, how great! Praise be to Rnuangili and Rudalapay, as lofty as Dawu Mountain.
Pala-I—lay! Lhialevene luiyia pinasu lhikulavane.
Oh, how great! Praise be to Lhialevene of the cloud leopard people.

Every hunter and hero wore hawk-eagle feathers and lilies and raised their heads to sing about how they had become heroes. Esai, who could not lead the song, sat in the corner keeping harmony. A great hero sat beside him and passed his cup to Esai, that he might enjoy a hero's glory, and said, "You, too, are a hero. It's just because your grandfather was a hero that you refuse to wear the feathers."

"I'm not qualified and disgrace my ancestors."

"You are a great hunter so there is no need to be so modest."

"If there was an opportunity to go to war in this day and age, I'm sure you would be a great hero."

"I regret this more than anything else." The hero took the hat of hawk-eagle plumes and gave it to Esai to wear temporarily, saying, "Please wear it, with me beside you, no one will say anything."

Somewhat embarrassed by the old man's good intentions, Esai shrugged his shoulders and accepted it, saying, "Won't I have my day?"

The old man encouraged him to sing a song about his hunting. Esai could not refuse.

Pala-I—lay! Kadura ku sangate inavalhuane.
Sing! I've never dared count myself among the glorious lily bearers.
Pala-I—lay! Vaevanga ku adrisiku suininu li.
Sing! Unable to wear feathers in my life, I am a disgrace to my ancestors.

That night Esai remained with the celebrants wearing lilies. Drunk, he actually lay down, oblivious to all. Some thought he hadn't showed the appropriate respect, had violated a hunter's principles and spirit, and wanted to reason with him, saying, "Why does Esai not respect us? Wake him up and ask him." He behaved with the attitude of one wishing to give Esai a teaching.

"What else do we want to say to him?" asked the old man speaking for Esai.

"Does anyone deny his accomplishments? The only thing he hasn't done is brew wine to announce that he will wear the lilies."

The people he had taught to hunt as youngsters picked up their *ahma* to carry him home. His uncle went with the group and scolded his nephew's wife, "He hasn't yet worn the lilies because you do not love your husband. That's what everyone is saying. I never encouraged him when he was young, but it is nearly thirty years, as you well know! Do you delight in having your husband scorned and insulted?" After speaking his mind, the uncle turned and left. Although Debolan didn't utter a word in protest, she was sad and wept in her heart. In fact, every year at the approach of the ceremony, she always mentioned the matter of wearing the lilies, but he would put her off by saying, "My ancestors Daili and Langepao were great hunters and they never wore the lilies. Why should I?" He would continue, "When I die, you must remember one thing—you must not put lilies on me but use creepers instead."

"Then you don't care that I am always scolded and criticized behind my back?"

"I won't attend next year. Listen to me for the sake of our love."

"I know you love me, but that's not the way to go about this. Just don't pay attention to what other people say," he warmly pleaded. Debolan felt it was very difficult to be a wife of someone from a younger generation.

One night Esai had a dream. "I was standing under a very high waterfall. The gushing torrent fell through the air with an ear-splitting roar. The sunlight struck the watery mist, and I stood under an arching rainbow." It was the first time in his life that he had had such a dream. Waking early in the morning, he immediately went to see his uncle and told him of his dream. Earnestly, and in all sincerity, his uncle said, "If you continue to hunt, you will probably reach new heights." He tried to comfort him, but he knew that the dream was a bad omen for Esai. He changed the topic so that Esai would not notice his serious expression.

He had just reached middle age and was no longer the man he once was and, although he would like to reach new heights using whatever means and all efforts, game was becoming scarcer because of the decline in nature. For hunting one had to go east of the Central Mountain Range to between the headwaters of the Taima and Zhiben Rivers. To make this long trip meant wasting a lot of time and energy.

His interest in hunting had gradually diminished and he was more intent on looking after his family. Those were the calmest days of his life and were hard to forget or get used to. Later, in a more balanced frame of mind, he considered going hunting again, perhaps for the last time. Then, unexpectedly, he shot two bucks. He felt he had achieved his ideal best. Was there to be another high point in his life? He had long forgotten his strange dream. For his uncle the dream had brought to mind only the dangers that face a hunter in the forest. For that reason, when he saw Esai calmly passing his days at home, he thought, "The child has escaped."

His wife waited for the year she could see the glorious lilies on her husband's head at the lily festival. The millet she and her husband had sown in the field they had cleared was ripening. By the time the field had been harvested, the big day she had waited for had nearly arrived.

One morning as the time was drawing near, a lot of things were needed, and they could only be purchased with a trip to the east. Among the things needed were salt and matches, but most important was to go to Dalumake to see if he could buy a cartridge rifle. After he and his wife discussed the matter, she prepared two deer whips, deer antlers, and food for several days. As she prepared his bag, she exhorted him, "Remember, buy needle, thread, and embroidery cloth so that I can embroider the wedding dresses for the three girls, since they are already of age.

He hurriedly wolfed down breakfast, shouldered his bag, and said goodbye to his family. This time he would make the trip alone and, being so excited, he didn't take into account what the birdsong meant. Or perhaps, as he thought, "After decades, it's the same road. What is there to worry about?"

Stepping lightly, he hunted as he journeyed east. Following the old path, he reached his destination in four days. Upon arriving at the house where he and his friend stayed previously, the headman's oldest son was as friendly as ever, but the father was nowhere to be seen.

"Where is our *ahma*?" asked Esai.

But the nobleman hesitated, as if unwilling to speak. Finally, he replied, "Our *ahma* is no longer with us."

Deeply saddened at the news, Esai, replied, "Is life so short?"

The nobleman invited him to a bountiful supper, after which he took him to see a friend to find out what he needed. That evening they successfully obtained a *kalubung*, or five-cartridge rifle. Esai and the nobleman were both very excited and celebrated with drink until midnight. The following day he went to Balhangau to buy the embroidery cloth, thread, and needles his wife wanted. He was especially mindful of his pregnant daughter-in-law, so bought a piece of cloth for he would soon be a grandfather. Swaddling clothes were necessary, and his daughter-in-law probably had her needs as well. Regardless of how long the journey was, he no longer felt pressured.

On the morning of his third day there, he set off with the rifle he had wanted for so long but that had been so difficult to obtain and a number of gifts. The nobleman had also given him several days of food for his trip home. He bid farewell to the nobleman and, not liking good-byes, set off toward home on the path by which he came.

On the day he was anticipated, his wife waited for him at home. He had still not returned by nightfall. The following day he again failed to show up. That evening everyone gathered at Esai's house. His uncle made a suggestion:

"If he doesn't come back tonight, the young men should go out first thing tomorrow morning and search the mountains."

"They can form two groups: one to go into the mountains on the high road, the other group can enter the Central Mountain Range via Dadugulu," said an elder. At midnight he still had not returned home.

"Villagers, please listen!" The elder stood outside Esai's house to make an announcement. "All young men will mobilize tomorrow morning and head east along the two ancient paths to look for Esai, who has probably disappeared." He continued: "Prepare sufficient provisions and the gear you will need in the mountains."

All the women had gathered around Debolan to comfort her. Another night went by and her anxious hopes turned to sadness. By that time a number of young men had already taken up torches and, like will-o'-the-wisps, had entered the forest. The people who watched them depart prayed, "Esai, have patience, friends are coming to your rescue."

An old woman said, "Esai, we are still waiting for you. My grandchild."

"Your wife and your beloved children are waiting for you to come home."

"Spirit of my child, come back!"

A group of woman faced east and prayed for his return day and night. Night followed night; his people and relatives in the area all waited for his safe return.

On the third day of searching the forest, a man finally returned and everyone was hoping for good news.

"We haven't found him yet." They knew then that he might never come back.

The member of the search party recounted to them, "He decided to go to visit Kalawan, his *ahma*, by going via Dadugulu, so he changed his route and took the old lower eastern path to the flat upland on the eastern side of the Central Mountain Range. We located his tracks there, but we lost them turning west and, try as we might, we were not able to pick them up again. The search party is continuing, but they are almost out of food."

More people were sent to search. Day followed day and he still did not return. More people were dispatched, and the search went on for more than a month without success. Disheartened, the elder made an announcement shattering everyone's hopes: "Our beloved Esai! Our great hunter!" he said, wiping his tears away, "is never coming back."

Everyone began to wail, "Esai! Our beloved Esai! Where are you? Why have you forsaken us?"

"We still hope for his return, but it has been more than a month since he left. Judging from the situation, our hopes are diminishing." Speaking for the family, he apologized to the searchers, "You did everything you could. *Shabao* for your efforts, but he is now with our ancestors. We are sure that he has witnessed your concern, and takes comfort."

His poor family—especially his wife and six children, who were now orphans—was not able to witness his return. It was heart-rending to see how his family embraced and wept. Those standing by them recounted his life:

"He was the nicest person."

"He knew how to take care of women and children who were in trouble," said one woman.

"He was a greatest hunter of his generation," said the elder.

"Though more than worthy, he never wore the lily."

"This family is short-lived and they all die by accident."

"Everything in life is predestined," said the headman, sorely grieved. His best friend Jiamanle was the last to offer his condolences, "Esai! My best friend! My *talia lalay li*! How can you bear to forsake your beloved Debolan? Your children?" For a moment he was unable to speak. Such a strong man was reduced to tears.

"We thought that a great hunter like you would live forever." The sad song and sighs were heard from the stone house.

"For this reason, I think you are still hunting. We still are waiting for you to return and we will wait forever." Outside, spring lightning flashed and the thunder boomed. A cold rain began to fall and an odd wind whipped up. Each gust brought the smell of gunpowder. The old shaman stood up and addressed those present, "This is his destiny, do not be sad!"

It rained without letting up. Near dusk, it suddenly cleared and the setting sun shone on the eastern mountains. A huge brilliant rainbow arched over the sacred land where alone the rain fell and thunder sounded. Suddenly his uncle remembered Esai's strange dream.

The arched rainbow and the strip of evening clouds slowly vanished. The children, huddled in a corner, wept, accompanied by the grief-stricken cries of his wife:

Thalhalhai li! Yiainsu?
My love! Where are you?
Mangangerece-nga kai sadramate su!
The good food we prepared for you is grown cold!
Mua baisi-nga kai lalalake ta, kai ta lhagilhagi su, kai saka cekele ta!
Our children, your friends, and our people who await your return are hungry and thirsty.
Aii! Mua lebe ku sa drengedrenge lhi mayiayianga ku ama peaelaela pakela kela matatakemane.

Aiyi! The news of stone columns falling in the courtyard, shaking the earth to sky's edge.
Saka tapisaraku ku silu li, Saka kaolhava aku ku makae dredretane li.
My glass bead! I have dropped you! My ceramic vessel, I have lost you unintentionally!
Aii! Ngua tukadre tagarausu li lhi puinu aku talu kai dredreme li
Aiyi! My Northern Wu Mountain falls, my soul has lost its support
Ani tumane amiyia su ki la vavalake pai daidadikily
And your children are left orphans with no one to look after them.
Aneane ku asudralhuane su ku lhi pau lecege bulhu?
Whom do you believe will now teach your children the straight path?
Kia kadradrimit aku lhi taruauaungung aku kadruanga su ka tilivare li
You make us search in the dark as if no moon shone in the sky
Mua lebe ku sapakataleare, kai naku thingale lu lhiki kaliara aku luigane.
As if all the stars had fallen, with no idea when the sky will grow light again.
Aii! Na Thalhalha ili! Kai sa kia libake li musuane, kai lhikaela ku ta chubungane li
Aiyi! My love! I swear I steadfastly await you
Mukalava musuane miyiaku ka mialhealhe ku kalavalava ki lhau
The way I wait for the sun to appear in the east in the morning
Pakela lu mamilhing.
Forever.

Essays

The Mother of History

PA'LABANG

As If She Lived Outside of History

Mother is seventy-nine this year. She has lived through tumultuous times of great change—two world wars, the Japanese occupation, the acute social changes in Taiwan and mainland China, and the developments, by leaps and bounds, in scientific technology. She witnessed them all. Mother is like all elderly indigenous people—peaceful and serene. She just shut her eyes as if none of it mattered, as if she lived outside of history.

From an early age, I liked to ask mother about her past. I could never accept the lack of a sense of history among the Puyuma people. If ever I have loved or understood the Puyuma or other indigenous people, then without a doubt my mother was responsible. From the events of her life as she recounted them, and the attitude she developed toward life, I was able to piece together the fragments of a dim tribal memory and thereby grasp the wisdom and philosophy of my people. For me Mother's history is the history of the Puyuma. She made me realize the depth of my own history.

The wide and multifaceted world itself exists as an historical truth. But does that mean that the marginal world is any less true? Though the marginal world is weak by comparison, it can still help us understand history because it is true and possesses a hidden virtue. These are thoughts that come to me whenever I think about mother's life.

The Promise of No Regrets

Tivitif is my mother's Puyuma name. It means "no shortage of grain." When my grandmother was six months pregnant with my mother, my grandfather died. And my grandmother died when my mother was twelve. Mother took her four half brothers and sisters to stay with my great-aunt. Her life was uncertain until my great-aunt died at the age of forty and she took charge of the household.

Whenever my great-aunt and great-uncle are mentioned, mother's eyes invariably fill with tears. As an orphan she was grateful to the two old people, but also feared and respected them. She remembers quite clearly many details of their lives and the things they said. Sometimes she sings an old Puyuma song that the old people were fond of hearing. The song—and her tears—allowed me to glimpse the harmony of life as well as the mysteries of the Puyuma, which have been passed down for thousands of years.

There are many indications that the decision to bequeath the family property to mother was made by my great-aunt in her later years. As in other large families, the inheritance process was rather complicated and full of twists and turns. Mother said it was my great-aunt's steadfast will and her own devotion and diligence that were behind the decision. These are the most important aspects of my mother's character.

Mother, as I remember, was always busy. Even today she works under the scorching sun to hoe the garden, mend a fence, or do some embroidery. She always said that labor tempers the will. This is perhaps the result of her experience as an orphan.

In compliance with my great-aunt's demands, when mother was thirteen she quit the "aborigine school" that was set up by the Japanese and immediately went to work in the fields. Her regrets at having never finished school made her determined that her six children would complete their educations. When mother was seventeen my great-aunt and great-uncle arranged her marriage with my father. To this day she has never had second thoughts about the decision.

One event left a deep impression on me. In the late 1950s a Catholic missionary came to the village. My great-uncle, who was the head of the village, weighed the situation and decided the village would convert to Catholicism. Mother was against the idea at first, fearing it would destroy our traditions and customs. My great-uncle felt Catholicism would bring modernization to the tribe. He pointed out that the church would respect the tribe's customs and traditions. My mother submitted to my great-uncle's decision in the matter. "A promise is a promise, you cannot be of two hearts," he said. The following year the entire family was baptized. The same year my great-uncle died of a heart attack. The first Catholic funeral ceremony was held in the village. I remember that day. Mother stood by Great-uncle's coffin. He was dressed in traditional Puyuma clothes. She appeared particularly calm and pious; that same look appeared later in her religious life.

Society changed, and the Catholic Church declined in the village. People are no longer enthusiastic about it, and some have even changed religions or have no beliefs at all. But mother has never changed. She still prays before dinner and before going to bed. For years she has risen at four or five in the morning to read the Bible and say her rosary. I don't know how well she understands the tenets of the Catholic Church, but I do know that if people keep a promise and never waver they already approach the holiest realm of religion. Even when I am away from home I know with certainty that she prays for me every day. That closeness is the deepest feeling I received from my mother.

Profoundly Mysterious Transmission of History

After quitting school at the age of thirteen, mother joined the village *misahor*, or hoe brigade. Traditionally, Puyuma boys of twelve or thirteen years of age are sent to the *palakuwan*, or lodge, to complete preparations for entering society. There is no systematic plan for the socialization of girls. The hoe brigade fulfills this need. When the busy summer season arrives, the women customarily form a hoe brigade and do all the farm work as a group.

The hoe brigade is usually organized by an older woman with leadership ability. First thing in the morning, she calls the hoe brigade together and then they set off. The group organizer is responsible for calling rest breaks, encouraging the workers, and leading the group in folk songs to ward off fatigue and the effects of the hot sun. The hoe brigade works until evening, when they go home and take care of the household chores. By working together the women cultivate friendship and learn how to get along with others. Experience and knowledge are handed down to build character and strengthen morals. In other words, the hoe brigade is not just a labor force—the character of a Puyuma woman is molded through collective labor.

Mother herself underwent this same character-building training. Her richest legacy from the hoe brigade is a vast knowledge of Puyuma myth, legend, history, and an ability to sing the ancient folk songs. Mother joined the hoe brigade when she was young and later became a hoe brigade leader. Because she had a great deal of contact with older women when she was young, mother became a very typical Puyuma woman.

Strangers

The character of the tribe changed radically after the 1950s. The men's lodge system began disappearing, and it also became more difficult to organize the hoe brigades. The socialization of Puyuma men and women became less traditional. They faced a completely alien culture, and the world they were familiar with was rapidly vanishing. Several years ago mother organized a *muhamud* (a traditional celebration held after the hoe brigade completes its work) with all the women in the village. The once joyous celebration was filled with a solemn atmosphere. When they started to sing the old songs, they began to cry.

Tribal society has declined, much like traditional Han society, with the emergence of modern industrial society. The fates of both being inevitable, there was not much anyone could say. But the concurrent disappearance of the Puyuma language made the older Puyuma people strangers in their own land. They could not communicate with their descendants (their descendents speak only Mandarin), nor could they enter the "new society." They had no choice but to isolate themselves in their own world, as if the world outside did not exist.

Mother can speak Japanese. This was a useful tool in earlier days because most "Taiwanese" received a little Japanese education. Later, after the Mandarin movement and an anti-Japanese policy were fully implemented islandwide, the number of people mother could converse with was greatly reduced. I will never forget when we got a television set. Mother would sit in her rocking chair with her eyes glued to the TV set in front of her. The look on her face was a complex mixture of curiosity, conjecture, confusion, and perplexity. She really wanted to understand this world. If we brothers and sisters had time, we would sit with her and explain things. If we were in bad moods, conflict was inevitable. After arguing, she would stare dejectedly at the TV and then doze off. Perhaps there was greater certainty in the world of her dreams. After father passed away, mother's lonely figure appeared sadder than ever.

The summer before last, when my older sister became seriously ill, mother accompanied her to a large hospital in Taipei. One time my sister wanted to eat noodles. To make her happy, mother went out in search of a noodle stand. She wanted to ask passers-by for directions, but, much to her consternation, she couldn't express herself. Fortunately, she met a kindhearted old woman, who, half-guessing what she wanted, showed her where to buy noodles. When mother returned to the hospital, my sister didn't feel like eating, but she knew how much effort mother had expended, so she forced herself to eat a few bites as tears fell into her bowl.

When I was studying in Europe, mother was afraid I wouldn't understand the letters she wrote in Japanese, so she learned our language using the Latin alphabet. For a seventy-year-old person, that required a lot of determination and fortitude. Every time I received a letter in her small, cramped, poorly formed handwriting (they were naturally full of spelling errors), I would see her vividly in my mind asleep in front of the TV set, and I'd feel utterly worthless.

Who Is the Landlord?

A people without a written language or a history is easily forgotten. Mother had no hatred for and rarely criticized the "main actors" on the stage of Taiwan's history. She always felt her own people were backward and should be more open to advanced society. I think it was Great-uncle who influenced her in this regard.

In 1963, when my oldest sister graduated from college, she initiated a revolution in our domestic ways by marrying a man from mainland China. After that, with the exception of one of my sisters and an older brother, we all married people from elsewhere: Henan, Jiangxi, Zhejiang, and I myself married a Taiwanese woman. Mother often said that this was perhaps the future of Taiwan.

Of course mother doesn't understand the complicated background to all the political and social transformations and conflicts since the 1970s. Once, I asked her what she thought of the people from mainland China, Taiwan, and Japan. Her reply gave me much food for thought. She said, "The Japanese are to be respected and feared. They obey the law, have a sense of honor, and they stick to their word. I don't like their severity, but their contributions to the tribe can't be denied. The Taiwanese are selfish and pragmatic, and we always get the short end of the stick in dealing with them. The mainlanders are a little kinder. Hasn't Taiwan made a lot of progress in the last forty years? I don't understand their quarrel. Aren't they all Chinese?"

Mother's criticisms are simple and emotional. She cannot distinguish among the complicated factors of power and the distribution of wealth. She gripes about the Taiwanese because forty years ago the indigenous people had enough of their bullying, which was much worse than it is today. During the Japanese occupation the Taiwanese considered themselves Chinese and therefore superior to the indigenous people. Forty years later they changed their identity and call themselves Taiwanese in order to demand more power locally. This is probably what lies behind my mother's criticism of the Taiwanese as being selfish and pragmatic. Surprisingly, I later discovered that many indigenous people harbor the same feeling. I know for a fact that they cannot understand basing the Taiwan nativist movement on notions of province or region. Taking the settling of old scores as the starting point for the restructuring of power will only add to the crimes of this land.

Mother of History

I have relied on mother's history to grasp the history of the Puyuma people. Her sorrows are the sorrows of the Puyuma. Every time I see her serene and peaceful face, I see the twilight of the Puyuma. Her small responses to the wide world during her life have helped me see through today's illusions. I believe that unless we all have the courage to forget, like all indigenous people, we will never be able to come together and create our own history on this land. Perhaps the indigenous people will one day be the mother of Taiwan's history!

Wooden Clogs

PAIZ MUKUNANA

AT A CERTAIN age everyone becomes nostalgic. As it is commonly said, "Young people live in their dreams; middle-aged people live in reality; old people live in their memories." It's true. I don't know how many times I've seen an older person put something down and immediately forget where they put it, but they could remember events from their childhood as clearly as if they had just occurred. There was once an old person, eighty or ninety years old, who could spend all day talking about his childhood and his mother in such a lively and vivid way that you would have thought he was a seven- or eight-year-old child being peevish with his mother to elicit a display of affection from her. No wonder he is so adorable despite his age.

Why do I have so many memories from childhood? Am I really that old? I might not be old, but I do like to recall memories of a bygone age.

I arrive at the old street in Xinzhuang to make some purchases for the New Year. As I walk, I examine the goods used during the New Year holiday piled high in the stores. Anything anyone might want to eat, use, or wear is available. Suddenly I hear a sharp and loud knocking that seems very familiar but also somewhat far away. I turn to look for the source of the sound when I see an adolescent girl wearing Japanese *geta*, or wooden clogs, which I haven't seen in ages. No wonder the sound seemed so familiar! But it seems like ages since I have heard them. Her clogs were exquisite and, judging from the look of them, were probably imported from Japan.

This old street at this moment in the afternoon before dusk and before the night market opens is a completely different scene from the hubbub after dark. Hearing the sound of wooden clogs at such a time comes as entirely unexpected. It might wake the old shop owner sleeping in the broken-down chair in the shop doorway. Or perhaps it will thrust him, as it does me, back into the memory of a time when everyone wore wooden clogs and they could be heard everywhere.

Remembering the time when wooden clogs were worn doesn't mean I like to wear them. You could say I don't like them, especially the kind with a thong worn between the big toe and the second toe, the kind my *ahmo* ("father" in Zou) liked to give the family. When I was little, I preferred to go barefoot after bathing rather than wear wooden clogs. Before bed I'd wash my feet again, slip on the clogs, and go straight to bed. It's probably because my toes were so small and bony that the thong would make them hurt. Unfortunately, in a time of material poverty, it was as my husband says: "Poor people eat whatever they can and use whatever they can, but when they have money they can have anything they want." It's true; there's no other choice. But at this moment what resonates in my memory isn't wearing wooden clogs but making them.

I must have been eight years old at the time. Ours was the only family living in the valley. Outsiders rarely came except for the seasonal purchase of dried bamboo shoots, palm fiber, and other mountain products. One day, when I was playing with my brothers and sisters, a group of people shouldering carrying poles descended the mountain path above our bamboo house.

"They are not *Zou* (the word used by the Zou when referring to themselves or other indigenous tribes)," shouted my little brother. The people of our village always carried things in baskets on their heads or their backs for better maneuverability on the narrow mountain paths. We children were all scared to death because strangers were so seldom seen, especially ethnic Chinese. I scooped up my little sister and, along with my younger brother, ran desperately for our bamboo house, shouting: "*Budu*, *budu*, there are *budu* (Zou for ethnic Chinese)." My *ahmo* heard me shouting and came out to greet them as they arrived at the open space in front of the house. We children poked our heads out from the door and windows, our eyes wide as we watched to see what the *budu* wanted.

It was a few years after the war had ended and we hadn't learned a new language with which to communicate. In addition to Zou, which we spoke with our own people, all we knew was Japanese. My father spoke Japanese with one of the *budu* while the others stood around and talked among themselves. *Ahmo* came in and told us that the *budu* wanted to make wooden clogs. We young clods replied, "Make wooden clogs? They came all this way to make wooden clogs?" We knew what they were, but we didn't know what they were made of. My *yinuo* (Zou for mother) said, "You cut down *budu* trees (*budu* tree is Zou for the tung oil tree, probably because it was introduced by the Chinese) to make them."

I hurriedly asked my *yinuo*: "Which *budu* trees?" I asked because the ones on that mountain were special to me. My *yinuo* replied, "The ones above the Japanese road." The Japanese road was built during the Japanese occupation period so that the Japanese could better control the Zou villages. The Zou were ordered to build a road connecting their villages, and they were ordered to use it. It was supposed to be level and wide enough for a jeep. The Zou behaved themselves under the harsh Japanese policy, but, after they left, the Zou, who preferred to run wild like the goats and deer, forsook the winding Japanese road for the comparative convenience of the small mountain trails. Their souls were as free as the broad sky and could live as they always had.

You know my heart was pained to hear that the grove of *budu* trees above the Japanese road was going to be cut down. The end of spring and beginning of summer marks the season when the *budu* trees put forth their white blossoms. The mountain is a gorgeous sea of white. And when you stand on the mountain ridge to the right, and a gentle breeze blows up through Zhujiao Valley, the white flowers covering the mountain move in wave after wave (at that time I had never seen the ocean, but my uncle who had seen it told me about it). It is so beautiful.

After October, time permitting, all of us, young and old, would shoulder our baskets and, amid the *budu* grove, look for the ripe fruit from the trees that had fallen between the dry leaves. The fruit was round like the native guava and prickly. But at the height of autumn the ripe fruit on the trees would break open and the seeds would fall to cover the slopes .One fruit contained as many as five seeds the size of chestnuts. Seeing the husk on the ground, you would look a little more closely among the dry leaves to find the seeds. The gathered fruit would be piled at home. When anyone in the family had time, they would use a nail or a spoon to pry out the seeds to dry in the sun, after which they would be taken to the store in the village and exchanged for goods. Year after year it was the same life and work involving the *budu* trees: enjoying the white flowers in early summer and gathering the fruit in autumn. I heard that the oil extracted and refined from the seeds could be used to prolong the life of airplanes, cars, and various machines. I guess that's what it was used for; I don't really know.

But for some unknown reason, when I was a teenager, the village shop refused to purchase the seeds gathered by the village families because the businessmen from outside no longer wanted them. Only later did we learn that this was because imported oil was better. But this happened after the making of wooden clogs.

Naturally, I couldn't voice my displeasure because my *ahmo* had already come to terms with them. Although there were other *budu* groves, they had already set their sights on this one, probably because it was closer and more convenient. Moreover, it was a huge patch that covered an entire mountainside. Nor could I, a child, have a say in the decisions of adults. All I could do was stupidly poke my head out the door and see what could be done with the *budu* trees.

Once my *ahmo* had come to terms with the representative, the *budu* took their machetes and saws and headed off to the groves of spotted bamboo and cassia bamboo. It didn't take them long to cut down and carry back the bamboo because different kinds of bamboo grew all around the house. Then they constructed a workers hut and a long bed out of bamboo, a cook stove out of stones, and hammered together a rough table. They then unpacked all the things they had carried with them—blankets, tools, eating and cooking utensils, and food that they each arranged. We watched all the goings-on stupidly, without moving, as if we were specimens pinned there. One minute my *ahmo* came out to talk with them, another minute and they came looking for my *ahmo* to ask him something, then my *ahmo* went out again to tell them something. My *yinuo* stayed inside taking care of household matters. Occasionally she would call me to help her, but I'd soon be back, stuck at the door peeking at what the *budu* were up to.

Around dusk several of them carried some firewood back from the forest and started to cook dinner. When everything was done, they placed a piece of pork and some other things that I couldn't see clearly from where I was standing, lit some incense and worshipped. I knew how the *budu* worshipped because I had heard my *ahmo* talk about it. The Zou worship the gods in a different way. Suddenly a horrendous ear-splitting racket was heard. As old as I was, I had never encountered anything like it; my little brother and sister were wide-eyed with fear and dared not cry. I scooped up my little sister and dragged my brother over to my *yinuo*. I was so scared I almost fell. My *yinuo* said, "Don't be afraid. It's just *bagujigu* (Japanese for "firecrackers," for which no word exists in Zou). That's the way the *budu* worship." In a short while the one who spoke with my father came in carrying some pork and some candy and thanked us for our help. Since the war had just ended, Japanese was still the common language, just as Mandarin is today. I was still pretty young, but could understand some Japanese. Seeing the candy, my brother and sister and I forgot our fears of a moment ago upon hearing the firecrackers.

The *budu* arose early the next morning. After breakfast they picked up their tools and headed off for the *budu* forest above the Japanese road. In a short while we could hear them chopping down the trees and their loud conversations. They took lunchboxes with them, so spent the entire day until dusk in the forest. When they finished working and returned to the workers hut, they all carried the wooden clogs they had made that day and piled them in the open space in front of the house to let them dry. They made two kinds of wooden clogs: one kind had a thong that was worn between the big toe and the second toe and the one-inch soles and cleats were cut from a single piece of wood. Wearing them, you are elevated off the ground, but they weren't heavy. The other kind looked more like modern-day sandals, with a strap over the dorsum of the foot. In the old days the former were worn by men while the latter was worn by women.

The *budu* were up with the sun to work and rested only when the sun went down. When the pile had grown so big that nothing more could be added, they would carry them to the train station at Fengqi Lake and let the train haul them down the mountain. At that time the train was the only form of transportation to the outside world. Jiuqihu was at least a two-hour walk one way from my home for these guys that worked in the forest. It was pretty tough for them, but I didn't care. Who asked them to come and steal the white waves of my heart?

When the entire *budu* forest had been cut down, it was time for the wooden-clog-making budu to go home. I have no idea how many clogs they made, but the entire budu forest was gone and so were the white waves.

I seem to recall the *budu* who made clogs arrived in autumn and left in a little over two months. They hadn't been gone for long when another group of *budu* arrived. This group came to cut the cassia bamboo, because it was the right season.

"Why do they want to cut the bamboo?" we asked my *ahmo*. My brother and sister and I were no longer curious about the budu because we had been around them every day. "They want to cut the bamboo to make wooden clogs," replied my *ahmo*. "Wooden clogs can be made out of bamboo?" asked my older brother who had been away at school when the first group of *budu* workers arrived.

"The bamboo has to be cut into thin strips and pressed flat after which it can be glued to the surface of the wooden clogs. Colorful pictures can be painted on them, making them even prettier." Who cares? In school or on the mountains, we all went barefoot. So who cares if they are pretty? I asked myself, unhappy at having lost the white waves.

"They are suitable to be worn only by city dwellers on the flatlands," said my *ahmo*.

Of course we had no choice but to wear the many pairs of rough unfinished wooden clogs that the boss of the first group had left for us. For a thong, my *ahmo* used his craftsmanship to string a cloth or palm-fiber cord through holes he had bored through the wooden clogs with a red-hot poker and tie a fast knot at the bottom. In this way the clogs could be worn. Everything about my father was wonderful—he was responsible, honest, diligent, and respectful of the aged. He was a father worthy of respect. The only thing about him that upset me was that he made no distinction between boys and girls. I had to wear those clogs. But that's the way it was. When the boss wanted to give them to my *ahmo* before he left, my father had to have that kind.

The cassia bamboo was cut, leaving an open slope, the same as when the *budu* forest had been cut. But my *ahmo* said, "The bamboo will grow back. The soil where the *budu* forest grew can be worked and we can plant millet and potatoes. We can also replant the *budu* trees. They grow fast and in six or seven years will blossom and bear fruit again. So my *ahmo*, who was so conscientious and diligent when it came to his family, also had his own plans. Think about it. In six or seven years I'd once again be able to see the white waves. With food to eat and something to play with, a child could be filled with hope.

The following year I learned that my *ahmo* had sold the *budu* trees and the cassia bamboo so as to build a new house, otherwise there would have been no money to start construction.

After the plastics industry took off, the mountains and valleys were filled with plastic goods, including all shapes of lovely plastic sandals. Gradually, everyone forgot about wooden clogs. When, occasionally, I see a pair of wooden clogs, the memories come flooding back and I long for the days of my youth in the valley and that endless stretch of white waves.

The Sound of a Flute in the Mountains

RIMUI AKI

AT THE BEGINNING of the month I return to the mountains for a short stay.

There are four distinct seasons at home. In late spring the branch tips put forth tender new green leaves that tremble gently in the breeze. The air is cool and pleasingly fresh.

In the gentle afternoon breeze my daughter Anni and I walk barefoot down a small mountain path; the grass and trees are all like old friend we haven't seen in ages; the leaves wave, greeting us. As we walk I teach my daughter the Atayal names for each plant.

Here they are all my old friends, from the moss that clings to the ground to the fir tree that towers into the sky. As we walk we nibble on a blade of grass, eat a tree leaf, chew on a wildflower, or suck nectar from a blossom. Anni admires me deeply.

The whole way the faint sound of a flute seems to float on the breeze. It is a softly melodious sound, very faint but gently beautiful and as natural sounding as chirping birds or purling water. It is clear to the ear, but somehow ethereal.

Who is it? Playing the flute, so leisurely and carefree, in this warm afternoon breeze.

We follow the sound down a path through a bamboo grove and, turning a bend, a vista suddenly opens up before us. It really is "a trackless place where mountains and rivers end but where a village suddenly appears amid bright flowers and shady willows." It is Uncle Shaka's wood, and the whole slope is terraced with fields. The fallow ground is covered with cogon grass, and when the gentle breeze blows the mountain is filled with waves. It is breathtakingly majestic.

Beside the bamboo grove next to the fields sits a low tiled house. It's an old house of red roof and mud walls. Camellias grow all around the house. One beautiful red one, though it grows deep in the mountains where it cannot be appreciated, blossoms with each flower trying to outvie with the next.

A young girl with long hair sits upright on a small bench, a book open on her knees and a flute in her two hands, totally absorbed in playing a melody. If I could paint, I would do a watercolor titled "The Sound of a Flute in the Mountains" or "Flute-playing Girl" and hang it in a simple wooden frame. She resembles a mountain sprite in her loveliness.

She is Ting, the eight-year-old daughter of my cousin Leisa, who died two years ago in an auto accident. Concentrating on her flute playing, Ting fails to notice us standing behind her. The book on her knees, which is her sister's piano textbook, is opened to a tune titled "The French Doll," but that is clearly not what she is playing, a song the likes of which I have never heard. Unwilling to break the beautiful spell, I stand silently behind her, but . . .

"Mom, she is playing it wrong. It should be rui mi rui so, says Anni, as if discovering a new land. She has studied the piano since she was five, so she knows the staff and notes. She never makes a mistake, but, seeing me so enraptured with the music, she has to point out Ting's mistakes to me.

"Huh . . . it's just something I made up!" Ting discovers our presence and is at a loss as to what to do. She immediately closes the book, stands, and greets me: "Auntie!" She smiles, embarrassed, and eyes Anni who has just corrected her.

"It doesn't matter. You play so well. Your auntie was entranced and walked over to listen." I really understand her sense of failure in front of Anni.

Many years ago I was sent to the village to attend junior high. The first day in English class I was scared out of my wits listening to my classmates saying their perfect A, B, C, D. I had never encountered anything like it in the mountains, and, what's more, all the kids had already memorized the alphabet in the cram schools during summer vacation.

"You didn't prepare for English class?" my teacher asked, surprised, in the same tone of voice that Anni had just used. My heart sore, I wept and shook my head.

God knows, like all other mountain kids, I spent the summer swimming, climbing trees, stealing bird eggs. Every day was spent playing. Who knew what the flatland kids were doing?

At home I was an outstanding student. But at the junior high of three thousand plus students, I was lost in the crowd, and from the very first day of English class I lost my self-confidence . . .

Seeing Ting in front of me, I can't help feeling a tender affection for her.

I caress her hair (which was uncombed, and unbraided; it just hangs there). "Where's your mom?"

"She . . . she hasn't been back in a long time . . . " Her long lashes hang downward.

I am upset with myself for having asked. After Leisa died, my cousin's wife often went off to work. At New Years I saw her returned to the mountains dressed in fancy clothes. It's said that she works in Jilong and rarely comes home. Ting and her brothers and sister live with their grandfather.

The cold moonlight seeps through the curtains like water. Though night in the mountains is quiet, I can't sleep. In my mind's eye I see the little girl sitting upright playing the flute from the back, and the long drawn out sound of her flute wafted on the breeze.

Such a lovely little girl; such a beautiful melody. Will she explore the world of music later? I think of my childhood playmates . . .

Ahbate was a good drawer and liked to carve his pictures on the trees and bamboo. He once gave me a piece of chalk, which became a long and exquisite dragon.

I recall one day on the way home after school I watched Ahbate climb a vine and draw on a rocky face next to a gardenia. He used pieces of red brick, charcoal, and colored stone he had picked up to draw lively pictures of people, fish, birds, and beasts. I was filled with admiration.

After I grew up I saw the same kind of painting at an exhibition of Chagall's work at the Sun Yat-sen Memorial and was moved in the same way.

Later Ahbate went to work as a form builder on construction sites. I wonder if he thought about the wishes of those years as he climbed up and down the scaffolding . . .

"When I grow up, I want to be a painter!" he had said, with so much anticipation.

Of course, not one of us kids believed him, because he often played hooky, his studies were terrible, and he never represented our school in any sort of drawing competition. He wasn't a good student, and such activities were reserved for good students.

I often represented the school in academic competitions for drawing, recitations, public speaking, and composition, because I was "good." But I still don't have the makings of an artist. Ahbate was unfortunate.

Houla Tiemu was a natural muscleman. With his bare hands he could pull down an iron basketball hoop and then set it upright again.

Naturally, he never received the training to become a champion weightlifter, because after junior high he earned money by hauling bamboo. A few years ago he lost his life when his motorcycle went off the road and into a deep ravine after he had been drinking.

Limeng Walang, who was very beautiful, was able to create dances in the second year of primary school and organize a song and dance party and gathered all of the village kids and wrote a play and performed for the adults. At fifteen she was married off and is now the mother of four. Whenever I see her plump body and her hair in a casual ponytail go to the store to buy salt or oil, I sigh that such a talented girl today is . . .

The spring breeze brings warmth, and everything comes alive and is flourishing and full of hope. Anni sleeps soundly beside me and, though she is half Atayal, she has never experienced the sadness of her mother, who has suffered as a minority.

If the lifestyle and culture of the Han Chinese are the only choices on this island today, may I ask if the indigenous people have ever been given the opportunity to compete fairly?

If an indigenous person is to succeed in society, the first thing they must do is learn the rules of the game as established by the Han Chinese; otherwise there isn't the slightest chance of success. But, unfortunately, it is precisely the established rules with which we are unfamiliar.

I look at Anni's soundly sleeping face and listen to her regular breathing. Tomorrow we will return to Taipei so that she can receive her first-place award in American English recitation.

But why? On this night of thin clouds and a pale moon, I toss and turn, unable to sleep, thinking of Ting, my childhood playmates, and the fate of my beloved people . . . I sigh softly, upset for what has been lost.

Let's Go for a Big Feast Outdoors

ADAW PALAF

EARLY IN THE morning, young and old alike hopped about like sparrows in the workshop getting together pots, *katipay* (red glutinous rice), *ta'pila* (wicker baskets), and *pah* (wine), which were then loaded into two trucks. First we drive to meet at a friend's house in Zhunan and from there set off for the mountains around Nanzhuang.

Arriving at our destination, the adults dip their index fingers into the wine in their cups and sprinkle it for our *Tatu'asan* (ancestors) in heaven and the *Kawas* (spirits) on earth while chanting:

"Safeguard us *Tatu'asan* in heaven and *Kawas* on earth and allow us to fill our baskets with vine tips and wild vegetables."

Afterward they drain their cups. The men head off for the distant mountains for wild vegetables; the women build a fire under the bridge over the river and cook the red glutinous rice . . . and the children play in the water. Another *kapah* (young guy) who just got out of the army and I go to net fish.

We cast our nets several times without catching a fish (just some small ones that we toss back). Just when we are sitting weak and weary on the rocks doing nothing, we see a *matu'asay* (old person) and two kids starting a fire under a large tree. They look like Amei, so we hail them in our language and wade across the river.

"Any fish?"

"No, *Faki* (term of respect meaning uncle), not much luck today."

"It can be that way, *kapah*."

He is peeling some . . . *vow*! *facidol* (breadfruit).

"Where'd you get the *facidol*?"

"They came from the Xinzhu elementary school, *kapah*. My *kadafu* (son-in-law) got them.

"Where did the two of them go, *Faki*?"

"To pick some wild vegetables, *kapah*."

The golden *cucu* (breast) shaped fruit was tinged with the blush of a young girl. I was so excited that I held it in my hand and played with it for a long time . . .

Chatting, we learn that they were from Maogong in Hualian. Her *kadafu* is living in Xiangshan where he works as a form builder. I introduce us as bricklayers in Xinzhu from Ji'an, Taibalang, and Gaoliao.

After he finishes peeling them, we help square them and remove the cores after which we pull apart the sections by hand, wash them in water, and then put them piece by piece in a pot of boiling water to cook along with a little salt.

After it is cooked, we sample it. The soft, yellowish, stringy flesh is plain but tasty. The red fibrous skin is blossom sweet and the seeds even more so when you crack them in your mouth and eat the kernels . . . *vow*, it's really fragrant.

"*Aray* (thanks), *Faki*, we're going to take off. Hope you can join us over there under the bridge for some *pah*."

"*Aray*, *kapah*, we'll see you there," he says, smiling.

We can hear the singing before we get to the bridge. My cousin's wife sees us coming and runs to see the fish in our basket.

"Oh, you men!"

Then they sing:

The kadafu fishes, fishes by the sea
His girl comes to see him
He has two big fish baskets
He has two big rice buns
But he's sound asleep
A close look in his basket shows
He has no fish
Hi-ya-hu, hi-ya-hu
No fish in his baskets
Such a kadafu, with not even a fish

Being sung about by the women that way, we hurry off to dry our nets on some boulders and lie down. Only then do I notice the jade-green bamboo grove and fir forest . . . in this mountainous region of the Saisiyat, the wind is cool. Really, and it has been ages since I breathed fresh air in the dusty construction site. This is the first outing I've had since I started working for my cousin Malang (he's the boss of the bricklayers).

No matter how far the mountains or high the trees, the vines always grow higher and sway in the breeze . . . as if calling us to touch its surprisingly prickly stems and enticing us to suck on their sweet sap . . .

My watch says it's past two, and, just when I'm wondering why the men haven't returned, I suddenly hear their shouts and see the little kids run to greet them. They come back, their baskets full of mostly rattan heart, but some are carrying *sokway* (a kind of bitter melon). The women are happy to soon be busy peeling and slicing and chopping. And after a wash it is all dumped in the two big pots to cook.

Everyone is sitting or squatting on the ground, grabbing the steaming red *hakhak* (cooked red glutinous rice) from their *ta'pila* along with the home-salted pork and wild vegetables. We all drink sharp and fragrant *bah*. Everyone is eating with relish and talking and laughing . . .

"Is there any more rattan in the mountains?" asks a quiet *kapah*.

"Yes, there is," says thirty-year-old Haluo from Zhunan.

"Don't the Saisiyat eat it?"

"It's not that they don't eat it, they just think it is too bitter. Actually, all people eat their share of bitterness, but the Ami really love it. In other words we are a 'totem' people."*

"What is a totem?"

"A totem is the object of worship in primitive religion. The totem of the Rukai and the Paiwan is the hundred-pacer snake, like the dragon for the Chinese or the flying fish for the Yami. But we Ami . . . "

We shake our heads and he continues:

"Actually, to this day I still don't know what our totem is. Rattan is needed to make grass huts, weave baskets, string *fasiyaw* (an octagonal kite with a string that hums in the wind made of *teng*), and we plant it in our yards and on the slopes . . . rattan is our hope, happiness, and our totem, so the Ami are a totemic people."

We all continue eating rattan heart and drinking *pah*.

"We have twenty or thirty kinds of wild vegetables, right?" my nephew, who has studied in junior high, asks.

"More than that—at least double that," replies my cousin's husband, who is over fifty.

---

* There is an untranslatable play on words involving the character *teng* for "rattan" and *tou-teng* for "totem." The wordplay works only in Mandarin and for this reason the Ami *dogec* is not used, the only instance in this essay where a plant name is not given in Ami in the original.

"Actually, there's no way to calculate if you want to be very accurate," adds my aunt. At that moment five men and women and their kids slowly walk over to us. I tell everybody about meeting the *matu'asay* while fishing in the morning. Everyone is happy.

"There's not much *facidol* here; hope everyone can have a taste."

"*Aray, Faki.*"

Malang helps them set down the pot, which everyone quickly surrounds. Between lowering his head and lifting, the pot has been licked clean. Malang rubs his lips with the back of his hand and says, "It's been ages since I've had *facidol.* This time it was like tasting the *adigo* (spirit of the Amis). Come, let us toast them."

"*Aray, kapah.*"

Matu'asay says happily, "If you have work take your time doing it. No need to rush, because life is the most precious thing, especially since construction is *totemo avunai* (Japanese, meaning "so dangerous")! That's why our families all hope that we "ccay ponki a pida pata—loma" (bring home a basket of money)."

"Cheers."

For this gift of food, everyone has a good time and talks about how they sang and danced with joy all night in the worker's quarters after getting *lacidol* while working in Danshui, Beitou, and Shilin.

"Naluwan, naluwan . . . duyi yueyi heiyuehu-hai-yang . . . "

My aunt sings, and the men and women swarm around her and begin to sing and dance. The children run behind the adults and imitate them. Seeing this, the *matu-asay* says:

Wo Wo see Malataw, the spirit of heaven
Your people are singing, your people are dancing *Wo Wo*
Wo Wo (chorus)
Dance *kapah* dance out of that ancient dream
Wei-ha-hai

Smiling contentedly, everyone sings and dances, the Naluwan dancing and singing echoes in the quiet valley, attracting a lot of curious Saisiyat people. The kids dance their dances, childish and lively. The adults consider themselves rich beyond compare. The men's hero dance (no one knows where it originated) is so comical that the women are in stitches watching them. The women's dance is a combination of the cha-cha and traditional Ami dance steps that changes continuously . . .

After dancing the *niuwaniu* dance (weed-pulling dance), the harvest dance, and just shaking booty . . . after dancing more than ten dances, the sun is setting in the west. Everyone holds hands, forms a large circle, and invites the Saisiyat to take part in the *mi-hahai* (harvest ceremony).

Matu'asay loudly proclaims:

Sing, *kapah*
Sing out the exhortations of the Tatu'asan
Wei-ha-hai

The little girls, who stand in the middle of the circle, offer *pah* to one adult after another. Everyone sings more loudly, following the lead singer, and dances with more energy . . .

Ahma'ao ama (dad)
Ha-hai
Is this a dream?
Ha-hai
Is this a dream?
Ha-hai
You take us brothers to work in the wilds
Ha-hai
Cidal (the sun) is directly overhead, the sweat runs down our backs
Ha-hai
Far away you point to the place
Ha-hai
Want us to go to fill bamboo buckets with water
Ha-hai
The river is clear, the water good to drink, you stress
Ha-hai
The water we carry
Ha-hai
Is muddy
Ha-hai
An enemy must be roiling it at the source
Ha-hai
Hurry, *patayen* (kill him), take his *tagal* (head)
Ha-hai
Be our *ahma,* use a stone ax
Ha-hai
See the *tagal* he holds in his hand
Ha-hai
So it is our respected *ahma*

Ha-hai
. . .
Kaka' ao kaka (brothers and sisters)
Ha-hai
I didn't do it on purpose
Ha-hai
I was in a reedy ditch catching fish with electricity
Ha-hai
Saw something huge wriggling in the water, winding away
Ha-hai
It must be an eel, I thought happily
Ha-hai
I pursued and zapped it
Ha-hai
I heard a scream of pain; it shot up and ran
Ha-hai
That *paga kaka* swayed and shook
Ha-hai
Falling from the short skirt of *kaka*
Ha-hai

I don't know when the crescent moon appeared in the sky—everyone was singing and dancing, unwilling to stop. After the bonfire goes out, we drive back to Xinzhu, singing all the way . . .

A Large Stingray

SYMAN RAPONGAN

JUST AS BEFORE, I always get the urge to go spearfishing every afternoon around three. If I don't go down to the sea during the day, then I must go in the evening. If I don't get in the water at all, I'm at a loss as to how to idle away the day. From the roof of my unfinished house, I can see the ocean current around J-Langoyna (cape, promontory). Today the waves are not surging violently, but the tide should be pretty strong according to the lunar calendar. I figure I have the stamina to handle it.

"Syman, are you going down to the sea? It's going to get dark soon," says my father.

I really don't feel like answering, just to avoid him throwing cold water on my growing urge, so I set off directly on my bike. The only thought in my mind is to spear five or six black-tongued unicorn fish, to show respect for him, and three or four blue-barred parrotfish for my mom and my plump woman. I assume that would make the day worthwhile.

Black-tongued unicorn fish school near the ocean's surface during the winter. Weak and minute plankton can often be taken in amid the seaweed in the ocean channels—in even greater numbers when the cold current occurs. The black-tongued unicorn fish especially likes places where the current flows unimpeded and they can all swim into the current. At around four in the afternoon they swim inshore where they rest and spend the night in rocky caverns.

When my father was young, these fish were incredibly easy to spear because there were few divers and the fish were not afraid of humans. All a person needed was good lungs and you could spear as many as you wanted. But today the fishing boats from Taiwan come to the waters around Lanyu, where they blast for fish and poison them. Nowadays, the minute a fish sees a diver it's gone. After all, fish too have an instinct for self-preservation.

Still, we can still spear a few black-tongued unicorn fish, just not so many as in the past. On this December day in 1993, when I arrive at my spot (it is a Yami taboo to mention the names of fishing places so as to prevent evil spirits from following and scattering the fish) I notice that the tide is not very strong because it was high. Although my diving spot is only five meters from the shore, there is a fault shelf twenty meters down on which coral grows. The terrace above is the same, attracting a plentiful number of finger-sized tropical fish. Their beauty and grace is difficult to describe. They are unafraid, because the Yami do not hunt and eat them.

I sit without moving on top of the reef examining the movement of the water and rinsing my mask. Judging from the height of the sun in the west and taking into account the trip home, I estimate I have a little over an hour for spearfishing. I dive to the fault shelf and lie prone in wait for the fish. The visibility isn't all that great, but there is lots of plankton in the water to attract fish like yellowback and goldband fusiliers. As I lay motionlessly on the reef waiting for my prey, they circled my head, sometimes clockwise and sometimes counterclockwise, like flies. I find it difficult to shoot because of the underwater current and the fact that there are so many fish, and they are extremely skittish. Second, since the fish are of the same genus, they all look about the same, neither beautiful nor ugly; the only real difference being in size. As a result I fire without hitting anything. After I do spear one, though, they all depart to look for plankton elsewhere.

I wait in the same place for the unicorn fish to appear. The tide was rising and the sky darkening. The current is running from the west to east, so I figure the unicorn fish will soon be schooling to swim out to the channels to spend the night. Sure enough, in a few minutes I begin to make them out. The next time I dive to the bottom, I hope that they will soon be within range. The fish like to swim against the current, darting up and down to eat the plankton. Occasionally they descend to the bottom and nibble on the seaweed. The first time I dive they do not swim toward me with their usual curiosity, but when I ascend to take a breath I so scare them that they swim off to a distance.

The next time I dive I blow some bubbles to pique their curiosity, but to no avail. And at that moment I am swept by a wave of fear the likes of which I have never experienced before. Although I often go diving alone, even at night, and have never been afraid, my own unlucky presentiments surprise me. I look all around me, and see nothing out of the ordinary, but I am still possessed by that inexplicable sense of fear. When I look up I am startled to see a large stingray directly above me.

Damn. So that is what made me afraid. Looking at the stingray, I immediately recall a story about stingrays discussed by some men older than myself. Once, when my cousin and some of his friends were spearfishing, he was enveloped by a stingray and was unable to surface to take a breath. He was afraid of it because it was too ugly to touch and also because it had a poisonous tail. To preserve his life, his only means of defense, his only choice, was to shoot it. He shot the stingray and, in addition to a huge amount of blood (For the Yami it is taboo to come in contact with the blood of ugly fish such as sharks, eels, morays, and stingrays, because it symbolizes death or disease for one's close realtives), it seemed to go crazy and beat my cousin savagely with its wings and knocked him against the reef with the force of a typhoon. His body was jabbed and lacerated by the coral. He said that, by the time he reached shore, he couldn't stand, and he was so dizzy he couldn't see anything clearly. He was unconscious for a full two to three hours. Fortunately, he had companions to help him. There, right above me, is a stingray, its wings at least three meters long. Its shape and white underbelly disgust me, and to me it was a thousand times more ugly than a moray. So, clinging to the coral, I slowly inch my way toward shore. And, being supersensitive, it follows, keeping pace with me. If I try to surface, I'll run right into its underbelly. I started to get nervous. Although I am underwater right off the shore, I am in a fault zone, and the worst thing is that it won't let me surface and its wings are already hitting the reef. I have been underwater for about fifteen seconds, but, due to the tension, my breaths were short. But I have to think of some way to get rid of the demon. If I spear it, it will drag away my spear, and I am really averse to seeing the evil thing's blood. In desperation, I shout underwater with all my might. It is startled, as if cursed, and swims away.

I breathe a sigh of relief and surface and immediately climb onto shore and rest. I thank my ancestral spirits for protecting me. But within five minutes the stingray is back. I watch it from shore. It is easily two meters wide, a medium-sized one. It swims to and fro in front of me. I look for a stone with which to hit its head, figuring one the size of a coconut will knock him good. When it swims directly in front of me, I take aim at a spot between its eyes. Taking advantage of my superior position above, I hit my target with a "pok." The water shoots up in a spray, and, though momentarily stunned, it unfurls its wings and flees, one wing above water and the other submerged. It brings its wing down on the water's surface with a loud slap, stirring up some impressive waves before it dives. Go and die I say.

Proudly, I smoke a cigarette to calm myself. The sun has already fallen below the sea, but I am still intent upon spearing some fish, because my net bag contains only one yellowback fusilier. I dive in the water again, but not a fish is to be seen. There are no parrotfish for my mom, and the one in my bag is to be fried for the kids so there are none for my dad either. I decide to swim elsewhere to spear some fish. As I swim I think about what just happened and feel a lingering trepidation. If I can't spear any unicorn fish, I can shoot some dumber fish so that my parents at least will have fish soup to eat. If I come back empty-handed, they will have their doubts about my abilities. They'll call me as a "degenerate Yami." I have no choice but to go on spearing fish.

When I spear a parrotfish, the fear starts to rise again. My father once said to me, "If you suddenly grow afraid while you are out spearfishing, don't hesitate to come ashore and return home, because it's an ill omen." Thinking of his words, I put my head down and swim back to where I had been. When I make my last dive and am lying prone on the reef, I look all around because the fear remained. Before I choose my prey, three white-bellied stingrays come swimming toward me—they are only twenty or thirty meters to the east. To avoid being toyed with by the three rays, and to preserve myself, I immediately surface and swim quickly for shore. Before getting to shore, I get a good look at them: beneath their eyes hang two sickle-shaped appendages of flesh, ugly to behold, between which are their mouths. They looked to be at least two meters broad and ugly beyond compare. They swim parallel to me as if to challenge me or to get revenge. The one I hit had gone for his brothers. They clearly are smart elasmobranches.

I climb ashore to get away from them, but they continue straight toward me and stop.

"The sea is your world, the land mine. I'm not getting in the water so you can't do anything to me!" I said.

When stingrays feed on the surface, they usually do so alone and they are carnivorous. I wonder what taboo I have violated for them to gang up on me and seek revenge. Blocking my way into the sea, they anger me. I am about to look for a stone with which to hit one of them. Watching them swim leisurely to and fro, I recall what my dad and my uncle once said to me: "Child, don't harm any strange fish you might encounter, because they are more intelligent than the average fish." Perhaps I dive too much alone and have slowly been influenced by their (Yami) pantheism. Influenced by my mother culture, I have come to believe that all living beings possess a soul, the existence of a kind of supernature. I put down the stone and say goodbye to the stingrays.

I don't say anything about this to my father. He would just stop me from going spearfishing again, and both my father and my mother would refuse to eat any fish I spear. They would do so out of fear that I might have an accident, because spearfishing is dangerous and I often go alone. In order to keep diving and to provide fresh fish for my parents who are nearly eighty, I keep my hardships and the strange animals to myself.

Wind Walker

SAKINU

ONE WHO LETS the wind move and pour in we call "a person who opens the way for the wind"; where the wind circulates and flows, we call the "wind's road"; the one who opens the way for the wind we call a "wind walker." The old hunter is speaking. "Open the palms of your hands and let the wind touch them. That is the language of Nature, words perceptible to human feelings. The wind is the language of Nature, and human feelings are a response to Nature. We call your father a wind walker. His two feet have carried him everywhere—he has seen everything and trod every inch of ground—no place is hidden from him. Your father exchanged his life for that. We say that the land and Nature give you a wind walker or "*kama,*" which means someone that can communicate directly with the soul of Nature and explain it to you," says the old man, pointing at the farthest crest of mountains visible to the eye.

As we follow the crest of mountains of father's hunting ground and enter the valley opposite, my father whispers to me, "This is my Discovery Channel."

"Discovery?" I ask, perplexed.

"Wait till dusk," my father replies, "and you'll understand. Keep quiet, don't make a sound." Pointing with his chin, my father indicates that I should keep my eyes on a large tree in a clearing by a steep and precipitous cliff close by.

My father moves ever so lightly and indicates I should get a good seat from where to watch the upcoming show. My father rubs camphor leaves on his body and face. I ask him: "*Kama* (father), what is that for?"

"There are too many mosquitoes here. By rubbing yourself with camphor leaves, they won't be able to find you. It will also make us invisible—the animals won't be able to scent our whereabouts."

"Invisible?" I say. How is that possible? Then father begins to move stealthily like a snake. He makes a blind of silver grass to conceal us by binding the flowering stalks to the rots behind or feet. I am really perplexed. I wonder what my dad, who is a hunter, is up to and what he means by Discovery Channel. I'm momentarily at a loss. Then my father thrusts his chin to indicate that I should look below the big tree in the clearing. I stealthily part the silver grass in front of me. Just as I am about to shout with joy, he forcefully pushes my face to the ground breathing with the earth. My father comes close to my ear and speaks softly and slowly, his voice seemingly at one with the air, as if everything has forgotten us. Only then do I realize that father has made himself one with Nature by following Nature's rhythm. Breathing with the earth, I slowly focus.

The sky at dusk gradually darkens; in a show of strength, the last rays of golden light penetrate the leaves, fall across father's hunting ground. Looking out through the narrow spaces in the silver grass, the light looks like that of a dance floor. As the last light fades, night taking the place of day, the cicadas begin to chirp, hastening day upon its way.

"*Kama*!" I shout to my father in surprise. But my father points to his mouth, indicating that I should be silent and stay vigilant. I am so excited because I have never in my life seen a whole herd of muntjac. My heartbeat echoes on the hunting ground. While motioning me to calm down, he criticizes me, saying, "Why get so excited? I can hear your heart beating and so can all the animals around us!" I took several deep breaths trying to keep time with the rhythm of Nature. When my heartbeat harmonizes with the rhythm of nature, my father says, "We are the hunted now. If you do not wish to be discovered, you must do your utmost to be in tune with your surroundings, in harmony with the rhythm of Nature; otherwise, you'll never see the traces of life hidden from your view by Nature. *Malici* (be still and don't talk)."

The muntjac are leaping in the clearing, their small tails swing unceasingly like pendulums. The pattern of the fur confuses my eyes. It's so beautiful . . . so beautiful.

"*Kama*, why are there so many muntjac here?"

"When autumn is nearly upon us," replies my father, "the muntjac will always gather here because they like to eat the fruit of ancient *Ra* (the name of the tree) tree, especially the young muntjac. It's heaven for them. After bringing them here, their parents tell them this clearing and the fruit are possessed and enjoyed by all muntjac. Last year at this time I came here to watch them meet, and while they're here they can propose marriage so that they can enjoy a wedding feast when they come next year."

"Son," my father murmurs, "when I was here last year some of the muntjac were still small, but now they are grown up." My father continues: "See the one with the broken horn. It was here last time. It is very old, perhaps the oldest. The blackest one is their leader." My father speaks as if he were checking the goats that he himself had raised. At dusk my father's hunting ground is entirely still. "*Dakeci . . . dakeci . . .* " call the muntjac. "They are telling other herds of munjac that this is their territory," explains my father.

Night takes over for dusk. A cool wind blows and a half-moon shines over father's hunting ground. The muntjac remain in the clearing, frequently gazing in our direction, their ears standing alert. Then they calm down. "Son, the night wind has carried our scent to the muntjac." In the night, the muntjac call constantly for their mates. The wind carries their desolate cries through the valleys and ravines on and on for great distances.

"Son, take a rest. Like us, the muntjac will sleep here tonight. As night deepens, the wind will grow colder." Fearing that any forceful movement or sound might disturb the deeply sleeping spirits and everything in Nature, my father urges me to move softly. The slumbering darkness becomes more sinister. The night is so still, so very still.

"Son, look!" My father nudges me with his shoulder and motions with his chin that I should look up on the cliff. But I see nothing. My father murmurs, "You're here, you're finally here. I've waited a long time for you."

I move softly and look in the same direction my father is looking. I am scared at the sight of a grayish-yellow shape with black spots surreptitiously gliding down the cliff. "*Kama*, it's a clouded leopard!"

"Son, that's what the Paiwan people call *liguliao*. The last time I was here and saw so many muntjac, I knew that a *liguliao* would certainly show up, just like the old people of the tribe told me. My expectations have been fulfilled; it is finally here."

"*Kama*, how did you know it would come?"

"Son, it arrived a long time ago. Night before last, it was resting on the cliff, waiting, and familiarizing itself with what was going on and the scents around it. It also knew when I arrived."

"When it saw us, it left for a while but doubled back at dusk, waiting on the cliff for night to fall. It knows that we humans are nearly helpless in the dark. The *liguliao* doesn't take us humans as the slightest threat. That's why the old hunters of the tribe always said that hunting the *liguliao* was the same as going into battle." *Kama* continued: "The old people of the tribe used to say that hunting a *liguliao* was very troublesome because we hold them in respect and there is a ritual required to kill one. Wearing a *liguliao* pelt is symbolic of its courageous death and bestows the same beauty and pride to the hunter."

"Son, don't make a sound—the *liguliao* of the cliff is already on the trunk of the ancient *ra* tree. Surprised, I look at the *liguliao* clinging head down on the trunk, its tail curling around a branch for balance. It looks as if it were walking on level ground, its body pressed close to the tree. It descends stealthily toward where the muntjac are beneath the tree. If I hadn't seen it all, from a distance I would have thought that the *liguliao* was just a protruding part of the tree trunk.

It's then that the muntjac sense that something is amiss. They are constantly looking around without being aware that the tree that produces the fruit they love to eat poses a great danger. My pulse begins to race as if I am about to witness a killing that I am powerless to prevent. The forest grows quieter, making it seem to me as if everything were pausing to watch the most brilliant part of the program on the Discovery Channel.

My father and I hold our breaths and control our heartbeats, but they seem to pick up speed to accompany the rhythm of Nature. As the *liguliao* selects its place, it fixes its eyes on us through the silver grass for several seconds. Its sharp eyes seem to tell us this is its prey and its hunting ground. Because my eyes blur under its sharp gaze I am unprepared when it pounces on a muntjac below the tree. The moment I am about to shout, my father's large hand closes over my mouth, allowing only the minutest sound to emerge from between his fingers. My face close to the ground, I scarcely dare to move my eyes. The muntjac pounced on by the *liguliao* struggles and cries out. I hear it cry "*ah-ming, ah-ming*" from a distance. Through the silver grass I see a muntjac that refuses to leave—it moves back and forth. "That's one of the muntjac's family," says my father. After a while even the lingering muntjac leaves the clearing.

As I turn my eyes on the *liguliao* beneath the ancient *ra* tree, I am surprised to find that it is nowhere to be seen. My father passes a branch before my eyes several times, indicating that I should look straight ahead over the end of the branch. It's then that the moon seems to be blotted out by dark clouds. When my vision adjusts to normal human ability of "not being able to see a thing," my father wants me to listen. It's still on the tree from where it can be heard dragging the muntjac. I try to pierce the night's darkness with my eyes to spot its position. But after a while I hear nothing.

"*Kama*, is it gone?"

My father is silent a while before replying: "It knows the moon will come out again."

Once again the moonlight shines on the land.

"Son, it's in the tree."

"No it's not. There's only the muntjac hanging in the fork of the trunk."

"It's still here; it'll be back."

I fix my eyes on the muntjac in the tree, unwilling to take my eyes off of it lest I miss a chance to see it.

Then, once again, the land is enveloped in blackness. "It's back in the tree. Do you hear it?" my father asks. I am about to ask my father how come he knows so much about its every move when I can faintly hear the sound of the muntjac being dragged over the bark. Finally all I hear are the dry leaves fluttering and the twigs and fruit falling to the ground. "*Pai-si*" is the last sound of the night and the only sound the *liguliao* left in my memory.

"It leaped onto the cliff, son; it's on top." I look hard and, before I see its shadow, I pray to heaven and the spirits of my *VuVu* (ancestors), let me see it one more time, OK? I press my hands to my chest and pray: one more time will be enough. I don't know if heaven was moved or my ancestors promised it, but when the moonlight slowly rolled back the black night covering the land, I can vaguely see it pacing the cliff top. "Son, do you see it?" my father asks. Absorbed, I don't reply. I wait to see, but, by the time the moonlight shines again on the land, the *liguliao* vanishes over the cliff and does not reappear.

"It's gone, gone far away. This is its place; it knows that we are in this silver grass blind." My father loosens the grass on his heels and allows the wind—the cool night wind—to move again, to blow on our faces and bodies. I roll over, reclining on the *liguliao's* land, thinking to myself: this belongs to it. My father tells me that the old hunters of the village told him that the dead soul of a hunter is transformed into clouded leopards because he is unwilling to leave the land he knows, understands, and is accustomed to. The dead soul becomes a clouded leopard to forever guard the life of the land. The old people also say that the clouded leopard is the high priest of Nature. It can call down a storm when the land needs water; it can stand on the mountain crest to let the heavenly gods know to send rain. When the land needs to the wind to awaken its slumbering life force, it can climb the highest cliff and shake its tail to inform the heavenly gods. It knows in advance about natural changes by seeing crises concealed beneath the soil.

"Really, *Kama*?"

"That's what the old people used to say. Otherwise how did it know when the moon was going to disappear so that it could climb into the tree unseen under cover of the darkness and then disappear before the moon reappeared? The old people are always right. It will be a sign to one's descendants. Son, one day when I am no longer here, if my *VuVu* (descendants) have the opportunity to see a *liguliao*, tell them that it is the soul of their grandfather."

"*Kama*, will the muntjac return here?"

"Why not?" replies my father. "Here birth and death are the cycle of life in obedience to Nature and accepted by the land." Father twists around, and out of curiosity I ask, "*Kama*, what are you doing? Why are you twisting around that way?" My father answers: "I'm returning the land's warmth to it and covering my scent with earth." When we get up to depart I look back at the clearing under the ancient *ra* tree. A moment ago a surprising natural drama was enacted here. I began to wonder if the muntjac really would return. My father seemed to understand what was on my mind. "Son, what you should as is will the clouded leopard return." Will we see it again and be witness to a place where the ecology strives for balance. Furthermore, we ought to worry whether today's hunters have the same attitude, ideas, and methods as the clouded leopard. That would be sufficient because it guarantees the continuation of life. It is the natural life process bestowed by the land: one must have respect for the life one takes."

On the way back we pass by the hunting hut an old hunter who is a friend of my father's. Before we arrive my father says, "The old hunter is here; I detect his scent." A barking dog is heard far away at the hut. As we approach the hut the old hunter asks, "*Di-ma shun*? (Who is it?)" My father replies, "*Digaiyang.*" "Ah, *Difinali'an* (wind walker)."

It's early morning and the day hasn't broken yet. A cool breeze blows. Father tells him about the clouded leopard we saw. The old man holds a walking stick and, in his native tongue, says, "This is their place. I too saw them in the past, but I'm old and can't match their rhythm. It's been ages but I never told anyone *yimara, yiruwa, liguli* (there are clouded leopards here). This was our secret."

"*Di finali'an*," the old hunter calls my father wind walker, "*di shun* (you) *di'a'en* (this old hunter) has hunted the *liguliao*, *nudachu* (this will be our secret."

"Gaiyang," says the old hunter using my father's Paiwan name, "hunting the *liguliao nimijia da paiwan da kayi* (we Paiwan people say that the meaning of *liguliao* is 'moves as swiftly as the wind, agile and difficult to spot—as soon as you so much as glimpse it, it is gone.'"

The old hunter speaks to me: "*dishun da kama*, we call your father *finali'an*, wind walker, the meaning of which is 'this place is his' because no one knows this place better. Your father knows every place; there is no place he has not been."

The old hunter looks off into the distance and mutters to my father, "We call *dishun* (you) *finali'an*, or wind walker. In Paiwan *liguliao* means 'as swift as the wind'. If you see one it confirms that wind walker is accepted by the land and Nature."

"*Gaiyang* (my father's name), *dishun daahra* (your child) should be called 'follower of the wind.'" Smiling, I reply, "*bulai* (great, not bad)."

"*Sacinaci'er* (very beautiful)," The old hunter smiles sweetly. It's a memory that will always be with me.

Father and the Land

NEQOU SOKLUMAN

"HAVE YOU AGREED upon a price for the land?" The surveyor had just left and I sat with my father in the shade of a tree beside the field. A gentle breeze stirred the deep green maple leaves.

"Not yet. I wanted to get it surveyed before discussing price. Your older brother thinks eight hundred thousand, but I think that'll be hard. I'll take whatever I can get for it. If it's not enough, we'll have to think of something else." Looking straight ahead into the distance, Father put down his hammer.

The economy hadn't been doing well of late and money was short. Everyone in the village had the same idea: if you had to sell land, it was best to sell it to your own people, because a price could be negotiated and then there was the possibility of getting it back later. But, after looking for a buyer for a while, only one from the flatlands could be found.

"As long as our own people are living on the land, we can get it back. Being in the right frame of mind is most important. To overcome difficulties, you have to think clearly and know where the problems are. Your older brother told me this via your mother. Everything happened so quickly, and I'm so nervous that I haven't slept well for a week. I don't know what to do. Fortunately your mom is here and together we have decided to sell this piece of land. What else can we do? In any case, he is my child. I can't just ignore him. I'm still strong enough to go out and make money to get the land back." If I had been in his shoes, I would have been too weak to say anything, but here was my sixty-five-year old father speaking with such firmness. An expression like "the rain fell throughout the night with the roof already leaking" was inadequate to describe our recent misfortunes. Every so often some new difficulty would befall our family. The year before last, my second brother was crippled in a fall at Grandma's house, then came the September 21 earthquake, which destroyed out house, and then, while we were living in temporary quarters, mother had a stroke after drinking too much on a cold winter night. With all the difficulties after the disaster, my dad and my older brothers had a fight and, in a fit of rage, my dad drank a can of pesticide. Fortunately he survived and heaven saw to it that there were no complications. And with the sluggish economy, my brothers and I lost our jobs one by one and were forced to return to the village. And now, without any forewarning, we have a seven hundred thousand yuan debt to be paid within a month. It's as if each time we try to take a step forward, we are forced back ten steps by our problems.

The debt stemmed from an incident eight years earlier involving my oldest brother. He was a truck driver and, out of fatigue from overwork, he caused a big pileup on the freeway and had to compensate. Actually it's not as if we never knew it was coming because my oldest brother had always been allowed to run wild. It was only a matter of time before things exploded like a hidden land mine. Actually our difficulties were accumulated over a long period of time, like the problems of my second brother and my mom, all of which were the result of excessive drinking.

"Dad, has this land lain fallow since we planted broad beans year before last?" It was neglected during the earthquake and the economic downturn. The weeds are waist high, and I have to keep my eyes peeled for fear of stumbling on a poisonous snake or something.

"Your mother and I decided that if the village really wanted to get involved in tourism, then we thought we would build a few traditional wooden houses where tourists could stay and we could make a little money. We never expected such an unavoidable problem. Tourism is a topic the village has been discussing for years. It is an idea proposed by Youhani, who is a member of the Council of Aboriginal Affairs. He says that the village environment would be a big tourist draw and that we can build a world-class tourist village. At first, most people were opposed, because it was so completely different from the agricultural or labor work that they have done for years and to which they are accustomed. It seemed like a cock-and-bull story. Everyone is busy. They get up early and get home late. They don't have a lot of time to think about such things. Most people have the notion that a harvest can be had for a minimum of labor. But, in the digital age, this notion is worthless. Most villagers don't receive the compensation they should receive for their labors. For example, some bosses will delay on some pretext or another, and the simple villagers don't know what to do. Sometimes a boss will just take off and not pay anyone for their labor. Later, the value of village crops declined. For example, plums sold for at least around thirty yuan per *jin*. It was the most substantial and most reliable income every year. Every family made quite a bit at harvest time. The kids all had the most spending money in their pockets at that time. We would work after school. Two or three kids with bags would pick the plums up off the ground that everyone else had missed. In a couple of hours we could gather anywhere from three to five *jin*. One or two hundred yuan made us feel rich. But in recent years the price has fallen to around five yuan a kilo. Not only that, but in order to sell them they all have to be picked by hand, be at least two centimeters in diameter, and be unblemished. A lot of villagers have trees laden with fruit they can't sell. It's enough to make a person cry and harden their heart to chop down their trees so as to try growing something else.

People realized the seriousness of the situation only recently. Traditional agricultural wasn't sufficient to keep food on the table, and, if things continued in the same fashion, it would be just as Professor Youhani said—we'll become ever poorer. Tragically, when the tribespeople pursue a material life they tend to lose their collective life in which the joys and hardships of life are shared. People become closed up in themselves and as soon as an advantage is at stake they attack one another like mad dogs. It is hard to work together and they lose their spirit of harmonious coexistence with Nature. Wilderness areas are overdeveloped and Nature counterattacks and the villages exhibit all kinds of ailments.

"It's unavoidable! Maybe we can improve our home or use it for tourism. Weren't pears once planted here, Dad?"

"Yes. So you remember!" I remembered that that piece of land was once covered with a pear orchard. That was before I went to primary school. It wasn't just this land of ours—all the dry land neighboring ours was planted with pears. My playmates and I were always reluctant to leave the place. Wherever you looked you'd see the yellow pears. We were like monkeys swinging from one tree to the next, eating our fill. Sometimes we'd play with the caterpillars we caught on the trees. And when the pear trees suddenly disappeared, replaced by high-value-added crops, so did the caterpillars.

The sudden disappearance left my young mind so confused that when I recalled them I wondered if they hadn't been just a dream.

I looked over toward the broken ridge. At one time there was an arrow bamboo grove there. The bamboo stalks from there were straight and hard. When I was a kid, my playmates and I would take saws, knives, and penknives and fight our way in. We would clear a path with our knives and then cut down the thicker, unblemished stalks with our saws. With our knives we'd remove the small branches at the nodes as well as the tender tops. Then we would upend a section of bamboo, place our knives on the node-end, and rotate the bamboo back and forth until we cut through to the hollow center. Then we would insert a plunger of bamboo, about eight centimeters in length, which would have to be able to be pushed in and out of the larger tube. Finally, we would moisten the old newspaper we had brought along and tear off a good bit of it and roll it into a ball that would then be inserted into the thick section of bamboo. Then the bamboo slip would be pushed in with force, compressing the air in the tube, shooting out the paper wad that had previously been inserted with a loud pop. Our *teqong* (bamboo popgun) was finished. We wiled away our summer afternoons playing army with our bamboo guns. But today you cannot tell there was once a grove of arrow bamboo there. The sound of firing *teqong* has also long departed.

The village has changed a lot in recent years, and a lot has disappeared. And what has disappeared will be difficult to recover. How could it disappear? Because it is out of step with the times.

"Frankly, your father has never lost. It's you, my children who have lost. If your older brothers had not had problems, we wouldn't have fallen this way. When you were little I could still buy land. Each one of you grew up and we were beset by one problem after another."

"That's right!" Actually, that's the way things were, I thought to myself. Compared to the older people of the village, the young are a lost group [losers]. We fell in the crack between the old and the new. With the village in our hands, I'm afraid that the village will be lost. We lack the stubborn fighting spirit of the last generation and we can't keep up with the changeable and treacherous world around us. We are caught in a dilemma.

"Don't lose heart. After this passes we'll go out and work and make money. I can do even more if I put my mind to it. Really. If heaven blesses me, I'll still be able to buy back some land." Father smiled as he spoke. I admired my father for being able to say such things in the face of such adversity. It seems as if the moment our family encounters any difficulty Father is always able to be so positive. I think this is a lust for life.

Father takes of his hat and scratches at an abrasion on his forehead. He got it last week when he went to the bamboo grove on the other side of the broken ridge to cut bamboo shoots. He was careless; when he stepped on a loose embankment he slipped and hit his head. Although he is getting on in years, he is still busy. As always, he gets up early and comes home late. There is a time for work and a time for rest. Father built the livestock shed by the field, for instance, out of local materials he collected himself. It took close to a year to construct. Whenever he had a moment he would work on it, regardless of the weather. Looking at it, it is hard to imagine that an old man over sixty built it single-handedly. There is running water, a place to cook meat, and a place to sleep. There also are a number of orchids in pot that bloom all year long. Without fail, every morning father feeds the domestic animals there. And, sometimes, after he has had too much to drink and is afraid to return home, he goes there to sleep it off.

There is good reason for father to want to build the small wooden house here: it is a flat mesa that, while being level, offers a good vantage of the land below and the surrounding mountains, and transportation is convenient. It is peaceful and quiet and is naturally inspiring. The most important element in the vast scenic vista is Jade Mountain, thrust mercilessly upward into the sky, the sight of which makes even a child of the mountains like me sigh with admiration. Soon the land will be in someone else's hands; I really hate to lose it.

"Don't be sad, child. In the Bible you read about Job who was a wealthy man but who endured all kinds of hardships. He lost everything including his children and his wife. But he never relinquishes his faith. You see, God gave him more than he ever had before. I assume you know the story. Anyway, I'm still kicking, and what matters most is what you think." When it comes to keeping faith I have been influenced by my father. And, although he doesn't always go to church and likes to drink a cup or two, his life is one of firm faith. I've learned a lot from him.

"Let's go, child. We should be getting home." Father puts on his hat, picks up his hammer, stands up and sets off.

"Let's go!" I turn back to look at the piece of land, then look once more at my father's receding silhouette and smile.

Fish

TOPAS TAMAPIMA

It's August and Orchid Island is enjoying the sun's most loving attention. I spend all day working in the clinic and still feel its warmth. Even before the workday is done, my mind is someplace else, pulled away by the ocean breeze that comes through the window. I go into the dispensary to prepare a box of medicine before going to see an old fisherman of the Yeyin tribe. He has an unusual ailment that, when it acts up, is like a demon sticking nails in his joints.

I get on my motorcycle and ride down to the road that circles the island. The sea to my right reflects the blinding rays of sunlight. I dare not look directly at the sea's surface with my nearsighted eyes. I can sense its blue and its indescribable beauty. Occasionally, I squint to regard the leaves of the fat sweet potatoes and other vegetation as well as pursue some migratory bird I have scared up.

Reporting for duty at the Orchid Island Health Department at the beginning of last month, I excitedly tried to suppress an acute sensitivity. As if entering a strange new world made me dizzy with joy. Today I discover more lovely scenery such as the crystal clear sea by the road, the fresh air, the gentle faces, and all the other warm and fragrant sensations that only serve to heighten the mysteriousness of this strange land.

I turn the accelerator on the handle and increase my speed, continuing toward Yeying tribe.

A half a kilometer from the village, I reduce my speed. The village is on a slope facing the slanting sun. The sunlight reflected by the village makes it stand out. Groups of people are crowded around the houses. I wonder what kind of ritual they are performing.

I get off my motorcycle and walk into the village carrying the box of medicine.

Approaching one house, I see them slitting open the fishes' bellies. One person brings a fish's head close to his mouth and sucks, his throat and stomach contracting. Almost immediately, a smile appears on his face. They are eating raw fish eyes. I guess this must be why they have such good vision!

"*Guogaiyi* (how are you). What kind of fish is that?

"It is a parrotfish, *Guyishang* (doctor)."

"Would you sell me five of them?"

"No, I can't sell them."

"How about three, then."

He continues cleaning the fish without replying.

I'm stunned by his refusal to sell me the fish. I'd be willing to exchange the five hundred yuan in my pocket for some fresh parrotfish. I lower my head and slowly walk away, not daring to ask why he won't sell them to me.

I walked to another house where I was politely refused, saying that the fish had been a gift from a relative.

"I'd willingly sell them to you, *Guyishang*, but if a fisherman friend found out I'd be cursed and, I'm afraid, never be given another fish."

Accustomed to being able to buy anything I wanted with money, I suddenly discovered that money was of no value. Unwilling to be turned down again, I lowered my head and walked away from their joyful harvest and hurried off to the house of the patient I had come to visit.

I entered a traditional partially subterranean home and talked with my patient. I asked about his symptoms and diagnosed his ailment as caisson disease. Once again I gave him some medicine.

The patient, who was covered with linen cloth to ward off evil spirits, rubbed his arm after I gave him an injection and thanked me in the local tongue.

"*Guyishang*, would you like some fish?"

My patient seemed aware of my hopes. He weakly called to his son who was preparing the fish in front of the house and told him to give me two fish. I took the fish without the least hesitation and thanked him.

Leaving Yeyin Village, I slowly realized that sincerity is worth more than money.

Poems

Five Poems

MONANENG

To Wander

For my late friend Sajiyou

What does it mean to wander?
You had no idea
All you knew is that you had to leave
Hoping to find a permanent place to stay
At the tender age of thirteen
Still so innocent and unknowing
You went to work for twelve hours a day
Pawned to work as a welder in a factory
You bore the foul air and the long confinement
Not permitted to go out and with no wages
Your ID card held in the boss's safe
Once the three-year contract was fulfilled, you left
You ended up at a brick factory
Hauling bricks, you made more money
Strong as a wild mountain boar
In the stifling hot factory
You earned the praise of your boss
But you had to leave
Simply because you were unwilling to take
The lowest pay for the heaviest work
You went to the construction site to carry bricks, sand, and gravel

You said you got paid by the load
Anyway, you had strength and your freedom
But who would have guessed
Three months later the foreman embezzled the payroll
No choice but to pawn your ID card at a shipping company
You never stopped wandering
You worked as a hauler, sleeping in a truck
You worked in a steel factory, swinging a hammer, sleeping there too
You wandered to the vast ocean, hopped a fishing boat
Crossed the water to work in Saudi Arabia
Until a backhoe
Put an end to your wanderings
When it broke your back . . .
With your last breath you seemed to say
I understand. A man is forced to wander
And death is a release from worldly cares
Go, you wanderer
Wander to that unknown world
For perhaps it is a peaceful place

If You're an Aborigine

If you're an aborigine
Then wipe away your tears and blood
And, like a huge burning tree, light the road ahead
If you're an aborigine
Then sing out with your highland voice
In anger about your deep sufferings
Like desperate roaring waves
If you're an aborigine
Then set off the violence of your life
Like an explosive charge beneath the ground
Fiercely blowing open a pack of hypocrisy
If you're an aborigine
Then fear not the storm's tyranny
Stand tall like the mountain
Meeting all adverse blows
If you're an aborigine
Then when fate leaves you no way out
Do the only thing you can:
Fight with your back to the mountain

Shawumi, Come Back!

The frond tips of the betel palm
pierce the full moon
Its bright light streams through
the wooden window
Shining on me as I get ready
to go up into the mountains
Shining on my basket and curved knife
in the corner of the room
Basket on my back
Full of millet and taro
I gird my waist
Tie on the curved knife
inherited from my grandfather
I'm off to the mountains, the mountains
The cock's crow urges on my heavy steps
It's early spring, and the air is like
Millet wine just up from the cellar
Its bouquet joins my love song
On the path to the mountains
where countless insects sing
I'm off to the mountains, the mountains
Shawumi, oh, Shawumi!
I sing my love's name
No matter how many times the sun
rises and sets in the sea of clouds
No matter how many times the moon
waxes and wanes in the night sky
I never tire of singing
The name of my love
Shawumi, oh, Shawumi!
I plant the taro roots one by one
I sow handfuls of millet in the fields
Wait with excitement for a bountiful harvest
Carrying my curved knife and tinder
I cross one mountain after another
Shawumi, oh, Shawumi!
Singing your name again and again
Your name is food everlasting
Like the taro in the ground

Like the millet in the fields
Shawumi, oh, Shawumi!
A basket and seeds on my back
I cross one mountain after another
Guided by the cries of the owl
Searching the ancient myths and legends
Following the murmuring of springs
Thinking of Shawumi, who left long ago
Oh, a young girl bought with a military pension
When you think of your love here in the mountains
Do you sing this song again and again:
Who are you, who are you
Standing on the mountain
singing to me
Your figure and your song
More beautiful than a rainbow
Who are you, who are you
Standing on the mountain
singing to me
Your figure and your song
More majestic than a waterfall
Oh, your love's longings
Are hemmed in by the mountains
Bound by the murmuring springs
Day after day, mountain
after mountain
Through summer heat and storms
My browned body grows stronger
My thick hands and feet grow calloused
Finally, when autumn cicadas sing
in praise of summer
The taros are big and plentiful
The millet in the fields moves
in golden waves
Shawumi, come back!
Let us sing a song of joy for the harvest
Shawumi, come back!
Let me pick a taro leaf
Filled with sparkling dewdrops for a
betrothal gift
Let me brew a jug of sweet millet wine

We will drink it from traditional paired drinking cups
all night long
Shawumi, oh, Shawumi!
I carry a curved knife and tinder
With love and hope undying
One mountain after another
Singing your name again and again
Come back, oh, come back!
Come home, where millet and taro
are abundant!

I Really Don't Know

Sincere of heart
I awaited the harvest sacrifices
Though it was a bad year
I still had to pick the wild vegetables our ancestors liked to eat
As a way to welcome back their spirits
But three days after the harvest sacrifices
The court informed me
That I'd stolen the Forestry Bureau's property
I really don't know when the
Vegetables we have eaten for generations
Became public property protected by law
I really don't know what all this is about
When the kids ask me what the law is
And why we pick wild vegetables at the harvest sacrifices
My answer is
I really don't know

The Hundred-Pacer Snake Is Dead

The hundred-pacer snake is dead
Stuck in a transparent bottle of medicinal wine
The label on the bottle reads: *Aphrodisiac*
A teaser for the guys roaming the red-light district
The hundred-pacer snake of myth is dead too
The Paiwan people once believed its eggs were their ancestors
But today it sits in a transparent bottle
Now the agent for promoting lust in the big city
When a man drinks the medicinal wine

And struts his false majesty into the red-light district
There, at the brothel door to meet him,
Is the descendent of the hundred-pacer snake:
A young Paiwan girl

Four Poems

WALIS NORGAN

Duckweed

"More and more like the floating duckweed . . . "
Someone returned to the tribe this evening
Amid bamboo fences scattered over the mountain
Pondering the pains and regrets over history
Too much rice wine to drink
Makes for incoherent babbling
Mizuno, you've lived a pretty good life
What makes you suffer so?
Your hut was completed before winter
The peach trees blossomed in the saddle of the mountain
In the second month
Someone married a girl from a different village
Everyone is overjoyed
So what is it that worries you?
"Three hundred years ago our ancestors
wove fishnets and caught fish
Large sailing ships from the west appeared
blocking out the sun
Fifty years later they shunned the farmed plains
Returning to the forests to hunt
Aside from fighting over land
We lived in peace with each other
When the Japanese came, what was termed 'civilizing the savages'

Was in fact flogging, from the coast to the mountains
We've been like duckweed the last century . . . "
Someone returned to the tribe this evening
Rubbing the wound of history getting drunk
No one doubted his suffering
Perhaps he was mourning for his far-flung relatives
Perhaps he was angry at the destitution of the tribe
But not questioning justice and love
Though quietly drinking and talking
Though someone keeps leaving for distant places
Like a ripe fruit falling from the tree

Youth of Wushe

I don't recognize Tasiqisi's face
The 1930s are remote from today
Grandma says the pink cherry blossoms flower for him
That day he abandoned his books and returned to the tribe
Led the Atayal people against the canons
They all died in battle; Grandma told me to look at
The monument at the head of the road
The monument is mottled
Covered with lichen
But it's still difficult to cover Tasiqisi's hard work
At the end of the 1970s I graduated from the teacher's college
And was stationed at the front lines; two years later
I took up chalk and taught in school far from home
Constantly I complained about the wastewater and air pollution
And the problems with public transportation
I'm certain that if you came to the city
You'd be bad tempered too
The cherry blossoms still shimmer in winter
Tasiqisi gradually grows vague
The monument is still covered with lichen
The city performs and plunders
I still have to make a living
In the 1990s I'm still hoping to meet a nice girl and get married
Having a son would be nice
(The world's population is exploding)
Peaceful in old age, if you were me
I think you'd want the same

Down the Mountain

At the station on the way to Baling Mountain
A woman squats quietly and humbly
While her children run around without worries
They all look very happy
They are going down the mountain to shop
Using their harsh Mandarin and perhaps
Some gestures too.
It's the spring of 1985; I'm at the station
I saw farmers from the plains in the 1960s
Going to the city, often quiet and ill at ease
In the city I never speak Atayal
I do my best to scrub my dark skin
I do my utmost to suppress my savage blood
And even suppress my childhood memories
I've learned to chat happily with others
Tie a bow tie and drink coffee
They softly pat my shoulders praising me
I suddenly felt weighed down
Today, many years later
At the station on Baling Mountain
Familiar as before, the sound of a woman
Her sadness and the innocence of the children

He Makes Another Survey

This is 1996, but it's like being back in the days when the island
belonged to the Japanese emperor.
On the hundredth anniversary of the survey
this light-brown hard-cover book is offered, your eyes
are silent, the publishers are all strangers.
Strangers, strangers hoping for the *Ai* of Laolaoshe.
Your phonetics teacher is there; she'll teach you how
to greet strangers—*logah da gwara*;
she'll lead you into the world of the indigenous peoples:
cautiously to drink sweet rice wine, eat salted meat, and take
detailed but confusing field notes.
You close your book, willfully put on wings,
Quietly fly away from the air-conditioned conference room
To Hungtou Island, at one time a possession of the Japanese emperor.

You arrive at Hongtou Island, discovered by Chou Yuchi
Two hundred years ago; you arrive smiling
with perpetually happy flying fish, looking for that hundred-year-old
notebook, in which is penciled the date Nakajima Fujitaro
had his accident.
Nuclear waste is stockpiled nearby. They dance to drive away the
demons.
It seems that the spotted colored paper
Was the white flag waved by the grandson of Mr. K, who gave the
report;
He wields a pen instead of a sword and studies your taped dictation.
Strangers, strangers, only the likenesses of the old people
breathe to the pulse of the Pacific Ocean.
In the dark night of a dream they take a dugout canoe south
to trade with their relatives far away, to exchange greetings,
to exchange news as before.
The news is a bright song: on the shore
A banner waves above the Taidong Hall that says "drink and song."
On your lips is the smile of the native peoples
Encouraging you to go barefoot the way you like; the fifteen tribes
Of Malanshe you like are scattered like stars over the Peinan Plain.
On this day, following the voices, you find your lost dance steps,
Following the voices, your clansmen arrive at the ruined
Ceremonial grounds
Loudly singing "Return to Nature," so popular in Atlanta.
The old vocal cords of Mr. and Mrs. Kuo Yingnan, born less than
A hundred years ago,
Struggle to be heard across the Pacific,
Like sonar insistently seeking dignity in the sea bottom of history.
The dignity of history follows the route of the survey around the
mountains;
Out of sadness your wings grow tired and you land on the northern
coast;
A gravel truck passes through Santiaochiao, leaving a cloud of dust,
And in the haze
The leaning stone walls of the church don't hear the pious chanting
of Shijiushe in Tamsui; strange names are written on the bus route
sign:
Nankan, Tingsheh, Fulung, Hoping Island, Shihmen, Hsiulang,
Tachih, Tienmu
(Oh, I feel you still like the old romanized

Pingpu names, thousands of traces preserved); you thought
you had returned to the wild forests, just as I thought
I could by following your diary full of pity for Formosa.
As you sleep peacefully in your book, I silently read
The names of the tribal communities shining like stars:
Maoshaowengshe, Tatakanshe, Litsushe, Paijieshe,
Kuilunshe, Wulaishe, Takekanshe, Zhutoujiaoshe,
Shiba'ershe, Shitoushe, Bagualishe, Mabilahaoshe,
Wusonglunshe, Meishe, Dehuashe, Bushe, Heshe,
Xiaolongzhuang, Zhulaodongshe . . .

TASI-ULAUAN PIMA

Remembering the Little Souls

In the tenth lunar month the silvergrass flowers are falling in profusion
The time for making sacrifices to the Little Souls is at hand
Don't know if the Little Souls have been informed or not
The blessings and disasters, the joy and anger of the past
All have become a whisp of smoke
The Saisiat repent everyday and have waited year after year
The Saisiat have knotted the silvergrass, inviting the Taai home for a visit
Together let us revive and old dream as we recall and ponder the past
Amid the flowering stalks of the silvergrass
The Saisiat remember the words of the Taai
The Saisiat haven't forgotten the arts taught by the Taai and the
Instructions from the Taai on how to farm and hunt
The Saisiat dare not forget the exhortations of the Taai
Recounting the past when we joyfully pursued one another
Through the fields, farming, hunting, offering sacrifices, and
Entertaining the spirits
How regretful the Saisiat lost grip, allowing the Taai to drown
The Saisiat shouted their remorse and suppressed sadness
The tragedy of the Broken Tree Bridge
Oh, Souls of the Taai, it was all the fault of the Saisiat
The Saisiat will not forget the lesson of the death of the Taai

The spirits of the Taai touch me, raise me, look at me, and advise me
But really, the Saisiat didn't do it on purpose
We deeply regret letting the Taai drown and become ghosts
With our own eyes we saw you disappearing along the Sekai River
And would always keep you in out hearts
The complaints and vengence of the Taai frightened the Saisiat
Always are the hearts of the Saisiat troubled and ill at ease
Oh, Souls of the Taai, the Saisiat were unable to see you
The Saisiat knotted the silvergrass inviting the Taai to accept
Their apologies
Don't forget our agreement, the Saisiat piously welcome your
Descent from Heaven
The Saisiat have prepared food and drink for you and your
Favorite Roro fish and shrimp
Please follow the Sekai River and allow the Saisiat to reverently
Welcome your arrival
The Saisiat have prepared song and dance to entertain you
To pass a beautiful evening in a scenic place
The Saisiat wait quietly to serve the spirit of the Taai when they
Descend from Heaven as appointed
Let us mend old wrongs at the Broken Tree Bridge and build
A new bridge of understanding in our hearts
Let the enmity between us be forgotten, so we plead with you,
The Taai

Two Poems

ADAW PALAF

Young People, Sing and Dance!

There was a time when the blue, blue sky was our *niyaro* (tribe)
Shining brightly like a huge, huge mirror.
There was a time when the high mountain fields were our *niyaro*
Shining with primordial solemnity and glory.
There was a time when the big rivers and vast sea were our *niyaro*
Washing away all that was unclean.
There was a time when the gatherings of men were our *niyaro*
Listening to our ancestral myths and learning solemn adult ways.
There was a time when the *mi-ilisin* (harvest sacrifices) were our
  niyaro
Expressing our gratitude to *Malatao* (chief god of the Amis) and our
  ancestral spirits
Through dance and song.

But the moment the darkness covered the heaven and earth, when that foreign civilized power burst in accompanied by a high-class religion, our *kakarayan* (celestial body) and song vanished from the fields; no one listened to the ancestral myths after the men's house was toppled; every place was filled with the gas of the asshole government, and the solemn *mi-ilisin* were seen as superstition. Our fences, those with form and those without were broken down plaguing our *fagcalay* (beautiful) *niyaro*.

Young people, dance!
As noble as Ali mountain

Towering amid the clouds
Young people, charge yourselves!
Let that primordial energy fill you
Brave as a bear
Young people, bathe yourselves!
Clean as *kakarayan*
As benign as the sweet fragrance of the papaya
Young people, lie down
Let the Xiugumi and Puyuma rivers and the sea
Sing lively but softly as they always have, young people
Like the sound of nature
When the *bali* (wind) blows caressing the land
Young people, dance vigorously
Pounding and whirling
When the *wakes* (whirlwind) dances madly

Asking Him to *Mi-kadafo**

Surely brave and upright Parol (male name) is waiting for me
Waiting for me to *mi-kadafo* him
But I have so many performances in
The huge and stately . . .
When we were kids we grazed buffalo together
On the grassy banks of the Mataian River
He pitched a grass hut and I gathered wild herbs
He netted fish and I made the fire . . .
The *cidal* (sun) high overhead
The buffalo entered the river—
Naked, we swam
Or we danced and sang in the cool shade of the trees
Or we slept holding one another, flying on the wings of dream
Red clouds appeared over the Central Mountain Range
Holding me, Parol and I rode a buffalo home
He inhaled the fragrance of my body
I listened to his many stories
As the trains increased
So the buffalos decreased
I heard

---

* *Kadafo* means son-in-law or daughter-in-law. Adding the prefix *mi-* makes it into a verb meaning "to marry."

The tearful buffalos
All went to the slaughterhouse
Couldn't be helped, despondent
Later
Parol left for the far sea
I wandered to the city
Ha-hai (yeah)
We have been apart so long
Parol ought to be coming into port
Shouldn't he be back for the initiation ceremony
And the drunken *mi-ilisin* (harvest sacrifices)?
A pretty "lover's bag"
On his back
Containing my rich hopes
And my abundant affections
Has just—
Been snatched away by a lovely young woman
The victor shouts:
Parol is my *kadafo*
Don't you try to change his *tagal* (head)
On the last day of *padimo*
Ha-hai
I can't leave you, Parol, but
I have so many performances in
The huge and stately
National theater.

Six Poems

LAVULAS GEREN

Fists and Tears

You want to clench your fists and
Hold back your tears. Listen,
The joints in your fingers and the lines
In your palms act out your fate; look,
Tears through fire-red blood vessels
Depict this world

Withdrawn

Flowers no longer belong to the vase
Fish no longer belong to the fishbowl
Birds no longer belong to the birdcage
Animals no longer belong behind bars
God no longer belongs to the altar

On Rereading Bei Dao's Poem "Let's Go"

Across cracked fields on a day
The rats fight for food
Through the park
Where an old country fellow sleeps in the open
The flower buds just opened
Down the street

You wave eagerly
But only your eyes shout
Through the arcade where cockroaches
Appear and disappear
Hold the frightened children
Through the classroom, through the hallway
Shouldering the burden of chaos that
Has not yet returned
Across the stone steps laid with doubt
The green hills go on sprouting high-rises
Right and left, worrying people
Through pickling brine
Through cold wastes
Through falling betel nut flowers
Through the sobbing downstream
Down the town's only street
The broken bridge
Through the only mountain pass
Vines and fallen rocks
Waves and broken cliffs
Winding
Dizzying

The Zipper Song

Looking for that road
Which way does that bend?
Under the bushes, a cat arches its
Philosophical back
Everything watches, the wind pauses
The mountain's belly our *Vu Vu* (ancestors) groped their way over
The four seasons as yet undefined
Someone heard the crying of a beast's feet
The relatives across the river open their eyes and pray
The train carried away the women
The ancient tracks climb down beautiful cheeks
The small bells have been discarded
But it will be impossible to discard
the fatigue of traveling by night
The sickle probes unceasingly
Which way the road bends

The wind always changes direction
And all desire, unyielding as metal
Cries out together between 0 and 1
Looking for that road

The Plum Rains Still Not Here in the Sixth Month

Born this sixth month, this suspect sixth month
Can it be that the plum rains were spirited away
The wind blows brining news from the Pacific
Making one toss and turn all night long
Where did the plum rains go?
The hot sun topping the roof asks angrily
The reservoir, its bottom nearly exposed
asks embarrassed
The whole year asks with a mouth like a teacher's,
Tongue and lips dry and parched
The city as stifling as an oven,
flames leaping within
It would be better to drink sour plum soup
Than wait for the plum rains
Or simply freeze oneself with the chicken duck, and fish
As for the birthday, well the telephone lines
Sizzle with happy returns
—at this moment I'm longing to go home
For a long sweet dream under the longan tree
The sound of the cicadas hastening me to sleep,
The scent of grass filling my dreams
Who cares if the plum rains come or not
Who cares how long the draught will last
This sixth month

Through Hwa Dong Valley by Train at Night

1

Awake. The station name flashes by
Glimpsed on the guardrail through the window
Before I can pull myself up
The train is swallowed in the throat of night
Was that circle, that faint one
A light from Dakahan village?

2

The shadows of the betel palms vaguely discernible
Tabalang Ami language already has driven straight in
Through the screeching sound of the braking train
Interrupting the lingering sleepiness
The night market in front of the station is as bright as day
As if the festivities of the eighth month are being warmed up early

3

(Excuse me, tickets please)
Right and left, the conductor punches tickets
Someone sighs
Someone mutters a curse
Someone holds out his ticket in his sleep
Someone thrusts his ticket vigorously
One guy empties his pockets
Looks above, below, and all around his seat
The woman beside him with red fingernails
Curses him
—he'll have to
(Buy a ticket after boarding)

4

Waiting for the connecting train
Everyone seems to hold their breath
The silence increases the indifference
The anxiousness more suffocating
The surrounding darkness has swallowed everything
The air conditioner rattles, the passengers doze
But their toes long to be on their way
Wiggling in every pair of
Shoes

Five Poems

HAISUL

Forest

There are large flourishing trees
Cool spring water
And lots of different animals
This is my home
My grandparents lived here
Grandpa cut
The big trees
But they bravely sprang up again
The animals here
All know me
In the grass or in the trees
They look at me
The wind springs from the valley
Telling tales of my ancestors
It says
The shadows of my ancestors
Still float amid the white clouds
The brave spirit of my ancestors
Still hangs amid the big, old trees
But the footprints of my ancestors
Were overgrown by the grass a long time ago

Mother

Mother works hard
In the mountains
She sweats for me
All I have to do is study in school
But I can't
Thinking silently about my aged mother
Mother's black hair
Is turning white
I know
I colored her hair white
Her greatest anxiety
Is concealed in her white hair
I understand
Mother's cherished desire
Rests entirely on me
Her health and happiness
Depend entirely on me

My Feet When I Was Little

When I was little
My feet were the same as me
We hated to wear clothes
The sun did not like to see bare feet
So it baked
The asphalt road really hot
Hot enough to nearly cook my feet
Then the rain would fall
And my little feet would be happy
And run toward the water
Find a deep puddle
And go swimming

Time

Time flows with the river
Why does it never return?
Do you dislike this world?
Or did someone drive you away?

I try to stop you
But you pass through me without a trace
and are gone
Why?
My days drip in your heart
When will you return them to me?

Clouds

I want to pick you
Really, I really do
You are all sugary
Puffs and puffs of cotton candy
The sky is lucky
It can taste you every day
But me? I have nothing
I wish the sky would give me just one bite

MAISHU

Maishu's Song

The pure azaleas of Jade Mountain are blooming
From the meadows at Batong Pass all the way to
The old deserted hunting trail on Mabolasi Mountain
The cold breeze from the Malaxiaban River
And the sun floating above the Junda forest
The indomitable black goats stroll on the crags of Jade Mountain
Offering a beautiful winter impression
At the base of the scree-covered slope of Jade Mountain
and the steep and lofty peaks
Stands the fir forest with unequalled pride
I praise the scene with a mother's voice:
"Sing out for the primeval peace of the Central Range
With the Bunun respect for life and strength of wisdom."
Oh, stranger, your eyes have never beheld such expansiveness
All the sunlight and glittering streams converge in Bunun territory
in the Central Range
The millet on the slopes and the alpine lilies are the children dropped
  by the sun
Primeval freedom will follow the spirits into the arching heavens
Solemn lives traverse the Central Range with the clouded leopard
Oh, stranger, your soul must believe the Bunun words:
"The Junda mountains are the source of life in the Central Range
Listen, for the peace of the sea, the Junda River, the Danda River,

and the Luanda River promise to
Give the forests of Formosa to you as habitat
Friend from the sea, how could you discard Mother's promise
And yield to the temptations of the *hanidu* (evil spirits)?
"Go conquer the Central Range and the sea. Don't worry about the hundred-pacer snake
the mountain eagle, and the flying fish
Atayal of the Dabajian Mountain, Paiwan of the Nandawu Mountain, Zou of Jade Mountain, And Yami of the sun-washed sea have assembled
The will on the mountain peaks and seacoast, creating a world of language
Oh, stranger, your reason must awaken and call yourself back from the womb
Let all games bury the ocean trenches
So that we can watch as bright freedom fly through the will
Transcending time, space, and all differences
In the smiling air and the golden sunlight
And the fragrance of the high-mountain rose spread from the soil
Of Mother Earth
Oh, stranger, I want to be your *kafeiari* (good friend)
Let me sing in your soul or take the hunting rifle from my hands
Come, *kafeiari*, the beautiful forest and the blue sea are our *jina* (mother)
Come, *kafeiari*, I give you the right leg of this mountain boar
Come, *kafeiari*, after a cup of millet wine
We will wait for good news from you
On the cobblestone road that *Jina* so loves to walk

GUYOU HSILAN

Season of Meeting

Meeting Dananuoma*
June in the mountains the air unstable
In a car heading for *Yaya's* (mother) orchard at Mamei†
Clouds and fog roll over the peak of Dananuoma
Pressing down upon it
Like the ferocious face of a ghost
fleeing a hundred years of captivity
Yutas (grandfather) often mentions how the mountain that
Protects our people was once a battleground
In the days of fighting the Japanese
Winding and rugged, turning again and again
Like an old tortoise dragging its heavy shell
I clamber up to the peak
Just to go home in search of long-lost feelings
Clouds and fog roll over the peak of Dananuoma
Pressing down upon it

---

*Dananuoma is the name of a mountain and the site of a battle between the Atayal and the Japanese during the occupation period.

†Mamei is part of Yufeng Village, Jianshi Township, Xinzhu County. It is situated at the foot of Lidong Mountain and is the historic site of a battle with the Japanese during the occupation period.

The slight cold makes me shiver
Meeting Angels
June in the fields a profusion of flowers
Yaya is wrapping honey peaches in paper bags
Shovel, tribal blade, basket and her stooped back
With no regrets, her youth exchanged for sweat, tears,
and misery
What could equal such beauty?
Not wishing to startle her
I squat and from afar watch silently
If ever there was an angel in this world
Then surely she who has never complained is one
Meeting Azaleas
Every spring when the azaleas blossom on the opposite hill
Yaya is accustomed to shouldering her basket and going there
To pick wild herbs
Whenever she passes that sacred place where she and *yaba* (father)
plighted their troth
I always see her linger long on the hill
As if I saw her a bashful girl twenty years earlier
Shyly waiting for her sweetheart under a tree
Her eyes have not lost their glow because of age
Her tears, like stars in the night sky, are bright and clear
Finally she understands that pain and suffering separate
the living from those in heaven
This year under that tree I smell
The fragrance of flowers on gusts of cold wind I close my eyes
And can almost see *yaba* and *yaya* happy hand in hand
And my tears, like the stars in the night, are bright and clear

IT TA-OS

Sacrifices for the Little People

In all humility sacrifices are made to the east
Banana leaves filled with good food to atone for our sins
Are offered to the grieved souls making their way upstream
Hearkening to the endless sadness and prayers
The wooden mortar carved and polished out of ancient wood
shakes and rolls
Sonorous exhortations shake the mountains and the sea
The dark night, like a giant python, devours
Love and hate, kindness and enmity, increase and destruction
The sacrificial song, weeping and plaintive,
penetrates the cracks of time and space
Striking and ringing the warning and cursing bells hanging at our buttocks
Caressing the fluttering sinners' flags on our shoulders, we run and spin
In that circular dance of torture and bestowal
The spirit whip cracks, tearing through the thick fog, damp
Look afar upon those unpredictably tender lives
Those tender lives as yet unseen
Concealing themselves amid the alders
As inconspicuous as the twining devil's rattan, tough and resilient
Bamboo containers for concealing grief and indignation, say
farewell to the Thunder Girl,

Forced to depart but leaving behind abundance
Amid violent waves of rumor and insult for
The Weaver Girl, the bright adornment of our people's costumes is sunk,
The sad dance suffused with Formosan sweet gum and poignantly
Mysterious, the repeated song and sentimental looks, deep and remote
The wind of forgiveness scatters the floss of the rattan fruit,
Sprouts the unending cycle of birth and death for the Saisiat
Tired and trancelike the parting sorrows, gathered together
Sentimental drunkenness cleanses flaws and meanness
Looking forward to another banquet promised by silvergrass knots
And to willfully display the boundless life of the tribe

PURDUR

The Sea

I choose this day of clear skies without end
To shoulder my fishing pole
and by myself saunter east to the coast
Enjoying the great outdoors, I loaf by the sea
At ease with all my troubles left behind
Clouds float in the sky
Birds fly through the air
Fish swim in the water
Close to the blue sea and sky
Leisurely and free of care am I
And at this moment so very content

DARKANOW RURUANG

How We Long to Go Home

The indigenous people wandering in the big city
Originally had few dreams
Our unique blood flows over our bodies
Not knowing if tomorrow will be the same
The indigenous people live in the dark when hurt
We want to go home
We have forced ourselves to pretend otherwise not knowing
If tomorrow will be the same
How we long to go home how we long to go home
But in fact you and I are the same
Young people earning money in the factories
Young girls forced into bed
Understanding that life isn't simple
Not knowing if tomorrow will be the same
What is the future of the indigenous people? It's
Still one of bitterness
I'm nervous about the answer not knowing
If tomorrow will be the same
How we long to go home how we long to go home
But in fact you and I are the same
The same

SIEPEP

Ripples on the Sea

In memory of my father on the Flying Fish Ceremony

Flying fish black wings still flying over the sea
In legend the flying fish maintains the channel of dialogue with the ancestors
The fins of the dolphin fish
Have carried Father's pride to the horizon
A silver helmet agate chicken blood
gifts Father offered in limitless gratitude to the sea
Millet and flint a sky bridge to summon the spirits of land and sea
Bringing blessings following the path of the flying fish
The flying fish is the fountainhead of the soil and spirit
The sacrificial rites are a life ceremony running through
silver helmet and agate
In the wings of the flying fish
Are Father's proud life and honor
Noble dolphin fish
Following the shimmering pieces of gold and silver
Father strew over the sea with honor
The wings of the flying fish that Father has become
the soul of the dolphin fish has become
Pressing forward in a boat there to meet on the horizon line

Notes on the Authors

Adaw Palaf (b. 1949) holds a BA degree in foreign languages from National Taiwan Univeristy's Night School. He has worked at a host of jobs including taxi driver, store clerk, and farmer. He has been involved in dance and theater for years and was a member of the dance troupe Yuanwuzhe for six years.

Auvini Kadresengan (b. 1945) holds a degree in management and taught management for years. In 1990 he returned to his hometown where he has been engaged in the preservation of Rukai culture and the restoration of traditional structures. He is an expert on the Rukai use of stone in building, and has published a number of short story collections.

Badai (b. 1962) is an officer in the Marine Corps and now serves as a military training instructor at the Hualian Teachers College. He began writing in 1989 and has won numerous awards for his fiction, including first place in the fiction category in the first China Motor Indigenous Literary Award for his story "Ginger Road."

Darkanow Ruruang (b. 1961) holds a degree in sociology from National Taiwan University. He taught English for a number of years in Pingdong. He later entered a theology school with the intention of becoming a minister. However, in the early nineties he became involved in the indigenous rights movement and in music. He founded the music group Yuanyinshe and is a singer. He has also tried his hand at fiction, essays, and poetry.

Guyou Hsilan (b. 1971) is a primary school teacher in Xinzhu. Her poem "Season of Meeting" won honorable mention in the Indigenous Voice Bimonthly Literary Awards 2000.

Haisul (b. 1969) began writing poetry when he was in junior high. He studied political science at National Cheng-chih University. He worked as a staffer in the National Assembly and subsequently earned his MA in political science with an emphasis on minority issues. After graduating, he worked for a year in the Executive Yuan before quitting to work on a Ph.D. in ethnology. He is currently doing research for his dissertation.

Husluma Vava (b. 1958) has a degree in education and has been a primary school teacher for more than twenty years. He has been involved in the preservation and promotion of Bunun culture for years. He helped edit primary school materials about Bunun culture for the Gaoxiong county government and has been active in teaching Bunun song and dance as well as in collecting and recording Bunun oral literature. He has published four collections of short stories and won numerous awards, including the prestigious Wu Cho-liu Literary Award (1998) for his story "The Hunter."

It Ta-os (b. 1957) works for the Namchow Group, a large international food concern. He is also the head of the Association for the Promotion of Saisiyat Culture. He has won numerous awards for his fiction and poetry.

Kowan Talall (b. 1941) served as a police and customs official. His short story collection *Yuwai menhhen* (Traces of dreams in foreign lands) was published 1971, making it the earliest book published in Taiwan by an indigenous author. He has published police stories, love stories, and is at work on a novel.

Lekal (b. 1964) is a graduate of the Gaoxiong Maritime Academy. He currently works on a high seas fishing vessel. His grandmother was a shaman and his father a minister. His story "Elegy" won second place in the first China Motor Indigenous Literature Award in 2000.

Liglave A-wu (b. 1969) cofounded Lieren wenhua with Walis Norgan. She attended Pingdong Normal School. She is a teacher. She is known for her writings on the plight of indigenous peoples, especially women. She has published several volumes of essays and stories, many with a feminist focus.

Lavulas Geren (b. 1956) holds a BA degree in philosophy from National Taiwan University. He is a high school teacher. His poetry has appeared in Shanhai wenhua and the *Epoch Poetry Quarterly*.

Maishu: no information available.

Monaneng (b. 1956) left home at the age of sixteen upon graduating from junior high school. At the age of twenty he lost is sight because of injuries suffered in a traffic accident. He has since worked as a masseur in Taipei. His poems about the plight of Taiwan's indigenous people and the handicapped attracted the attention of one of his clients, who saw to it that some of them were published. In 1989, his book of poems "Beautiful Ears of Rice" (*Meili de daosui*) was published, making it the first volume of indigenous poetry in Chinese published in Taiwan.

Neqou Sokluman (b. 1975) is a graduate student in the Presbyterian Bible Academy in Xinzhu. He writes both fiction and essays.

Pa'labang (b. 1953) holds a BA degree in Chinese from National Taiwan University, an MA degree in philosophy from Fujen University, and an MA degree in Chinese Studies from K. U. Leuven University in Belgium. He is currently the director of the Institute of Development for Indigenous Peoples and head of the Department of Language and Communication of Indigenous Peoples at National Dong Hwa University in Hualian. He has been a tireless promoter on indigenous culture and has served in both public and private capacities. He founded Shanhai wenhua bimonthly, the most important magazine devoted to indigenous culture. He is also the author of several volumes of essays.

Paiz Mukunana (b. 1942) has been a factory worker and a kindergarten teacher. She has published one book of essays and is a two-time winner of the China Motor Indigenous Literature Award.

Purdur (b. 1967) has a degree in architecture and is also a graduate of the Taiwan Police Academy. He works as a policeman. He is an award-winning singer with no formal training in music. He also enjoys painting and sculpture.

Rimui Aki (b. 1962) is a trained Montesorri instructor and has more than a decade of experience in preschool education. She currently teaches the Atayal language. She has published several collections of fiction and essays and has won many awards for her writing.

Sakinu (b. 1972) is a police officer. His work is deeply imbued with traditional Paiwan culture. He claims this is in large part due to the influence of older village storytellers and his father, who was a hunter. He has published two books of essays and has won several literary prizes.

Siepep (b. 1974) graduated from the Shixin University where she majored in journalism. She worked for a while at *Indigenous Voice Bimonthly*.

Siyapenjipeaya (b. 1946) farms and fishes and writes. He has been involved in the promotion and preservation of Yami culture and has worked at National Taiwan University and Academia Sinica as a translator of Yami oral texts.

Syman Rapongan (b. 1957) holds a BA in French from Soochow University and is now a graduate student in anthropology at National Ching Hwa University. After many years in Taipei he felt the need to return to Lanyu to find himself by reconnecting with his home and traditions. His first book was a retelling of the myths and legends he heard recounted by the older Yami. He has focused more on writing in recent years and has written a number of volumes of essays that have proved highly popular. He also won the prestigious Wu Cho-liu Literary Award in 1999.

Tasi-ulauan Pima (b. 1955) holds an MA in Chinese from National Zhengzhi University. He has written extensively about Bunun customs and traditional literature. He has taught at all levels of public school. His poem "Remembering the Little Souls" won first prize in the 2000 China Motor Indigenous Literature Award.

Topas Tamapima (b. 1960) graduated from Gaoxiong Medical School. He served as a doctor on Lanyu Island where he was known as the Schwitzer of Lanyu. He is now a physician in Taidong. He is one of the best-known indigenous writers in Taiwan and has published short stories, essays, and a memoir of his days as a physician on Lanyu. His story "The Last Hunter" won the prestigious Wu Cho-liu Literary Award (1987) and he was also the recipient of the Lai Ho Literary Award in 1990.

Walis Norgan (b. 1961) graduated from the Taichung Teachers College. He now teaches primary school. He is a prolific author of essays and poetry. His earliest interest was in poetry and he was an avid reader of the works of famous second-generation poets such as Yu Guangzhong, Luo Fu, and Yang Mu. After encountering the poetry of Wu Sheng, the nativist poet, his own view of poetry changed drastically, becoming more attuned to social engagement. In 1990 he founded the magazine

Lieren wenhua (Hunter's culture), devoted to indigenous culture. Two years later the magazine was restructured as the Research Center for Indigenous Culture, which collects and analyzes indigenous social and cultural information. Walis Norgan has also won a number of literary awards.

Yubas Naogih (1943–2003) received an MA degree in Chinese from Taipei Normal University. He was a junior high-school teacher for thirty-five years. He was equally at home in Mandarin as he was in the Atayal language. He published four collections of short stories. Alarmed at the disappearance of Atayal culture, he was also involved in Atayal linguistic research.

GPSR Authorized Representative: Easy Access System Europe, Mustamäe tee 50, 10621 Tallinn, Estonia, gpsr.requests@easproject.com

www.ingramcontent.com/pod-product-compliance
Lightning Source LLC
Chambersburg PA
CBHW020947310726
48980CB00001B/91

* 9 7 8 0 2 3 1 1 3 6 5 0 1 *